THE ALDEN
COLLECTION

Isabella Macdonald Alden

● ●

As In A Mirror

CREATION
HOUSE
BOOKS ABOUT SPIRIT-LED LIVING
LAKE MARY, FLORIDA

Creation House
Strang Communications Company
190 North Westmonte Drive
Altamonte Springs, FL 32714
(407) 862-7565

Originally published in 1897

Unless otherwise noted, all Scripture quotations are
from the King James Version of the Bible.

CONTENTS

5

INTRODUCTION

nder the pen name "Pansy," Isabella Macdonald Alden exerted a great influence upon the American people of her day through her writings. She also helped her niece, Grace Livingston Hill, get started in her career as a best-selling inspirational romance novelist.

As Grace tells it in the foreword to *Memories of Yesterdays*, her aunt gave her a thousand sheets of typing paper with a sweet little note wishing her success and asking her to "turn those thousand sheets of paper into as many dollars.

"I can remember how appalling the task seemed and how I laughed aloud at the utter impossibility of its ever coming true with *any* thousand sheets of paper. But it was my first real encouragement, the first hint that anybody thought I ever could write. And I feel that my first inspiration came from reading her books and my mother's stories, in both of which as a child I fairly steeped myself."

Another time, shortly before Grace's twelfth

birthday in 1877, Isabella had been listening to her as she told a story about two warmhearted children. As Isabella listened, she typed out the story and later had it printed and bound by her own publisher into a little hardback book with woodcut illustrations. She surprised her niece with the gift on her birthday. That was Grace's first book.

Isabella Macdonald was born November 3, 1841, in Rochester, New York, the youngest of five daughters. Her father, Isaac Macdonald, was educated and was deeply interested in everything religious. Her mother, Myra Spafford Macdonald, was the daughter of Horatio Gates Spafford (1778-1832), author and inventor. Isabella's uncle, Horatio Gates Spafford Jr., penned the popular hymn "It Is Well With My Soul" after learning that his wife had survived a tragic shipwreck; his four daughters were lost at sea.

Isabella was taught at home on a regular daily basis by her father. As her guide and friend, he encouraged her to keep a journal when she was young and to develop a natural affection for writing. Under his direction she acquired the ease and aptness of expression for which her writings became known. When she was only ten, the local weekly newspaper published her composition titled "Our Old Clock," a story that was inspired by an accident to the old family clock.

That first published work was signed "Pansy." Isabella acquired that name partly because pansies were her favorite flower and partly because of a childhood episode. She tried to help her mother get ready for a tea party by picking all the pansies from the garden to decorate the tea table. Not knowing the flowers were to be tied into separate bouquets and placed at each lady's place, Isabella carefully removed all the stems.

Years later, while teaching at Oneida Seminary, from which she had earlier graduated, Isabella wrote her first novel, *Helen Lester*, in competition for a prize. She won fifty dollars for submitting the manuscript that explained the plan of salvation so clearly and pleasantly that very young readers would be drawn into the Christian fold and could easily follow its teachings.

Isabella wrote or edited more than two hundred published works, including short stories, Sunday school lessons and more than a hundred novels. She had only one manuscript rejected. At one time her books sold a hundred thousand copies annually with translations in Swedish, French, Japanese, Armenian and other languages.

She usually wrote for a young audience, hoping to motivate youth to follow Christianity and the Golden Rule. The themes of her books focused on the value of church attendance; the dangers lurking in popular forms of recreation; the duty of total abstinence from alcohol; the need for self-sacrifice; and, in general, the requirements, tests and rewards of being a Christian.

Reading was strictly supervised for young people then, and Sunday schools provided many families with reading material. Thus, Isabella's fiction received wide circulation because of its wholesome content, and readers liked the books.

Her gift for telling stories and her cleverness in dreaming up situations, plus just a little romance, held the interest of readers young and old. Isabella was known for developing characters who possessed an unwavering commitment to follow the Master. She portrayed characters and events that anyone might encounter in a small American town during the last quarter of the nineteenth century.

A writer in *Earth Horizon* (1932) acknowledged that "whoever on his ancestral book shelves can discover a stray copy of one of the Pansy books will know more, on reading it, of culture in the American eighties [1880s] than can otherwise be described." Some of the customs of the times in which Isabella wrote may seem peculiar to readers today. But to understand the present culture, we need to know the beliefs and practices that have existed in the past.

Isabella believed wholeheartedly in the Sunday school movement. She edited a primary quarterly and wrote primary Sunday school lessons for twenty years. From 1874 to 1896 she edited *The Pansy*, a Sunday magazine for children, which included contributions from her family and others. An outgrowth of the magazine was the Pansy societies which were made up of young subscribers and aimed at rooting out "besetting sins" and teaching "right conduct."

For many years she taught in the Chautauqua assemblies and, with her husband, was a graduate of what was called the Pansy Class, the 1887 class of the Chautauqua Literary and Scientific Circle— the first book club in America. The Chautauqua assemblies were an institution that flourished in the late nineteenth and early twentieth centuries. They combined popular education with entertainment in the form of lectures, concerts and plays and were often presented outside or in a tent.

Throughout her career Isabella took an active interest in all forms of religious endeavors, but her greatest contributions came in her writings. She wanted to teach by precept and parable the lessons her husband taught from the pulpit, in Bible class and in the homes of his parishioners. Her writing was always her means of teaching religious and moral truths as she understood them, and her method was to tell a story.

Her husband, Gustavus Rossenberg Alden, was a lineal descendant of John Alden, one of the first settlers in America. He graduated from Auburn Theological Seminary and was ordained soon after his marriage to Isabella in 1866. He served as a pastor in churches in New York, Indiana, Ohio, Pennsylvania, Florida and Washington, D.C. The Aldens moved from place to place for health reasons and to be near their son, Raymond, during his years of schooling and teaching.

Amidst her many and varied responsibilities as a minister's wife, a mother and a prolific author, Isabella found time to play a significant role in her son's career as a university professor, an author and a scholar in Shakespearean literature.

Her final years were marked by a series of trials. In 1924, after fifty-seven years of marriage, Isabella's husband died. In that same year her last remaining sister, Marcia Macdonald Livingston, Grace's mother, died. A month later her only son, Raymond, died.

About two years later she fell and broke her hip. Although in much pain and discomfort she continued writing until the end. Her final letters were filled with thoughts of going "Home": "Isn't it blessed to realize that one by one we shall all gather Home at last to go no more out forever! The hours between me and my call to come Home grow daily less...."

Isabella Macdonald Alden died August 5, 1930, at the age of eighty-nine in Palo Alto, California, where she and her husband had moved in 1901.

The following year *Memories of Yesterdays*, her last book, edited by her niece, was published. In the foreword Grace describes her aunt:

"I thought her the most beautiful, wise and wonderful person in my world, outside of my home. I treasured her smiles, copied her ways and listened breathlessly to all she had to say....

"I measured other people by her principles and opinions and always felt that her word was final. I am afraid I even corrected my beloved parents sometimes when they failed to state some principle or opinion as she had done."

As Grace was growing up and learning to read, she devoured her aunt's stories "chapter by chapter. Even sometimes page by page as they came hot from the typewriter; occasionally stealing in for an instant when she left the study, to snatch the latest page and see what had happened next.... And often the whole family would crowd around, leaving their work when the word went around that the last chapter of something was finished and going to be read aloud. And how we listened, breathless, as she read and made her characters live before us."

Originally published in 1897, *As in a Mirror* tells the story of a young author, John Stuart King, who is challenged by a Sunday morning sermon to search for truth. It is our hope that your love for honesty and straightforwardness will be deepened through reading this new release from the Alden Collection. And, like the thousands of families who read and were helped by Isabella Macdonald Alden's books in her day, you too will be influenced to "right feeling, right thinking and right living."

Deborah D. Cole

THE CHARACTERS

John Stuart King
Arnold Fletcher, King's friend
Dr. Talbert, pastor
Elizabeth, King's fiancée
The Elliotts:
   Roger, father
   Sarah, mother
   Helen, older daughter
   Corey, son
   Anna, younger daughter
Susan Appleby, hired help at the Elliott farm
Winnie Houston, Helen's friend
Laura Holcombe, Anna's friend
The Marvins:
   Mr. Marvin
   Mrs. Marvin
   Nannie
   Kate
   Lillian
   Alice
   Nell
Rex Hartwell, Nannie's fiancé
Squire Hartwell, Rex's uncle
Rob Sterritt, local boy
Jack Sterritt, Rob's brother
Thomas, schoolboy
Augustus Sayre Hooper, college boy
Judge Barnard, lawyer
Dr. Warden, Rex's friend

CHAPTER I

A SERMON
THAT BORE FRUIT

he day was so warm that irregular Sunday worshippers remained at home as a matter of course. And even those who were fairly regular in attendance found the weather sufficient excuse for staying away. Yet two young men, who belonged to the latter group, were exceptions. Possibly they had gone to church because the great stone building where they worshipped looked darker and cooler than their respective rooms. In any event, they met in the pew they owned together and smiled a languid greeting upon each other.

The only person who did not seem languid was the pastor. Apparently the heat had created energy within him. His voice rang out among the half-empty pews and echoed down the aisles in a way that occasionally startled a sleepy member into sitting erect. Perhaps the pastor had to be vigorous and denunciatory in style to keep himself awake. Or perhaps something had occurred recently to set his heart athrob with sympathy for a class of persons for whom, as a rule, little sympathy is felt.

The good man's text was, "I was a stranger and ye took me not in," and his first sentence, "The negative form of that statement is true to the experience of today." A series of incisive statements followed concerning the ordinary method of dealing with the modern tramp. The sermon could not be called a plea for the tramp exactly, for the speaker frankly acknowledged the tramp's general worthlessness and deplored the habit that a "very few, very lazy people" had of giving him money. But he declared that the average person used neither judgment nor charity in dealing with tramps.

There were men and women who would dive into filthy streets and alleys in search of the lost; who would give whole afternoons to seeking out and ministering to tenement-house sufferers; who would go, even on days when the thermometer stood as high as it did today, to jails and prisons and other poorly ventilated places to try to teach the depraved. Yet these same men and women would turn away from their doors, with a harsh refusal, a hungry man who asked for food, and without a word of inquiry about what had brought him to that state or the slightest attempt to win him to a better life. Tomorrow, the next day or the next week, when his desperate need had made a criminal of him, they would visit him in his cell and do what they could toward his reformation. But not one crumb of prevention were they willing to give to the poor tramp at their doors, whose worst crimes, as yet, might have been poverty and laziness!

The pastor grew eloquent as he continued. He cited some thrilling instances that had come to his recent knowledge. He affirmed that the Lord Jesus Christ, who came to save the lost, would be ashamed to meet two-thirds of the people who bore His name because of their treatment of His starving, tramping poor. He did not plead for indiscriminate giving; he begged no one who was listening to him to be so foolish as to go away and say he had urged the giving of money to tramps. He would even be careful about giving clothing that could easily be exchanged for liquor.

But a bit of bread to be eaten on one's doorstep, followed at least on such a day as this by a draught of cool water offered in a decent cup and a few words of inquiry, sympathy or exhortation accompanying them, could not drag any poor tramp much lower than he was. And who could say but that the opportunity might be blessed of God and the seed dropped bear such fruit that bread-giver and bread-eater might rejoice together through eternity?

Was it not at least worthwhile to stop and think about this army of hungry, half-clad opportunities who tramp past our doors continually? Were we ready today to give account to Him who said, "I was hungry and ye gave me no bread," concerning how we had treated even the least of these?

The two young men who had met in church were not sleepy. In fact, one of them sat erect and looked steadily at the speaker, his eyes kindling with deepened interest as the sermon grew more and more emphatic. His entire attitude expressed keen attention.

"How that man can get up so much energy on such a day as this is beyond me to understand." This was his companion's first sentence as, following a brief prayer and a single verse of a hymn, the organist roused himself and roared and thundered them out of church.

"It was the subject that energized him," said the young man who had listened intently. "Upon my word, he handled it well and in an original fashion."

"Dr. Talbert is nothing if not original, you remember. What puzzles me is why he chose a regular broadside for such a melting day. I should have thought that something quiet and soothing in its nature would have been more in keeping."

"So that people need not have been disturbed in their slumbers, eh? I didn't discover on looking around that there was any need for special consideration on that ground. They slept very well. What a trial it must be for a man like the doctor to pour out eloquence and energy on a company of sleepers!"

He added with renewed energy to his friend. "Seriously, Fletcher, weren't you a good deal impressed with his way of dealing with the problem? It seemed to me that he had not so much found some new ideas, perhaps, as he had dared to speak out on an unpopular side and tell the individual what was his duty. We deal with this matter by organizations nowadays, you know — Associated Charities and the like. The average man and woman, who know these organizations only by name and never lift a finger toward their work, feel somehow that their responsibility has been shouldered and there is nothing left for them to do but moralize."

"Oh, he talked well," his friend agreed. "Dr. Talbert always does. I told you last week he was more worth hearing than any speaker in town. You have heard so little of him, you see, that you haven't gotten used to the style, and it makes a deep impression. He didn't come until after you went abroad, did he?"

"He came the Sunday before, but I didn't hear him. I went with my mother to Dr. Pendleton's church that day. No, I have heard Dr. Talbert only a few times. Is he always so impressive?"

"He is always high pressure, if that's what you mean. I haven't decided yet whether he is really more impressive than a quieter man would be. Doesn't some of it impress you as mere oratory?" challenged Fletcher.

"What do you mean by that? He's an orator certainly. But I wouldn't use the word *mere* in connection with him. Do you think he doesn't really feel what he says?"

"Oh, some of it he feels, undoubtedly, as much as circumstances will admit, probably. But I would like to be a tramp tomorrow morning and call at his door to see how he would apply his sermon."

"How do you think he would?"

"With his Monday morning shoes, very likely," Fletcher replied with an indolent laugh. Then, seeing his friend was waiting for something more serious, he added, "Not so bad as that, of course, but I really would not expect any more consideration from him because of that sermon. You see, King, there's a certain amount of — what shall I call it? idealism? — to be taken into consideration when one listens to a sermon, especially when the speaker is an enthusiast like Dr. Talbert. One cannot pin him down to actual hard fact. He must have a chance to soar, to make statements which, the next day, in cool blood, he would naturally tone down a little."

"I don't believe it," said King emphatically.

"There is a great deal of surface talking done in this world, I know. But I like to think that from the pulpit we get verities, not only in doctrine, but also in the statements that belong to everyday life. I mean, I like to believe the speaker is intensely in earnest. I may not think as he does, I may consider him utterly mistaken, but I want him to believe every word of every sentence he utters to the depths of his being. Nothing less than that could command my respect."

"Who is idealizing now?" laughed his friend. "I thought his views were held steadily within the line of common sense." As he spoke, he halted before the door of an apartment house where his own handsome rooms were situated. With a cordial invitation to Fletcher to enter, which was declined, the two separated.

Fletcher would saunter three squares farther and let himself into a fine house on the corner, where his father and sisters were already awaiting him. King would seat himself in the elevator to be taken to the fourth floor front, where he lived in luxurious apartments quite alone.

Speedily dressing in the coolest possible attire, King drew an easy chair in front of a window where a faint suspicion of a breeze occasionally hovered. Contrary to his habit, he had neither book nor paper. The walls were lined with many rows of well-filled shelves, and a searcher among them would have found every choice book of the season, as well as the standard volumes of the past. A bookcase devoted to standard magazines was crowded almost to discomfort, and the large study table was strewn with the very latest in newspaper and magazine.

Mr. King was obviously an omnivorous reader,

yet not one of his silent companions appealed to him. He did not look sleepy; on the contrary, that intent look he had held in the church was still on his face. Some problem had confronted him and insisted upon being thought about. It kept his mind steadily at work during that entire afternoon, with the thermometer in the nineties.

He went out to his boardinghouse for dinner as usual, but he carried that thoughtful, preoccupied air with him and came away again without lingering for music or conversation as he sometimes did. He lay down for his Sunday afternoon nap, but sleep did not come. Instead, he stared at the ceiling and continued his thought.

He had just dropped into that same easy chair again, still without book or paper, when he heard a tap at his door. His friend Fletcher appeared in answer to his invitation to come in.

"Awake, old fellow?" was his greeting. "I knocked softly for fear of disturbing a nap. It was so hot earlier in the day that a fellow couldn't sleep. Don't you want to go around and hear Dr. Waymouth this evening?"

"Take a seat," said King, glancing about for another empty chair and motioning his friend toward it with the familiarity of long acquaintance. "No, to be entirely frank, I don't. It seems to me that I have had sermon enough for one day. I cannot get away from the morning one. It has stayed with me through this entire afternoon."

Fletcher laughed genially. "Dr. Talbert is going to be too strong a tonic for you, I'm afraid," he said. "You will have to change your church relations and go to Dr. Pendleton's. You are a high-pressure type yourself and need soothing, as I told you this morning."

"We are all too much in search of soothing potions at church, I'm afraid. No, you're wrong. I believe I need rousing. Wheel that chair up here and let me talk to you. I've done a tremendous amount of thinking this afternoon. I tell you, Fletcher, that sermon needs to be thought about. It dealt with a problem that demands solution. Do you know how many tramps there are in our country annually?"

"Well, I've never really — "

"I thought not; the figures are appalling! I was reading some statistics on the subject only last night, but they didn't impress me much until I heard Dr. Talbert. What do we know about the poor fellows? As the preacher said, we pass them by with a smile or a sneer, then go on our well-fed way and think no more about them. Who is trying to reach them in any way? We haven't the least notion how we would feel if we were put for a single week in their positions — homeless, moneyless and without decent clothing."

"Many of them leave good homes to tramp about the country," said his friend.

"Don't you believe it," King said earnestly. "A certain percentage of them are scamps in search of adventure, no doubt, but I believe the great majority tramp from stern necessity. How is one going to learn how to help them unless he can enter into their lives? I'm planning to write a book with a tramp in it. I've been gathering materials all this spring, and I thought I was nearly ready to begin work before I heard that sermon. Now I'm sure I know nothing about them. I'll tell you what I'm going to do, Fletcher. I'm going to turn tramp!"

Fletcher leaned back in his chair and laughed. It wasn't loud laughter, but a succession of low, amused chuckles that died down and then bubbled up again as though he could not get away from the absurdity of the idea.

"Laugh as much as you please," said his friend good humoredly, "but I'm in dead earnest. I've thought it all out. Since hearing Dr. Talbert this morning, I've decided that I've studied exactly one side of the problem and that it would be an impertinence to try to write about it before studying the other. Do you remember Charles Reade's old book, *Put Yourself in His Place*? There's a vast amount of common sense in that title. I'm going to attempt just that thing. I have the whole summer yawning before me. Mother and Elizabeth are in Europe and want to remain there until next spring. There's nothing to hinder my turning tramp tomorrow, and in all seriousness I mean to do it."

Fletcher ceased his laughter and began trying to dissuade his friend from taking such an erratic step, though he had little hope of succeeding. "Look here, King, have you forgotten that man Wyckoff and his two years of experience?"

"Certainly I haven't forgotten him. And I have no doubt that when he gets ready to give his experiences to the world, he will help materially in solving some of its problems. But he tramped for himself and will know what he is about when he begins to write. That's exactly what I mean to do. Moreover, it's a slightly different phase of the matter that I wish to consider, I think."

Fletcher was not surprised at this answer. In all the years he had known John Stuart King, that young man had been noted for carrying out his projects, many of them unreasonable enough in appearance, to the very letter. Fletcher had no doubt that he would do the same with this idea.

The subject was thoroughly canvassed that evening. The church bells tolled in vain; the hot day reached its ending; darkness and a measure of coolness fell upon them; and still the two sat and talked.

"Well," said Fletcher at last, "if you will, you *will*. I knew that before I started. But mark my word, you'll be thoroughly tired of your bargain before the season is half over, and you'll know no more about the 'true inwardness' of tramp life than you do now. It's all a farce. You can't be a tramp. A man who knows he has a fortune to fall back upon at any moment cannot feel as the poor tramp does, and it's folly to try."

"There's truth in that," the other said so thoughtfully that his friend turned and looked at him anxiously and was sorry he had said it. John Stuart King was capable of willing away his entire fortune to the first charitable institution he thought of, once convinced it was actually in the way of his plans.

"There is truth in that," he repeated. "I can only approximate the conditions. But it shall not be a farce. I will not use one penny of my money while I tramp over the country. I will be hungry and ragged if necessary, if I cannot find work enough to feed and clothe myself. It's the honest tramp who is doing the best he can with his environment that interests me, and an honest tramp I'm going to be. Anyway, I'll help myself to write my own book, and that's a great gain."

CHAPTER II

In Search
of Truth

he third day following that warm
Sunday, a tramp made his way
slowly down one of the principal
business streets of the city. He
walked with the slouching gait com-
mon to that class of people, and he avoided looking steadily into the eyes of anyone he met in a
way also characteristic of the majority of his kind.
His hair, which was brown and plentiful, was
tossed about in wild disorder, and the slouch hat
he wore pushed well down over his head was very
"slouch" indeed.

His dress was cleaner than that of many tramps.
One noticing him carefully would have decided he
had made an almost painful effort to be clean and
would therefore have considered him as belonging
to the better class of unfortunates. Still, the dress
had many defects. The sleeves were much too
short and badly frayed; they had been out at the
elbow but were decently patched with a different
material. A calico shirt was buttoned high about

the neck, and that also was clean, but collarless. The shoes were decidedly the worst part of the outfit, or maybe the shabby trousers that dangled above them.

John Stuart King looked furtively at himself as he lounged along, uncertain whether to feel elation or dismay at the success of his disguise. He had chosen a street with which he was least acquainted, yet from time to time he encountered people he knew well. For the most part, they passed him without so much as a glance. They recognized him afar off as one belonging to a world different from theirs, too common a world to awaken their interest.

As he grew bolder, he ventured once or twice to speak to men whose name and position he knew, asking for work. They were men who knew his name perfectly, would have recognized it anywhere, but did not know him well by sight. Without exception, they answered him curtly in the negative, without question or remark. They had no work for such as he. He might be hungry, they would agree, but it was undoubtedly his own fault, and in any case there were charities, breakfast missions and whatnot for wretches of his stamp. If their faces expressed any thought of him at all, the tramp concluded they were negative thoughts indeed.

One young lady's reaction alarmed him and made him feel his best course would be to strike out into the country as soon as possible. He had met her several times at receptions and parties, and as she passed him she stared in a startled way, even turning her head to do so. He heard her say, "How much that fellow looks like...." The name dropped from his hearing, but he was sure it was his own.

"The idea!" laughed her louder-voiced companion, and the tramp moved on more rapidly, his face flushing deeply. It gave him strange sensations, this incognito walk through the city of his birth. True, he was not exceedingly well known except in certain circles. Long absences during the years when he had changed the most rapidly had cut him off from the recognition of many. But to be able to pass those who would have been glad to call themselves his friends had they recognized him, and to receive no nod or glance of fellowship, had its startling side. Did the mere matter of clothes count for so much?

Then something happened to bring his speculations to a sudden conclusion. Yonder, approaching rapidly, was his most intimate friend, Arnold Fletcher. Now for the crucial test; if Fletcher passed him, then indeed he could not be himself. But he had not intended to test this on the public thoroughfare. How came Fletcher to be on this street at this hour? He was evidently in haste, for he came with long strides, looking neither to the right nor to the left. Yes, he was passing, without so much as a glance. Suddenly the tramp became courageous.

"Could you help me, sir, to find work of some sort, enough to earn my breakfast?" He said it rapidly, in the desperate tone he thought a fellow in his situation ought to use.

"Work?" repeated Fletcher, slackening his pace and bringing his thoughts back from — the tramp could not decide where. "There is work enough in the world, too much to suit my taste! The trouble with you probably is that you cannot do any of it decently. What kind of work do you want?"

"Any kind," said the tramp, but it was an unguarded moment. He felt such a thrill of satisfaction that his friend had responded, not merely passing him with a frown and a coldly shaken head, that he looked full at him and smiled his own rich smile.

"What!" said Fletcher, startled and apparently dazed. "Who in — upon my word! It can't be possible! And yet — well, if that isn't complete! Why, John, your own mother wouldn't recognize you!"

"Hush!" said King. "You talk too loud for the public street, and you're too familiar. The question is, have you any work for me?"

"Yes," said Fletcher, laughing heartily now. "What a scarecrow you've made of yourself, to be sure. At first sight I didn't dream it was you, and yet I was expecting to see you. I'll give you something to do; you go and call on Dr. Talbert — that's a good fellow. He'll have work for you — see if he doesn't — or a cup of coffee and a sandwich, or something of the sort, which is better. He's bound to, you know, according to your theories. Just try it. I'll give a thousand dollars to home missions if you will, when I earn it."

"Hush!" said King again, this time in really warning tones. Two men were approaching whom they both knew. Fletcher took the hint, and as they passed he told King in dignified tones, "There is an Associated Charities station not more than a mile from here. You go down there. I don't know exactly where it is, but you can inquire."

One of the gentlemen glanced back with a superior smile and said, "Being victimized, Fletcher? Don't waste your time. The fellow needs the lockup more than he needs charity."

"You knew quite as much about the station as most of them, I presume," King said when they were alone again. "Never mind, I shall do without a breakfast. I'm going to leave town. I shall tramp as far as Circletown this very day, I think. Remember that one John Stuart will be looking there for letters. Good-bye, and thank you for your sympathy. It has done me good."

"John," said the other, detaining him with a hand and looking anxious, "Please give up this absurdity. What would your mother say? Above all, what would Elizabeth think of you? At least, don't go away without any money. Have you really no money with you?"

"Not a cent," King said with a genial smile. "I am honest, you see, and I'm doing nothing of which I need to be ashamed. I am simply testing for myself a way of life that is only too common. As for the anxiety of my mother and other friends, they are to know nothing about it, so they won't be troubled. If I come to downright grief, I'll remember you and your bank account."

"You'll be back looking after your own, as usual, within the month."

"Possibly, in which case I shall have accomplished all I care to in this line. I make no professions of having become a tramp for the remainder of my natural life. Good-bye, Fletcher. Wish me success, for you can't dissuade me."

Left to himself, our tramp considered for the first time the wisdom of following his friend's oft-repeated advice and calling on Dr. Talbert. True, he was a member of his church, but by no means was he well acquainted with the gentleman. He had but recently returned from an extended trip abroad and had only met his pastor two or three times at crowded gatherings. The chances that he would be recognized in his present attire were few. Why not test the practical nature of the discourse that had moved him so much? Not that Dr. Talbert was pledged to devote himself to the interests of every tramp he saw because he had chosen to speak unusual words in their behalf, but a word of sympathy or of exhortation, possibly of advice, would be likely to be given him. How did Dr. Talbert advise such men as he was representing himself to be? It was worth risking discovery to learn. Without further delay, he turned his steps in the direction of Dr. Talbert's handsome residence.

King had chosen an unfortunate day. That evening, Dr. Talbert would give his regular midweek lecture, for which he made as careful preparation as he did for the Sunday services. He was late in reaching his study, and he did *not* like to be disturbed once he was ensconced there. No one in his employ would be so rash as to call him down to see a tramp. But it so happened that an imperative summons had called him to the parlor and compelled him to show his visitor out, and the visitor had come on church business that had an edge in it for the pastor. (There is much such business of which outsiders know not.) The good man was frowning as his eyes rested on the forlorn specimen of tramp life who humbly asked for work, and his voice was harsh in reply.

"No, I haven't any work, and if I had, I would not give it to a fellow who doesn't know enough to go to the back door."

The tramp's face reddened. He had not remembered that there were back doors; he wasn't used to them. He tried to stammer an apology and repeated his willingness to do any kind of work for the sake of a breakfast.

"Breakfast!" repeated Dr. Talbert with an irritable glance at his watch. "It is much nearer dinner than breakfast time! My whole morning has been frittered away! No, sir, I haven't any work, any breakfast, or a moment's time to waste on you. My morning is gone already." And the door was literally slammed in King's face.

This was not Dr. Talbert's ordinary manner. He was a sincere man, and on almost any other occasion he would have tried to live up to, in a measure at least, his Sunday-morning eloquence. He would have been dismayed had he known with what an utterly disappointed heart the tramp turned from his door, saying to himself as he did so, "I believed in him, and he has spoiled it."

John Stuart King, the scholar and author, was not prone to make sweeping deductions on slight proof. But with the dress of a tramp, he had apparently taken on something of his surface character; at least, his heart felt very sore and sad at this rebuff.

He moved away slowly, moralizing as he went. Were Fletcher's cynical views of life the more correct after all? Was there no such thing as true sincerity in this world? He believed himself to be a lover of truth. He had personified Truth, admired and worshipped her, and written about her in a way that others had well-nigh worshipped. Fletcher had assured him it was all fine on paper, and important, too. Of course people must have ideals. But as for finding real flesh-and-blood specimens of Truth moving about, that was not to be expected.

King, on the other hand, had contended that the world held many whose daily lives were as carefully patterned after Truth as were his ideals. Had he been mistaken? He looked at himself and sighed. Then, as he caught his reflection in a plate-glass window he was passing, he laughed a laugh that had in it a touch of bitterness. The very costume he wore, having taken such pains to secure, taught him the same hateful lesson. He had visited pawnbrokers' shops and secondhand clothing stores without number and been almost in despair. The wardrobe of the decent poor was not apparently what he needed. Where was he to find his need? And then he had thought of trying a theatrical costume shop. Hurrying there, he had found exactly what he was searching for.

"Private entertainment?" the obsequious attendant had asked as he studied his customer. Then King had been complimented on his selection of character and assured that his part would be perfect. What a humiliating thought it was that to a degree, everybody was playing a part. No one was strictly and continually himself.

The bitterness went out of his laugh as he gradually saw that the matter had its comic side. Surely he should not be at war this morning against all shams when he had, for the first time in his life, dressed himself for as complete a sham as possible!

But I have a purpose, he told himself quickly, one that justifies the method. Neither am I planning to be a continuous sham. I shall lay all this aside very soon. I wonder if I'm half tired of it already? John Stuart, what you need is to get away from the city. You've always contended that the truest people in the world are to be found in the country. Now tramp out and prove it.

In all his cultured years that had been filled with opportunities, during no single day had John Stuart King learned more about human nature than on that first one of his new life. Men, women and children all contributed to his education. It was a new experience to him to have young and pretty women look at him with curious, distrustful eyes and cross the street to avoid too-close contact. Before twelve o'clock he was genuinely hungry, and he offered with some anxiety to bring pails of water from the "wells" that dotted the country through which he traveled, or to do anything else he could think of, for a dinner. Five times he was refused — once with hesitation and a lingering regret in the eyes of a woman who "hadn't anything to spare"; three times with cold indifference; and once with positive fire of tongue and slam of door. Being very hungry, he tried again, though he began to admit to himself that it would be easier to steal something.

The sixth woman gave him two pieces of very stale bread in a not-too-clean paper bag, and she added a bone that once had meat on it. "I'm afraid to refuse 'em," he heard her explain in a supposed undertone to someone inside, "for fear they'll fire the buildings or do something ugly. I've read of such things."

So even this was not charity! But the receiver ate it with a relish that daintier fare had not always found.

The woman looked at him occasionally and continued her remarks: "He ain't bad looking, not as tramps go. He don't look real mean, as some of 'em do, and his clothes is pretty clean and patched up kind of decent. I shouldn't wonder if he had a mother somewheres who had done her best to make him look decent."

Visions of his mother patching the clothes he wore were almost too much for the tramp's risibles. He ate the last mouthful hastily and moved on, philosophizing over the power with which he could describe the value of stale bread and bones where meat had been. For a full hour his sympathies were entirely on the side of the tramp. Then he met one so repulsive in appearance that he instantly justified the woman who had been afraid of him. It was a new experience to be accosted as he was by this one.

"Any luck that way, pal?" the man said, nodding in the direction from which King had come.

"I haven't found any work yet, if that's what you mean," King replied in the tone that in his former grade of life would have been called cold.

The man gave a disagreeable sneer. "Oh, that's your dodge, is it?" he said. "I can tell you I've had worse trials in life than not finding work. Did you spot any of the houses?"

"Did I what?"

"Mark the houses where they treated you decent and gave you coffee or lemonade, or something? You must be a green one! Don't you carry no chalk or nothin' with you to mark the places? Then you're a hard-hearted wretch. If you can't do so much for your fellow tramps as that, you ought to go to the lockup."

The healthy, clean young man found himself shrinking from this specimen with a kind of loathing. Would it be possible for him to fraternize with such as he, even to study human nature?

Then, curiously enough, at that moment, for almost the first time since he started out, he thought of the Lord Jesus Christ. What a lonely man He must have been!

CHAPTER III

FATHER'S TRAMP

he Elliotts had just risen from the tea table — that is, most of them had. Corey, the son of the house, who had been late, was still lingering, helping himself bountifully to cream that he poured over his sweet baked apple with an air that said he knew what a tasty treat he was preparing.

Anna, whose duty it was to gather the dishes and pass them out to Susan, the hired help, and who was always in a hurry, tried to hasten the laggard. "Come, Corey, you've had supper enough. If you haven't, you should have been here when the rest of us began. I'm going to clear off the table."

"All right," was the good-natured reply, "just leave the apples and cream. These apples are prime. I'm glad there's a big yield this year. Father?"

"Yes," said Mr. Elliott in an absentminded tone. He had the evening paper in his hand, and before sitting down to enjoy it at leisure, his eye had been caught by a paragraph that he stood still to read.

"Speaking of the harvest apples," said Corey, "makes me think of Jim and wonder who we're going to get to take his place. I stopped there coming home, and he won't be ready for work again this season, if he ever is."

"Is that so?" asked his father in a tone of deep concern. "I'm very sorry to hear it. Jim was a faithful fellow and did as well as he knew how, which you can't say about many. As to filling his place, I don't know. It's a bad time of year to be looking for extra help."

"We ought to have someone right away," said Corey, with his mouth full of apple and cream. Then came a knock at the side door, and the farmer, paper in hand, stepped forward to respond. A man's voice outside was heard asking something, and Mr. Elliott stepped out to him.

Anna, meantime, made rapid progress with the dishes, although she stopped from time to time to admire an illustration in the new magazine her sister, Helen, was examining. The summer dining room of the Elliotts was also their family sitting room, and Mrs. Elliott already had her sewing basket at her side, waiting to establish herself at her end of the table. Helen glanced up once from her book and said, "Don't hurry, Annie, the only rest Mother gets is while you're making the table ready."

"Annie is in too much haste for her finery to heed that hint," laughed the brother.

Then the door opened again, and their father returned. He went straight over to Mrs. Elliott and spoke in a half-apologetic tone. "Mother," he said, "there's an unusually decent-looking fellow out there, hunting for work. He didn't ask for supper, but I got out of him that he had had nothing since breakfast. You can manage something for him, can't you?"

"It's one of father's unusual tramps!" exclaimed Corey. "I knew it was. I saw it in his face." Both he and Anna laughed merrily, and the father's face relaxed into the semblance of a laugh as he waited for Mrs. Elliott to speak.

"Of course, Roger, if you say so. But you know you decided — "

"I know," he interrupted quickly, "but this man is — "

"This man is unusual," said Corey, taking the words from his father. "Don't you know that, Mother?"

Mrs. Elliott joined in the laugh. Every one of "Father's tramps" was unusual and must be made an exception to the stern rule that provided only a ticket to the Associated Charities Bureau in the city, two miles away. No matter how emphatically he declared that he had agreed with the board at their last meeting that it simply fostered vice to keep feeding tramps at one's door without inquiring into their condition; no matter how often he explained to Susan and his immediate family that it really must not be done at his house anymore; if Mr. Elliott answered the call of one of them, the man was surely fed and, if necessary, clothed and made as comfortable as circumstances allowed. The young Elliotts invariably laughed at this trait in their father and were always proud that it existed. Not one of them cared to turn deaf ears to the appeals of hunger.

Mr. Elliott turned back to his tramp, saying as he did so, "I will have him go around to the kitchen door. Give him some of that stew and a cup of coffee. He has had no dinner, remember."

Anna grumbled a little. "Dear me! Susan is in the milk room at work, and I shall have to go and feed him myself."

"Perhaps Corey will go out with you," suggested Mrs. Elliott a trifle anxiously.

Then Helen closed her magazine and arose. "I'll feed the tramp, Mother," she said. She did not care to have her pretty young sister, who was sometimes inclined to be reckless, gazed on by the bold eyes of a tramp. "Is he to have some of the ginger-cake and cheese?"

"Oh, yes," said Corey, answering for his mother. "And a napkin, Helen, and some of the choice grapes, and a finger bowl. Remember, he isn't one of the common kind."

Helen went away laughing and made ready a corner of the kitchen table for the stranger's use. She laughed again as she got out a small square of linen and laid it across the end for a tablecloth. It probably was folly, just as Corey thought, but she really had to make things neat and comfortable when a human being was to sit down before them. From the window she could see the tramp washing his face vigorously at the pump trough. He used the water as though it was a luxury, and he tossed back his abundant hair and bathed his head as well. Anna came out with a message from her mother and stood looking and laughing.

"He acts like a great Newfoundland dog who has been away from the water for a week!" she said and then added, "Helen, he has fine eyes. Just look at them. I don't wonder Father was taken with him."

"Run back, dear," said Helen, "and finish fixing the table for Mother. I know she's in a hurry to get to work, and you can hem that ruffle I was working on. Then I can baste it onto your skirt when I come in." She had no fancy for the child's lingering to study a pair of fine eyes.

However, they need not have been anxious. Mr. Elliott had no mind to leave his tramp to the care of either daughter. He saw Susan stepping briskly about the milk room and came himself to the kitchen with the tramp. By this time the table was neatly laid, and a generous portion of appetizing stew had been dealt out to him. The stranger gave the young woman in neat dress and with fair hair curling about her temples one quick glance. Then he gave himself to the business of eating as though he greatly needed the food.

"What is your name?" asked Mr. Elliott when the first pangs of hunger had evidently been appeased.

"John Stuart," was the quick reply.

"A good name. Are you a Scotchman?"

"My great-grandfather was."

"And a good, honest, hardworking man, I daresay. How came his grandson to be reduced to such straits?"

"Well, sir, you know the times are very hard. I've been looking for work as faithfully as a man could for the last two months and have found nothing but odd jobs here and there, enough to keep me alive."

"What can you do? What have you been brought up to do?"

The slow red mounted in the young man's face, reaching to his forehead. This question had been asked before but had never embarrassed him so much. Was it because the young woman was looking at him at that moment with earnest, interested eyes? On John Stuart King's study table at home was a small easel containing a fancy picture of a young woman with holy eyes and an expression that held a singular charm for him. The sketch was named "Truth," and its owner, studying it with his friend Fletcher, had once declared that the artist ought to have reached fame with that picture, for it was the very embodiment of truth.

"The embodiment of a fancy," his friend had replied. "You will never find such a face as that in real life."

Yet here was the face before him — at least, a striking likeness. In its presence the tramp felt that he could speak only truth. He answered presently in lowered tones.

"Nothing."

"That is frank at least," said Mr. Elliott with a little laugh. "I suspect you have at some time in your life run away from a respectable home. Is that it?"

"No, sir. My home is broken up. My father is dead, and Mother knows that I am out on a tramp."

"Poor mother!" It was Helen's voice, low and pitiful. She had hardly meant to speak the words aloud, but they breathed themselves out of her sympathy and reached his ear. Under the circumstances, the tramp should have felt nothing but amusement. The woman who was least in need of pity of almost any person of his acquaintance was his mother. Yet he gave the speaker a respectful glance of gratitude. He was grateful for the womanliness of it and for the effect it would have had upon him had he been in reality what he seemed. He suddenly decided to secure work at this house if possible or, if not, as near it as he could.

"How do you expect to get work if you're obliged to admit you don't know how to do anything?" was the farmer's next searching question, but he followed it with another: "Do you know anything about horses?"

John Stuart's eyes brightened. Here, at least, he could speak truth. Almost since his babyhood he had been around horses. He owned two, a well-matched pair, the envy of all his friends. He admired, yes, he loved almost any kind of horse, and his success in dealing with difficult ones had been a matter of surprised comment even when he was a boy.

"Yes, sir, I do," he said, his eyes kindling. "I know a good deal about them. I like them, and they like me. I can drive any kind of horse."

The supper, meantime, had been disappearing rapidly. Despite the figure of Truth that had stepped out of its frame and was looking at him with human eyes, the tramp was hungry. Nothing so thoroughly good in the way of food had fallen to his lot for many days, and he was making the most of the opportunity. Helen silently refilled his plate and replenished his cup. Then her father crossed to the dining room door, called his son and motioned him to stay in the kitchen while he went to hold a consultation. Helen followed him from the room.

"I've a mind to try him, Mother," Mr. Elliott said, going over to the table where his wife was sewing briskly. "We need help now, and we'll need it worse when Corey begins school again. He says he understands horses, and there's something about the fellow that makes me feel he's telling the truth. How does he impress you, Helen?"

"As a very hungry man," said Helen, smiling. But she added, "He hasn't a bad face, Father. I don't believe he is very wicked."

"But isn't it rather risky, Roger, a perfect stranger, and a tramp at that? You know the boy who drives the horses will have to take Helen back and forth, as well as Corey and Anna."

"Oh, of course I won't trust him in any such way until he has been thoroughly tested. He might drive the farm wagon, though, for a few days. I can tell in five minutes whether he really does know anything about horses. He's pretty tired. One can see that. I think we ought to give him some kind of shelter for the night, at least. And if he really wants work, I don't know how he's ever going to get it unless somebody trusts him. Will it be a great deal of trouble to get the woodhouse chamber ready?"

The thought of a tramp sleeping so nearby startled the farmer's younger daughter and her eyes darted up from the ruffles in her hands. "Oh, Father! You won't let a tramp sleep there, will you? He might set the house on fire and burn us all up!"

Her father laughed. "You must have been reading dime novels, Anna," he said pleasantly. "Tramps don't do that sort of thing much, outside of a certain class of books. I doubt if they ever do it when they're treated like human beings. If this fellow wants to get work, he will have every motive for behaving himself. And if he doesn't, it will be perfectly easy to slip away in the early morning without setting any fires. Do you object to his sleeping here, Sarah?"

"Oh, no," his wife answered quickly, "not if you think it's best. Susan can get the woodhouse chamber ready with very little trouble. If she doesn't get finished in time, Helen will look after it. Can't you, dear?"

"Yes'm," said Helen, with a quiet smile that she tried to hide from her giddy sister. These young people were often much amused with the deferential manner in which their father appealed to his wife, apparently leaving everything to her judgment, although they couldn't remember a time when she had not answered as now, "If you think it's best." "Your father thinks so" had been the law of life by which they had been brought up.

"When I get married," Anna once remarked, "I want to have a husband just like Father who will always say, 'What do you think, my dear?' "

Yet there had been times in Farmer Elliott's life, unknown to these children, when the quiet-faced, gentle-voiced woman had set herself like granite against some plan of his and had held firmly to "No, Roger, I don't think that would be right" until she had won him over. Invariably he had lived to thank her for having clear vision. There was no need, of course, for the mother to explain these things to her children.

Susan gave the woodhouse chamber the benefit of her strong red arms and executive ability, but before its new occupant was invited in, the daughter of the house visited the room. It was severely clean — that was a matter of course with Susan — and the bed was made up comfortably. But it was Helen who spread a white cloth over the small table, laid a plainly bound, coarse-print Bible on the cloth and fastened above it with pins a cheap print of a cheerful home scene.

Susan sneered at it all with the familiarity of hired help in the country. "Land sakes, Helen!" she said. "Them kind don't care for pictures. And as for the Bible, I don't s'pose he can read a word. If he can, he'd rather have a weekly story paper or some such."

"We can't be sure, Susan. I think he can read.

Most young fellows raised in this country learn to read and write in their childhood, you know. Perhaps his mother used to read the Bible to him. She may have sat in just such a chair as the mother does in that picture, and it may all speak to his heart. Who can tell?"

Susan sneered again. "I can," she said. "Them kind of things only happen in storybooks. Look how you fixed up for that Joe Wilkins, and what did he do but run away with the horsewhip and hatchet the first good chance he had? They're all the same. If I was your father I wouldn't have no such man around. But you'll get your reward for trying, you and him too, no doubt."

Susan's pronouns were mixed, but her heart knew whom to honor.

CHAPTER IV

"I Am Studying Truth"

he feelings of the "tramp" who finally took possession of that woodhouse chamber may be better imagined than described. Susan had remarked, as she took a final survey, that he "probably never saw anything so nice and comfortable in his life as that room." Susan's comments would have beggared imagination had she ever peeped into the bachelor apartments he usually occupied. The room contained a neat, old-fashioned, high-backed rocker, the cushion stuffed with sweet-smelling hay that could be renewed as often as there was to be a new occupant and a chintz cover that found its way to the washtub within an hour after the departure of the one who last sat on it.

Into this chair John Stuart dropped himself and looked about him with a curiosity in which there was more than a touch of tenderness. He had been a tramp long enough to appreciate the cleanliness, coolness and pleasant odors of this room. When he had occupied the "Sleepy Hollow chair" near the south window of his city home and planned this extraordinary outing, it had been early July. Certain business matters had held him in town through June, and it had been his intention to start vacation that next week; so he had started. Now the first days of September were upon them, and by ordinary calculations his vacation should be over.

But he told himself complacently that it had just commenced, although the experiences through which he had passed were enough to fill a volume. He had seen and studied all sorts and conditions of men. He had been hungry and had had nothing with which to satisfy hunger. He had been weary, with no resting place in sight. For the first time in his life, he had known what it was to suffer the lack of these common necessities. Some work he had found, though the fact that he had not been brought up to do any of it always told against him and made it apparently impossible for him to continue in the same place more than a day or two. In truth, this part of the experience had not troubled him, for he had found no place where he felt willing to tarry. Each day as he tramped on, he rejoiced in the thought that his plan did not include long stays anywhere. But this evening he felt differently. He was more than willing to stay at the Elliott farm.

He looked at himself with satisfied eyes. One of the hardest features of his self-imposed exile had been the difficulty of procuring a bath. He had prepared for himself a change of clothing that he had tied in a bundle and slung on a stick, as he had noticed that veritable tramps sometimes did. He assured himself that a self-respecting tramp, such

as he meant to be, could do no less than that. But
the difficulty of getting his clothing washed, properly dried and, above all, mended became simply
appalling as the weeks passed. More than once,
this difficulty had threatened the entire abandon-
ment of the scheme. But for a certain dogged perse-
verance peculiar to his nature, he would have
given up long before. Perhaps he would have done
so in any case had he not had days of exceeding
interest, during which he felt he learned more
about that strange, troublesome "other half" than
any amount of reading or any number of statistics
could possibly give him.

On this evening, for the first time since his new
life began, he had been offered the use of a bath.
"There's a place in the stable," Farmer Elliott had
said, "where you can wash up and be all fresh and
clean before you go to your room. My folks are
particular about that room. They keep it as clean as
they do the parlor, and they don't want anything
ugly brought into it. Have you got clean clothes in
your bundle? All right, then. I like that. When a
fellow wants to be clean and takes a little trouble to
be so, it shows he hasn't lost his self-respect.
There's a bundle of clothes in the stable closet. We
keep them there for times of need. If you need anything while your clothes are being mended, help
yourself. You are welcome to anything you find
there. I shall give you work enough to earn them
for yourself if you choose to do it."

John Stuart, as he listened, had felt his heart
glow with a feeling deeper than gratitude. Here at
last was a chance for a tramp to become a man. It
was the first genuine effort at helpfulness that he
had met. No, perhaps that wasn't quite fair. It was
the first common-sense effort. Others had tried.

Tracts had been given him, and advice, but not water and soap and towels. These he had found in abundance in the stable closet, along with certain garments of which he stood much in need.

He had been dismayed to discover that clothes wear out. He supposed he had had theories on that subject before, but to have theories and to realize them are two very different things. He sat in the sweet-scented chair and surveyed himself with satisfaction. He looked and felt better. Dr. Talbert had been right; tramps were horrid fellows. He wondered that anybody could endure them, but the treatment they received at the hands of the Christian public was calculated to drop them still lower on the social scale. There was an occasional Farmer Elliott, however, and he thanked God for him.

John Stuart looked over at the white-covered table. Susan was wrong; he appreciated it. Perhaps no table had ever looked to him more pure than that. Some of the places in which he had slept since July he did not think he was willing to describe even on paper. Tired as he was, he exerted himself and went over to the table to study the print pinned above it. The smile on his face would have made Anna declare him positively handsome.

Then he lifted the large, coarse-print Bible and took it back with him to the chair. The root of the difference between this Christian home and certain other homes he knew of was undoubtedly sunk deep in this old-fashioned book. He had not been reading in the Bible of late. It had not been remembered as part of the necessary furnishing of that bundle, and he had not come close enough to one to read. He was accustomed, not to daily Bible reading, but to more or less regular reference to the book. Was he not a church member? He was not sure that two months of his grown-up life had ever before passed without his having had recourse to its teachings.

He turned the leaves at random, as was his habit. He didn't have any fixed method of Bible study. The book had seemed to open of itself to Ezekiel. He was not familiar with that part of the Bible. Its imagery had always seemed too dense for easy understanding, and the time had never seemed to come when he could study it. But he paused this evening over a sentence: "And the word of the Lord came unto me again." He smiled over the fanciful appropriateness of the phrase. Probably Ezekiel had not been so long without that word as he had. What message had it for him? "Saying, Son of man, set thy face toward Jerusalem."

He read not a word further. He was not a romantic young man, nor one given in the least to whimsical interpretations of any writings, yet he felt slightly startled. It was not altogether impossible, of course, that the Lord had him in mind that evening and meant him to get His word from the book. Was it intended as a hint to him that while he had been busy studying human nature in new forms, with a view to writing a book that should have in it at least some startling facts, he had all but forgotten Jerusalem? Not that he had been distinctly irreligious. He had rarely laid himself down to sleep at night, even with the most inconvenient and incongruous surroundings, without going through the form of prayer. But more than once, he had been conscious of its being a mere form and had excused himself on the ground that a man in his strange circumstances could be pardoned for wandering thoughts.

That sermon preached by Dr. Talbert on that first Sunday in July had been the last he had heard. Not that he had not on each succeeding Sunday been within sound of the church bell, but the truth was that he could not bring himself to appear in church in the costume he was wearing. He told himself that he would attract too much attention and detract from the comfort of others by his presence. Moreover, as he thought of it this evening, he realized that the woods and the fields, the sermons he found in stones, and the music of birds and brooks had been more to his mind than he could imagine the services of the homely little churches being. So, without much consideration of the subject, he had simply stayed away and enjoyed it.

"Son of man, set thy face toward Jerusalem." Was it a message for him? Had he drifted away not only from the church, but also from — "Nonsense!" he said, pulling himself up sharply. "You're growing altogether too imaginative. That would do for an interpretation of some of those sour theologians of the past century, but not for me!" He closed the book and replaced it on its white table. He was too weary for Bible reading that night, he decided. But he got down on his knees and tried to hold his thoughts to something like real prayer.

And inside the farmhouse across the yard, Helen was on her knees in her room, asking at that moment that the stranger within her father's gates might not go from them without having had in some way a reminder of the bread of life waiting for his hand to lay hold of. She had placed the plain, large-print Bible in his room with a purpose, and she did not forget to ask that it might have a message for him.

Neither did Farmer Elliott forget the stranger who slept that night in his woodhouse chamber. Had the tramp heard himself prayed for when they knelt around the family altar, his heart would have warmed as it had not for many a day. The son of the house was impressed by the fervor of the prayer.

"That fellow out there won't fire the house tonight, Annie. You needn't be afraid," Corey said to his younger sister. "He can't after that prayer. He'd have to be good in spite of himself if he had heard Father pray."

"Why?" asked Anna brusquely, trying to cover up the feelings that prayer had awakened in her. "You've had Father's prayers all your life, and they don't seem to have had that effect on you."

"It's different with you and me," said Corey, laughing. "We are not lost sheep, wandering about on the bleak mountains. We're supposed to be safely tucked up inside the fold, you see." And he went away whistling sharply the tune of

Away on the mountains wild and bare,
Away from the tender Shepherd's care.

It did seem strange, and at times very sad, that with such a father and mother, and such an elder sister, Anna and Corey Elliott had never learned how to pray for themselves.

The next morning, Farmer Elliott said to his family, after watching John work a while, "He takes hold of the horses as though he had been brought up with them. Blixen took to him at once like a friend. I never saw a stranger that could do much with Blixen before. He must be a kind-hearted fellow, at least. She held her nose still, let him pat it

and turned her head to look after him. Jet likes
him, too. I told him Jet was inclined to be surly
with strangers. He laughed and said he never saw
a dog yet who didn't like him. And sure enough,
Jet walked right up and let him pat her."

"Father has set out to make his tramp one of the
perfect kind, you see," interposed Corey, "so correct in his life that even the horses and the dog
recognize it. Confess, Father, that you think of
keeping him all winter and trusting him to go to
the bank and everywhere."

Mr. Elliott looked over at his son and laughed, a
good-natured, companionable laugh. The family
relations of this household were perhaps peculiar.
Neither son nor daughters seemed to have the
slightest hesitation about making merry over the
little peculiarities of both father and mother. The
parents seemed always ready to meet them halfway, joining in the laugh at their own expense. Yet
it would have been hard to find a family where
genuine respect for both the father's and the
mother's opinions was more marked. Perhaps the
very fact that the parents were not too dignified to
laugh at their own weaknesses increased their
power over their children, who were keen to ob-
serve not only weaknesses, but also sterling worth.

"We must have someone to take your place,
Corey, when you go back to school." Mr. Elliott
said. "Why not John?"

"The idea!" said Anna, with her pretty nose in
an expressive curl. They all laughed.

Yet as the days passed, it became evident that
every member of the family liked John and that the
farmer increasingly trusted him. Certainly no
hired man had ever before given such entire satisfaction so far as the horses were concerned, and

Farmer Elliott confessed that went a great way with him. When they discussed the young man in the family circle, every member of the family had a word to say in his favor. Mrs. Elliott remarked that he seemed to have an excellent memory, that he had not forgotten a single commission that had been given him, though some of them were small and troublesome. Helen said it was a comfort to have a man who brought the horses to the door at the exact moment and was always on hand to receive them when one reached home. And Anna said he was the only man they ever had who knew enough to say "Miss Anna." The family laughed at this, but Anna stoutly affirmed that that was the way they always did in books, and she liked it. She thought it would be very much nicer if Susan were directed to say "Miss Anna," instead of shouting out "Annie" as she actually sometimes did.

"My dear," said Mrs. Elliott, laughing, "remember that Susan is a farmer's daughter like you, and she only comes here to accommodate us. I presume she would be willing to say 'Miss Anna' if you would agree to say 'Miss Susan,' but certainly not otherwise."

"Then," said Anna, "I wish we had a tramp for a girl in the kitchen, and I hope Father will keep John always."

Even Susan contributed to the general verdict in his favor. Having discovered, as she passed back and forth, that he was the subject of conversation, she said, "He's more particular to clean his feet when he comes into the kitchen than any fellow we ever had about. I'll say that for him. I wish Corey was as particular."

From all of this you can see that John Stuart was trying to do his best. Just what his motive was in lingering at their farm, setting himself studiously to learn a daily routine of work that could not be other than distasteful to him, he might have found it difficult to explain to the satisfaction of his friends, or even of himself. He could hardly insist he was studying human nature, for the sphere seemed too narrow. Yet every day he admitted to himself that he was more and more interested in the sphere of humanity now spread before him.

"I am studying Truth," he said aloud with an amused smile when he was alone in his room, and the form his meaning took justifies the capital letter. "I believe I have found Truth in Helen. The likeness to the ideal head increases rather than lessens as I see more of her. I believe she is the living embodiment of the idea — Truth in its purity and simplicity.

"Such a life ought to be a power in the world. I wonder if it is? Yet how can it be in such a circumscribed circle? Is she superior to her environment? I would like for her to be the heroine of my next book. Rather, perhaps, I would like my conception of her. What could I make her accomplish, I wonder, that would tell for good? How much I should like to see the girl herself set where she could reach people! I wonder if she is satisfied with her present sphere? I wonder if she realizes she has a sphere, or ought to have? How is one ever to learn?

"I profess to be studying her, yet an hour of conversation with her in the cozy dining room, I properly introduced, would tell me more about her than weeks of this sort of life. Or would it? I know hundreds of young women in that way, though not one who looks like her, I grant. But the home life ought to tell in some directions, circumscribed though it is. Let me wait and see."

CHAPTER V

Truth Under Difficulties

ohn Stuart was in the farmhouse kitchen at work on a door that wanted neither to open nor shut in a reasonable manner. Susan had called him peremptorily to the task as a matter of course. It was considered the duty of the hired man to be able to "fix things."

Fortunately for John, playing with tools had been one of the decided tastes of his boyhood, and he handled hammer, screwdriver and saw in a way to command the respect of even Susan, who was critical and could wield all those implements herself. Others were in the kitchen also. It was Saturday, and Anna had a task that she hated, namely, the washing of the breakfast dishes, while Susan did more important work elsewhere. Mrs. Elliott was giving personal attention to the bread, and Helen was hovering between kitchen and pantry intent upon a mixture that required eggs and flour and sugar and — the observant John could not decide what else. There was also a caller, a young girl from a neighboring farm, who, with the pleasant unconventionality that belongs to the country, had been allowed to come to the kitchen to chat with them all.

Her errand was with Helen. "I am so sorry!" she was saying when John began to give attention. "Can't you possibly go, Helen? It will be such fun for us all to be together in that house. What engagement can you have that cannot be postponed?"

The freedom of country life has also its annoying side. Perhaps in no other place are distinctly personal questions so urged upon one. Helen's face flushed a little over this one, and she hesitated, making a journey to the pantry before she replied. "I have no engagement, Winnie. I simply do not think it's best for me to go."

"How perfectly horrid!" exclaimed the young lady. "Do you really mean you don't want to go? I thought you would be the very one to help us carry it to perfection. Nannie Marvin is going — do you know that? And Rex Hartwell — that last doesn't need saying, I suppose, after I have mentioned Nannie. Oh, Helen, don't be horrid. Why won't you join us? Oh, I just believe I know why you won't; you don't like the games they play at those gatherings. There! That's it, I know, for you blush like a peony. Now I must say I think that's being too particular, don't you, Mrs. Elliott? If Nannie Marvin and Rex Hartwell can tolerate them, I think the rest of us might. You don't have to play unless you choose to do so. Please say you'll go, Helen. It will just spoil things if people won't join in heartily."

Helen found her voice at last. "I am sorry to 'spoil things,' " she said with an attempt at play-

fulness, "and since I am only one, I don't look for
any such disastrous result."

"But why won't you go? You haven't told me
yet. Is it because Rob Sterritt is to be there?"

"Certainly not," said Helen with dignity. "You
said you had guessed a reason. Why aren't you
satisfied with it? I believe it's well known that I
don't enjoy those games the young people are so
fond of playing, and I don't care to go where I am
sure to be urged to join in what I don't like, and
argued with, and pressed for reasons. I have no
desire to force my views upon others, and so, to be
entirely frank, I have determined to stay at home."

"Dear me, how foolish! Isn't she, Mrs. Elliott?
You will have to turn nun, I'm afraid — you're
growing so particular. What's the trouble with
those poor little games, anyway? I'm sure our
grandmothers must have played some of them.
They're better than dancing, I suppose. At least
people of your sort always think so, though I confess that I could never see the least harm in dancing."

If Helen Elliott did, she was apparently resolved
to keep her views to herself, much to the regret of
the man who was mending the door.

"Did you ever hear me say that I considered the
games better than dancing?" she said at last, still
making a noticeable effort to speak lightly. "But I
didn't mean to force you into a discussion. People
have to agree to differ, you know. Does Jamie go
back to college next week?"

"Yes, of course. Life is an utter failure to people
who are not in college. Anna may come on Tuesday
anyway, may she not? Aunt Amelia sent a special
invitation for her, and Kate will be awfully disappointed if she doesn't come. Kate is to have a

dozen or so of her young friends for her special benefit. You won't keep Anna from joining them, I hope?"

The eyes of the dishwasher flashed their keen interest in the reply, and Helen looked with a troubled air at her mother, who, intent on her bread, said nothing. Helen was forced to speak. "You must appeal to Mother in such matters, Winnie. I do not pretend to manage my sister."

"Ah, but everyone knows you do. Everything goes in this house just as Helen Elliott wants it to, doesn't it, Anna? Mrs. Elliott, Anna may come to the annual meeting, may she not? We want her particularly. There's to be special fun for the younger ones."

"Anna does not generally go out evenings without her sister," Mrs. Elliott said gently. "Her father does not think it best for her."

"There!" said the caller triumphantly, "I told you it would be just as you said, Helen. I think you are horrid, and I shall tell the others so."

She arose as she spoke and to Helen's obvious relief very soon took her departure. This, however, was the signal for an outburst from Anna. She hardly waited for the doors to close after their caller before she began. "I don't see, Helen, how you can bear to talk that way before Winnie! You know she'll go out and spread all over town everything you said, and a good deal you *didn't* say. What's the use of telling such people all you think? Why couldn't you just say you couldn't go to the meeting and were sorry and let that end it?"

"Because, Anna, I could go if I chose, and I am not sorry not to go. How could I have made statements that weren't true?"

The girl gave an impatient fling to her drying

cloth as she said, "I think you have run wild about truth. Everybody says such things, and everybody understands them. For my part, I think it's only common courtesy to say you're sorry when you can't do a thing that people want you to very much."

"So do I, dear, but in this case there was no previous engagement or any matter of that sort to plead. It was simply a decision on my part not to go. As for the reasons, she forced them from me by her persistent questions."

Anna was not to be convinced. "You could have said you were going to have company on Tuesday. Then you could have sent for Hattie and Rick to come and spend the day. It's easy enough to get out of things politely if one cares to be polite."

"Anna, do you really think that would have been getting out of things truthfully?"

"Yes, I do. It would have been true enough. An engagement you plan in your own mind is just as much an engagement as though you had already carried it out. Hattie and Rick are glad enough to come whenever they're sent for. Everybody does such things. Over at the Marvins the other day, Nannie saw the Wilson boys driving in and knew they were coming to call. She ran up to the meadow where her father was at work and told Nell to say she was not at home. I suppose you wouldn't have done it to save the entire farm, but it was true enough. Nannie's home isn't in the meadow lot."

"I am sorry," said Helen gravely, "that that is Nannie's idea of truth."

"It's everybody's idea but yours," persisted the agitated girl. "I wouldn't be tied up to such notions as you have for the world. It is perfect slavery. And you don't always speak the truth, either, for all your worship of it. You said you didn't pretend to manage me, but it would have been a good deal nearer true if you had admitted that you manage me all the time as if I were a baby. And I must say I don't like it."

"Anna!" said Mrs. Elliott in warning tones.

But the girl, whose eyes were now flashing indignation, set down the glass pitcher she was drying with a thud and said, "Well, Mother, I can't help it. It is just as I say. Father would let me go on Tuesday night if Helen wouldn't interfere. All the girls my age are going. Kate has invited them while the club is having their reports and things. She has a secret that is going to be told that night. There is to be no end of fun, and everybody in it but me. I think it is too horrid mean! I don't see how Helen can bear to put her notions in the way of my fun all the time. If that's the way religion works, I'm sure I hope I shall never have any."

"John," said Mrs. Elliott suddenly, "will you get a stick of wood for the sitting room fire, one of those large hickory chunks that are at the farther end of the woodhouse?"

And John, much to his regret, had to leave his unfinished door and do her bidding. Of course he knew why a chunk of wood was required just at that moment. As he selected it, he reflected that Helen Elliott evidently had a sphere and that it was a hard one to manage. It interested him to think that this encounter had been largely in the interest of truth. Helen would do still to compare with his ideal picture. Perhaps the artist who sketched it had understood what he was about, having studied to see what outlines a careful adherence to the soul of Truth would carve on the human face. Yet, as he chose an unusually fine log of wood, he confessed that he was in sympathy with both sisters.

He resolved to study the club meeting and learn why it was such an objectionable place. He could fancy surroundings that would in no wise be in keeping with the tastes of that singularly pure-faced girl, but why shouldn't the merry-eyed younger one be allowed to indulge the tastes that belonged to her unformed and rollicking years? Was Helen a bit prudish about it all, desiring to make a staid young woman, like herself, of a girl who could not be more than sixteen and had eyes that danced with prospective fun, even at their quietest?

It was growing very interesting. He had theories, this young man, with regard to this very subject. On what subject did he not have theories? He believed that young people in their unformed, kittenish years were often injured by being held too closely to occupations and interests that befitted only their elders. He would like to talk with Helen on this subject. He believed he could convince her quickly that — and then he pulled himself up suddenly and sharply.

Who was he that he should talk over education theories with Helen Elliott or anybody else? How certainly people would stare if they heard him attempt it. He had deliberately put himself outside the pale of all such efforts. What could he do in his present position for the betterment of the world?

But that was nonsense. Did he mean to hint by such reasoning that the laboring man had no opportunity in his sphere for benefitting others? On the contrary, he had believed, and he was sure the position was correct, that nothing was more needed in the laboring world than men who were examples to their fellows in all departments of moral life. "If we could persuade a few, even a very few, of our laboring men to be true to their higher instincts, to be clean and strong in every fiber of their being, we would see what a leaven would thereby be placed in that grade of life. We would recognize it very soon as the power that makes for righteousness."

That was the substance of a thought he had expressed somewhat elaborately in a careful paper presented before the Citizens' League in a certain town in his own state. He had believed in it thoroughly and had urged it as an argument in favor of hand-to-hand effort among the working classes. He believed in it still, but the trouble with him was that he was not a laboring man. He did not honestly belong to the sphere in which he had placed himself. Did the motive relieve the position from the shadow of falseness that rested upon it? He thought of Nannie, whoever she was, running to the meadow in order that it might be said she was not at home. Did his ideas of truth lie parallel with hers instead of with the ideal head that he had yet insisted was real?

He put all those thoughts away presently and gave himself to the business at hand. It would not do for him to be too particular about truth, not just now. He must rather take Anna for his model. Poor, little, bright-eyed girl! Was it reasonable to suppose that a frolic in which apparently the best people were engaged was an objectionable place for her?

The kitchen had changed considerably during his temporary absence. The dishwasher had vanished, as had all traces of that work. The bread-maker was tucking the last loaf of bread carefully away under blankets, and Helen was receiving at the side door a bright-faced maiden whom she called Nannie.

"I am receiving calls in the kitchen," she was saying cheerfully. "I intend to hover about my cake until it's baked. Susan has a talent for burning cakes, so come right in here. Oh, John, I can't have that great stick put in now. The oven is just right for baking. I will have my cake out in a very little while, and then you can build up the fire. Sit down, Nannie. What a pretty hat you have! It's very becoming."

"Now don't begin on my new hat and turn my head with compliments," laughed the caller. "You know very well I have come to scold you. I met Winnie Houston down by the lower gate. Not that I hadn't planned my campaign before I saw her. I had a sort of instinct how it would be, and I'm come to talk you into reason. Haven't you ever heard, my dear, that when people are in Rome they must do a little as the Romans do? We really mustn't hold ourselves aloof from these good people because we've had a few more advantages than they. Even Rex agrees to that, and he knows nothing about the country. He has never even spent six consecutive months of his life in it."

"Now, Nannie! Promise to confine yourself to common sense, won't you? The idea of my holding myself aloof from my neighbors! You know I don't. You mean to talk about the club meeting, I suppose. You will waste your breath. I told you two months ago I had attended that club for the last time, and I have seen nothing since to lead me to change my mind."

"Oh, I don't blame you for not wanting to attend

all the gatherings, but this is the annual meeting, you know. Winnie's aunt has opened her house, which is unusual, remember. I think you might want to go this time, just to see that old house at its best. They will be very much disappointed, and I am afraid offended, if you don't honor them."

John had not for the last fifteen or twenty minutes tried to work rapidly, but despite his slowness the door was done, and there was no pretext for lingering longer. He went away with reluctance. He had heard enough about this Nannie to want to study her. Besides, he was growing deeply interested in this prospective club gathering. Certainly he ought to be present. Evidently it would afford unusual opportunities for studying the social conditions of life in this region. But how impossible it would probably be to bring such an event about!

CHAPTER VI

VARNISH

n fact, the opportunity John sought was in process of preparation. He discovered early in his career as a hired man that schools formed an important part of the family life to which he now belonged.

Corey Elliott was a sophomore in a small college about thirty miles from his home. He had to be driven to the station two miles distant on Monday mornings and brought from it on Friday evenings. Anna was in the high school in the village and must be taken each morning in time for the nine o'clock bell, while Helen had nearly two miles to go in the opposite direction.

It made what Farmer Elliott called "lively work" of a winter morning. However it might be in winter, it was certainly pleasant enough work during the closing days of September. John Stuart found himself looking forward to the time when he might be trusted to take these drives.

It had given the hired man almost a shock to

discover that Truth, having stepped out of her frame, actually taught a country district school! Having decided, however, that this was part of her "sphere," he began to have a consuming desire to see her in it. He smiled sometimes to think how safely he could have conveyed her to her work in the neat little pony phaeton that was kept for her use. Occasionally he smiled almost cynically to think how readily he would probably be trusted to drive her there if he were in gentleman's attire and going about the work of a gentleman. In this, however, he did not do Farmer Elliott justice.

Mr. Elliott would not have entrusted his daughters to the care of strangers, no matter how well dressed they might have been. On Monday mornings, when Corey Elliott was at hand, the hired man was allowed to drive the double-seated carriage to the high school and the station. On Friday afternoons, he performed the same duty. Other than that, the father himself drove into town, while Mrs. Elliott sometimes, and Susan, drove the pony phaeton out to the little, white schoolhouse.

But on the Monday afternoon preceding the club meeting, a difficulty arose. Anna must be brought from school, a man was coming to see Mr. Elliott on important business, and neither Mrs. Elliott nor Susan drove the span of fine horses. John, passing in and out, intent on many duties, knew that an anxious consultation was in progress between husband and wife. He caught snatches of the talk.

"I have great confidence in him," the farmer said, whereat John wondered if he fully deserved the confidence. "He does his work with a painstaking care that shows him to be thoroughly conscientious."

Then his wife suggested, "Susan might go along

and do some errands, but that would seem sort of absurd." Her face brightened as she added, "Why, Roger, Laura Holcombe is coming out with Anna tonight to visit at the Houstons'. Winnie spoke to her about it yesterday. It will be all right for John to drive them out."

So John let the horses walk leisurely up the long hill while the two girls, quite willing to have the drive prolonged indefinitely, chattered in the back seat, growing so interested in their theme that they talked louder than they knew.

"It is a perfect shame you can't go tomorrow night! Everybody says it will be the nicest entertainment we shall have this winter. I would go if I were you! I tell you what it is, Anna Elliott. Everybody says it's odd that you allow Helen to manage you as you do. She couldn't do more if she were your mother. Why don't you insist upon going?"

"It isn't Helen!" said Anna with a touch of indignation in her voice. "Father said I couldn't go."

"Oh, your father! Just as though everybody didn't know it was Helen behind your father! He would let you go fast enough if it wasn't for her. People say you're a perfect slave to Helen."

"I should be obliged to people if they would mind their own business!" came the haughty answer. "It isn't any such thing."

"Then if I were you I would prove it. Why don't you plan to go anyway? Come in and spend the night with me. You've been promising to come this long time. Then we can go over to Mrs. Pierce's together and come back again when we get ready, and Miss Helen need be none the wiser. Do come, Anna. There's going to be such fun! Kate Pierce says it's the only entertainment she expects to give this winter, and she means to make the most of it.

There will be a whole lot of college boys there, too. Corey isn't one of them, so you needn't be afraid of meeting him. He was invited, but he said he had another engagement. Will you do it, Anna? I can plan it beautifully if you will."

The driver could not see the young girl's face, though he leaned over at that moment, ostensibly to take note of the action of the hind wheel, and tried to. Her face was turned from him, but her voice quivered with eagerness as she said, "Oh, dear me! I'd like to. Nobody knows how I want to go. But I suppose it's out of the question."

"Well, now, why is it? It isn't as though it was a disreputable place. Why, Anna Elliott, all the young people from the country around are to be there. It isn't simply that silly club, and why you shouldn't be in the fun as well as the rest of us is more than I can understand.

"Don't you see it's just some notion of Helen's that keeps you at home?" Laura conjectured. "Your father and mother wouldn't think of such a thing if it hadn't been for her. She doesn't like some of the games that the silly ones gather in a room by themselves and play, so she won't have anything to do with any of it! I call that silly, don't you? So what if she doesn't like the games? She isn't obliged to play them.

"I know what's the matter with her," she suddenly concluded. "Rob Sterritt caught her in a game of forfeits one night and tried to kiss her. It was all in the game, you know, but Helen has been mad about it ever since. Winnie says so. I know your sister is as good as gold, but don't you think she has a few real old-maidish notions? What hurt would it do for Rob Sterritt to kiss her just in fun? He worships the ground she walks on."

The spirited horses at that moment gave such a sudden start that even the preoccupied Anna turned her head to see what was the matter. The truth was that the driver had flourished his whip without knowing it. His eyes were flashing indignation over the thought that such a woman as Truth, even though out of her frame, should be subjected to the humiliation of a kiss from Rob Sterritt — whoever he was — in the name of fun. What a surprising country this must be into which he had dropped!

His desire to be present at the meeting of the club was growing stronger every moment. Before they reached the farmhouse, he decided he must be there, if for nothing else but to protect Anna from the Rob Sterritts who might be present; for to his indignation and shame, the young girl had been persuaded at last to help plan a system of deception so she could attend.

He couldn't hear all the talk, but he gathered from Anna's voice, and sometimes from her words, that she was not easy to persuade and that more than once she was on the point of abandoning the idea. Once she exclaimed indignantly, "I can't do it, Laura. You know I don't tell wholesale falsehoods."

"Falsehoods!" repeated the other. "Who wants you to? I'm sure I don't, either, and I don't think you're very polite to hint at such a thing. I would like to know what there is false about it! I invite you to go over to Kate's with me for a little while. I can't stay late. Father says I must be home before twelve o'clock, so we'll come back together, and you'll be doing exactly what you said — spending the night with me. And if they ask you at home if I'm not going to the club, you can say no, because

I'm not going *regularly*, not like the others. Mother doesn't want me to stay until late, because I have been sick, you know, and she's afraid I will get too tired. I'm to come away early, so it's not like really going. I never saw anything better planned for you, Anna Elliott! Even if your sister finds it out, she can't complain of such an innocent little thing as that."

And the sister of Truth was really deceived by such a film of truth as that thrown over a network of falsehood! The man on the front seat marveled much, and he was every moment more sure that he must in some way be one of the revelers. He also speculated. Had the elder sister been wise? Was she not, perhaps, straining at a gnat? Would it not have been better to accompany this lively young sister to the place of amusement and so be at hand to shield her from anything not desirable, rather than by her fastidiousness to drive the girl to such straits as these?

Then another line of thought came to him: Was there anything he could do? No, there was not. As John Stuart King, even with so slight an acquaintance with the family as two weeks would allow, he could imagine himself saying, "Have a care, Miss Elliott, for that young sister of yours. I have reason to think a plan is forming of which you would not approve," or some words to that effect that might put her on her guard. But he was learning to understand his present position well enough to realize that such a course now would probably be looked upon as an insult.

In the farmyard waiting to see him was a young man from the neighboring farm who was also a member of the committee of arrangements for the famous club meeting. He speedily made known his

errand. Could John Stuart come to look after everyone's horses during the meeting? Mr. Elliott had
agreed to spare him, if John was willing, and they
would give him as good a supper as the club had,
and fifty cents besides. He could even look on and
see the games, and the fun generally, as much as he
wanted to when the horses were all cared for.

Never was a job more promptly accepted. It was,
of course, extremely probable that Anna's plans
would in this way be suddenly overturned. The
hired man reflected that if she wished to keep her
evening's program a profound secret from her
family, she would hardly risk being seen by him.
But in this case, part of his object in going would be
attained. If he could shield the girl this way, it
might be the best he could do for her. But it turned
out that Anna heard nothing about his engagement. It was not, of course, a matter of interest in
the family circle, so no one mentioned it. And
Anna, being engrossed with her own affairs, forgot
to question what those boys from the Brooks
neighborhood wanted of John.

The next morning found Anna up unusually
early, making skillful and silent preparation for her
evening's sport. It was no easy matter to stuff all
the things she needed for the evening into her
small handbag. Several times she gave up in despair and declared to herself that it was not possible. Moreover, she was continually being made
nervous by sisterly offers from Helen to pack her
bag for her. Thus far her way had been made unusually easy. The invitation to spend the night
with Laura Holcombe had been so frequently renewed in the past as to occasion no surprise when
it came again. The Elliotts, being careful parents,
had not encouraged the fashion of the neighbor-

hood to exchange homes for a night, so that Anna's outings of this sort were limited. But the Elliotts knew that Laura Holcombe had been ill and so forbidden the night air for several weeks. They therefore judged that she had begged for Anna's company as a consolation in her disappointment at not being able to attend the club party. Mrs. Elliott's only remark had been, "Laura is obliged to content herself with you instead of the party, is she?" Anna had muttered some unintelligible reply and congratulated herself on not being obliged to "even *look* any fibs."

In truth, the Elliotts were really glad that the invitation had come at this time for their young daughter. They proved the completeness of their trust in her by not even thinking of the club party in this connection, although the Holcombes lived nearly across the street from the house that had been thrown open for the party.

Only John looked on with intelligent eyes at the unusual nervousness of the young girl and wondered sagely how many other embarrassing scenes she had been obliged to live through, and whether she had succeeded in escaping the falsehoods she had indignantly repudiated.

"Why, child!" Mrs. Elliott had exclaimed. "Must you carry so large a package as that? What can you be taking?"

"Oh, Mother, it's some books I've been promising to let Laura borrow."

"Books! It doesn't look like a parcel of books. Why did you tie them so carefully? They would have been less burdensome just laid on the seat, and John could have left them for you at the door this morning."

Anna had hesitated, and John, who was waiting

for her, saw the flush on her excited face as she said, after a moment's thought, "To tell you the truth, Mother, I have put my other dress into the package. I suppose you'll think it silly, but I thought I should like to dress up a little after school."

If the mother thought it silly, she didn't make any remark. Anna kissed her three times "for to-night and tomorrow morning" and went away happy in the thought that she had told the truth. She had held a little struggle with herself about the package, having been tempted to hint at fancy work or something of the sort, and she congratulated herself heartily on having escaped the temptation. I won't tell a downright falsehood, she assured herself, even if the whole plan falls through.

Yet she knew perfectly that her mother believed, and that she meant her to believe, that the package contained the handsome brown suit known as her church dress and would have been dismayed had she known that it contained, instead, the lovely pale-blue dress garnished with white lace that did duty on rare special occasions! Only the hired man's face looked grave. He understood the world and the dress of young people too well not to surmise the truth. It pained him more than seemed reasonable even to himself to see how easily the sister of Truth could satisfy herself with its mere varnish.

CHAPTER VII

LOOKING ON

ohn Stuart King, familiar as he was with the world and with what he had been pleased to call "society," made several discoveries at the annual gathering of the Bennettville Club. He had not supposed that such conditions existed as he found there. In his position as an onlooker there was abundant chance for the sort of study he desired, and he made good use of it. The gathering was large and, he could only think, representative. From the country homes for miles around had come the young people — boys and girls, many of them being by no means old enough to be called ladies and gentlemen, even had their manners justified the terms.

Two distinct classes of people were present: the intelligent, refined and reasonably cultured, and the "smart," handsome, slightly reckless young people whose advantages in the way of culture had been limited. Almost none present did not know to a certain extent how to dress. That is, they

had given thought and care and some knowledge
to the study of making themselves look pretty, and
to a degree they had succeeded. Some of the material was flimsy enough and, to the onlooker's
skilled eye, lacked details he was in the habit of
seeing. But the general effect as a rule was striking.
Bright colors were in the ascendant, of course, but
the wearers had some idea of harmony, and the
blondes and brunettes had instinctively chosen
their colors. On the whole, it was not with the style
of dress that the critic could find most fault.

When it came to the question of manner, there
were startling innovations upon accepted ideas.
The man who had been hired for fifty cents to take
care of the horses, and allowed between times to
look on, felt his pulse beating high with indignation long before the evening was over. It was the
position of the better of the two distinct classes that
excited his wrath. Some of these evidently moved
among the guests with an air of amused tolerance.
He readily selected the young woman Nannie and
her friend Rex from the others. They were apparently amused at many of the scenes. He overheard
snatches of talk when some of the guests would
meet at the end of a game that ought instead to
have been called a romp.

"I must say I don't wonder that Anna Elliott
wanted to escape this!" one gentleman said, half
laughing, yet shaking his head. "Some of the boys
are almost rough."

"Yes, but they mean only fun," another contended. "What's the use in trying to be so superior?
It's their annual frolic and a time-honored institution. I don't think they are ever quite so wild on
other evenings. Anna didn't escape it, you see —
or rather she did escape, I presume, and is here in

all her glory. How pretty the charmer looks tonight! Did you see her when Rob Sterritt tried to
kiss her? I'm surprised Rob would try his skill in
that family again. But Anna was too much for him.
I really think the child bit him. I do know she
scratched."

The sentence ended in a burst of laughter. What
would the two have thought if they had known
that just back of them, shielded from view by a
curtain across the doorway, was the Elliotts' hired
man, his face dark with indignation? Games? He
had wondered what they could be like to arouse a
lady's indignation. Now he saw.

Foolish games they seemed to be, for the most
part, having the merest shred of the intellectual to
commend them, and that so skillfully managed
that the merest child might have joined in them
heartily. But the distinctly objectionable features
seemed to be connected with the system of penalties attached to each game. These, almost without
exception, involved much kissing.

Of course, the participants in this entertainment
were young ladies and gentlemen. There seemed
to be a certain amount of discrimination exercised
by the distributor of the penalties, yet occasionally
such guests as Nannie and Rex and others of their
class would be drawn into the vortex, and seem to
yield, as if to the inevitable, with what grace they
could. John watched a laughing scramble between
Nannie and an awkward country boy who could
not have been over fifteen. He came off victorious,
for she rubbed her cheek violently with her handkerchief and looked annoyed, even while she tried
to laugh.

But the college boys were far more annoying
than the country youths without advantages. John

Stuart, looking on with indignation as he saw with what abandon these young men, who supposed themselves to represent the very cream of modern culture, rushed into the rudest of the carousing and scrambled as if for college prizes. There was an immense amount of scrambling and screaming and apparent unwillingness on the part of the ladies, yet one could not but feel that after all, as they were invariably conquered, they submitted with remarkable resignation.

Occasionally there was an exception. Anna Elliott, for instance, announced distinctly early in the evening that no one need put her name on for one of those silly games, for she would have nothing to do with them. As she might have known had she been more familiar with such scenes, this was the signal for putting her name on continually. But the boys who came in contact with her learned that, unlike many of the maidens present, she had undoubtedly meant what she said.

With the college boys she fared better than with the acquaintances of her lifetime. They speedily discovered that the prettiest girl in the room had a mind of her own. More than once her emphatic "No, indeed, I am not to be kissed on cheek or hair or hand, and you will be kind enough to understand it" held at a respectful distance a mustached youth who had just distinguished himself by "subduing" one of her schoolmates.

The boys who had been brought up in the neighborhood did not understand it, however, and thought it was ridiculous for "Anna Elliott" to put on airs with them. To her encounter with the objectionable Rob Sterritt, John Stuart had been not only a listener but a participator.

After the first scramble was over, and it had

been an angry one on Anna's part, during which the scratching and possible biting had taken place, most of the company supposed that Rob Sterritt had yielded the point and acknowledged himself worsted. But this was not his idea of valor. He followed the girl to the hall and began again.

"Come, now, Anna," he said. "Don't be ridiculous. It's all in fun, you know, but I must have my kiss, upon my word, or I shall never hear the last of it. I won't be rough. I won't, honestly. I'll just give you a delicate little kiss such as the minister might, if he was young enough, and let it go at that."

The young girl's eyes fairly blazed at him as she said, "Rob Sterritt, don't you *dare* try to kiss me! If you had any idea of what it means to be a gentleman, you would know better than even to refer to it, after what I've said."

He thought she was pretending. "I don't wonder you play the tigress, Anna. It becomes you vastly. You do it better than Helen. But then, of course, you know I must pay my penalty. It's a double penalty if I fail, and a good deal is at stake. Upon my word, you must."

It was then that John Stuart had stepped from his station just behind the door and said, "I intend to protect this young lady from whatever is disagreeable to her."

He had never spoken more quietly, but his low-pitched voice had reserve strength in it. His whole manner was curiously unlike that of the young fellows about him, and certainly impressive.

Rob Sterritt, a sort of accepted rough in the neighborhood — tall, strong-limbed, generally good-natured, priding himself on his strength and impudence — stood back and looked in unbounded astonishment, putting it into a single explosive question: "Who the dickens are you?"

"I am Mr. Elliott's hired man, and as such I consider that I have a right to protect his daughter."

"Oh, you do! Well, you insufferable idiot, there's nothing to protect her from. It's only a game. I understand it — you are here to look after the horses. I advise you to attend to your own business."

But he had walked away at once and left Anna to the hired man's care. Nothing had ever startled young Sterritt so much as the strange sense of power held in check that the brief sentence had conveyed to him.

Anna's face blanched. It was the first she had seen of John, the first she had known of his presence. "John," she said in a low whisper, "did they send you for me?"

"Oh, no, Miss Anna. I am here, as your friend said, merely to look after the horses. Your father gave me permission to earn an extra half dollar in this way. But I saw that the man was annoying you and thought I ought to interfere."

The color flamed into the girl's cheeks. The strangeness of her situation impressed her. Her father's hired man trying to protect her from her "friend"!

"He did not mean any harm," she said quickly. "It is a way they have of playing games. That is, some of the young people have that way. It's horrid! I never realized how horrid until tonight. Helen is right. John, you meant well, I'm sure, so I thank you, but —," she hesitated and then said, looking up at him appealingly, "they don't know at home that I'm here."

He did not help her in the least. She half turned from him as if in impatience, then turned back to say haughtily, "There are reasons I do not care to

have them know it just now. I don't suppose you
consider it a part of your duty to report that you
saw me?"

"I don't see that it is — at least, not unless I'm
questioned. Of course, if a question should be
asked me, the reply to which would involve the
truth, I would have to speak it."

She was growing angry with him; he could tell
by the flash in her eyes.

"Oh, indeed!" she said. "You are a worshipper
of Truth, are you? A remarkable hired man, certainly. Don't be afraid. I'm not going to ask you to
tell any falsehoods in my behalf. I don't think my
family will be likely to question you about my ac-
tivities. Are you always so careful of your words?
You would do for a disciple of — well, never
mind."

She had whirled away from him as she spoke.
He knew his face had flamed and was vexed that it
was so. Why should he fancy himself stabbed
whenever the truth was mentioned? So what if he
were acting a part for a little time? It was an innocent part, certainly, with a noble motive behind it
and with no possibility of harming anyone by the
venture. Had the girl meant that he would do for a
disciple of her sister? Would he? Would those pure
eyes of hers look with favor on even so laudable a
simulation as his?

In spite of himself, he felt a growing dissatisfac-
tion whenever he thought of Helen Elliott and the
wall he had built between them and any possible
friendship they might have. And yet, he also had a
growing determination to remain in just the position he was until he had demonstrated to his own
satisfaction certain truths that had nothing to do
with tramps.

Some truths he demonstrated that night. One was that certain country neighborhoods entertained themselves in ways that other country neighborhoods, where education and culture had permeated society, did not even suspect. Another was that some of the cultured people, either because of careless good nature, like Nannie and Rex, or because of far worse motives, like some of the college boys, fostered by their presence this unseemly condition of things.

Still another was that Helen Elliott had begun none too early to shield her beautiful young sister from the dangerous world surrounding her. That shield, however, was all too inadequate. He watched with a feverish sense of responsibility as the girl paced up and down the wide, old-fashioned hall beside a college youth whose face, he assured himself, he liked less than any he had seen. Infinitely less than Rob Sterritt's even. It was refined and cold and cruel. They were talking earnestly, Anna excitedly.

The watcher could distinctly hear every word she said. As the music in the next room grew louder and her companion raised his voice, his words, too, were distinct. John Stuart made not the slightest attempt to withdraw himself from hearing. He wanted to hear. He was there to learn. The tramp question was evidently not the most formidable one that threatened some grades of society.

Anna was still complaining of the games in school-girl superlatives. They were "awfully silly" and "perfectly horrid," and she was "utterly disgusted" with it all.

Her companion agreed with her fully. He had been surprised. He used to hear his uncle tell of such goings-on, but he had not known that the customs lingered anywhere. It was so bewildering to him that anyone should think for a moment of preferring such obsolete entertainments to the refining and elevating amusement of dancing. She danced, of course? Did she not? Now *he* was astonished. Dancing was the very "poetry of motion," she must remember, not that she needed it; every motion of hers was grace. He had singled her out from the first for this reason among others, and she would enjoy dancing so much. Might he ask why she didn't indulge? Was it possible that her parents could approve of such amusements as the games played tonight and yet object to the dance?

Anna winced over this — the hidden watcher could see it — and she struggled to be truthful. "No," she burst forth at last, "they by no means approve of entertainments like these. I have never been to one of these club meetings before."

The young man laughed pleasantly. He assured her he understood. She had escaped, like him, from the pressure of constant study for a little recreation and had found more than she sought. But she really ought to give herself the pleasure of a single dance just to convince herself of the beauty of the movements and the restfulness of the exercise.

He knew that a few good and rather secluded people still had some old-fashioned notions about the dance. They grew out of certain abuses of the past, he supposed. But really these were fast disappearing, and in cultured regions they had disappeared entirely. If he might only be allowed to promenade with her to the time of that delicious music, he was sure he would remember it all winter. Why, it made not the slightest difference that she didn't know how to dance. He could teach her the necessary steps in five minutes. She would take to it naturally, he was sure, as a bird does to song.

John Stuart's jaw tightened as he saw the two, a few minutes later, moving to the "time of that delicious music" down the long parlor that had been cleared for dancing. He knew young men fairly well — perhaps he knew college men and boys better than any other class of people. He didn't need to overhear the talk of two a moment afterward to assure himself that he had not mistaken the fellow's character.

"Look at Saylor with that bright-eyed gypsy in tow. She belongs to a very exclusive family," one said. "The older sister will not attend these gatherings. If her father were here, I could tell him that I would rather she be kissed six times by every country bumpkin present than dance fifteen minutes with a fellow like Saylor. Doesn't it make you shiver to think how he will go on about her tomorrow?"

That's what John Stuart overheard. He went out to the horses wishing he were John Stuart King, a certified protector of Anna Elliott.

CHAPTER VIII

SQUIRE HARTWELL

 little more than a mile from the Elliott farm stood an old-fashioned, substantial stone mansion. It was an object of special interest not only to the villagers a mile farther away, but also to the country people for miles around. John Stuart, on his first advent into the neighborhood, had had no difficulty in discovering its whereabouts. He, too, regarded it with interest, inasmuch as it was remotely connected with his own family. A somewhat eccentric old man, familiarly called "Squire Hartwell," had lived in this house quite alone, save for his hired attendants, for more than a quarter of a century. If public gossip concerning him was to be trusted, he was thoroughly disagreeable. In the spring of the year in which our story opens, the old man had died suddenly, and there were circumstances connected with the closing months of his life that had roused the neighborhood to keenest interest in his affairs.

Another name that had been commonly used for

him, as the younger man came to be known and liked, was "Rex Hartwell's uncle." That young person had been closely connected with him during most of his life. The country people had it that "Squire Hartwell had brought him up." That simply meant, however, that he had paid the boy's bills as a child in his old nurse's family where he was boarded and, later, at boarding school and college.

This was because the boy was the son of his only sister, who had died when her child was but five years old, and not because of any affection for the boy. He had held his nephew at arm's length during his boyhood, barely tolerating short visits from him in the long vacations and omitting even those as the boy grew to an age at which he might be supposed to be companionable.

Suddenly, however, almost immediately after Rex Hartwell's graduation from college, his uncle had decided to go abroad, taking the young fellow with him as his attendant. For a young man who had come up rather than been brought up, Rex Hartwell was a model in many respects. He had a warm heart and was so thoroughly grateful to one whom he had always looked upon as his benefactor that during their two years of travel, he devoted himself unsparingly to the old man's comfort, consulting his tastes in a way that had never been done before. For, despite his money, Squire Hartwell had lived a lonely and loveless life.

When the old gentleman suddenly made up his mind to return home, he brought Rex Hartwell with him, introducing him as his nephew and heir to those whom he chose to honor with such ceremony. He made no secret that he meant to leave his broad acres and railroad and bank stock to this young man.

"I have never told him so before," he said to the family lawyer, with whom he was as nearly confidential as with any person. "I had no notion of bringing up a fellow to swagger around and live for the purpose of spending the money I have worked hard for. I have kept him close and taught him the value of money. I think he will know how to take care of what I leave him.

"He's a very decent sort of fellow, if I do say it, and I like to think of the property's being held by one of the same name. If his mother had given him the full name, I should have settled it all before this, I daresay. But she had a soft streak in her and gave him his worthless father's silly name. 'Reginald,' indeed! Just right for a fop.

"Oh, his father was a decent enough sort of man," he admitted, "softhearted enough to be a girl, and with no business ability. A country doctor heavily in debt — and dying of overwork before he was thirty — that is his history. His son takes after the Hartwells. If he hadn't, I should never have tried to make anything of him. Well, now we're ready for business."

So the will was drawn, duly witnessed and signed. It left not only the old stone house that was almost palatial in size and the broad acres connected with it, but also factory stock and railroad stock and bank stock, as well as whatever bank account there should be at his decease, to his nephew and namesake, Joshua Reginald Hartwell. The gossips had it that the old man had used all his influence to induce his nephew to drop his father's name entirely in favor of the more sensible Joshua, but Rex had firmly declared that the name his father had borne and his mother had given him should be his as long as he lived. Not that he had any objection whatever to the name Joshua. And, yes, it could be placed first if his uncle wished. That would not matter in the least, as he would be Rex all the same.

To the simple country folk by whom they were surrounded, who counted their wealth by the few thousands that accumulated slowly, the young man was looked up to as a prospective millionaire. And deep was the interest they took, not only in him, but also in the fortunate young woman who had won his special regard. This was Annette Marvin, or Nannie as she was known in the entire neighborhood. Although there were some who perhaps envied her, it was, after all, a good-natured, kindly sort of envy, for Nannie Marvin was a favorite with old and young.

She was the daughter of a poor man whose farm joined Mr. Elliott's but was in every respect its contrast. Farmer Marvin had never possessed what the people of the neighborhood spoke of as "knack." His wheat and oats and barley and even his potatoes, to say nothing of apples and other hardy fruits, seemed to grow reluctantly for him and to hold themselves open to rot, rust, weevil and worm, and whatever other enemy of goodness hovered nearby to make advances. As the slow years dragged on, the Marvin farm was never very well worked, because there were not means with which to work it. The only thing that grew steadily larger was the debt that kept accumulating to pay the interest on the mortgage.

Years before his time, people spoke of Nannie's father as "Old Mr. Marvin." And then it wasn't long before they began to say, "Poor old Mr.

Marvin." He had a large family to bring up and educate, and "they were all girls, too, poor things!"

Almost without exception, people commended Nannie as a girl of good sense and unusual spirit. Then she suddenly struck into an entirely new path when she presented herself at the door of the old Hartwell mansion in answer to its master's advertisement for a "young woman to wait on the housekeeper."

Nannie Marvin had graduated from high school six months before, the best scholar in her class, and had spent the six months looking in vain for a chance to teach. Boldly she had declared that if there were no scholars for her to teach, she would see if she could "wait on" a housekeeper. The very girls who wouldn't have done such a thing for the world had sense enough to commend her. Not that it was unheard of for the daughters of farmers to accommodate other farmers in the neighborhood during busy seasons and go as "help." Susan Appleby, who reigned in the Elliott kitchen, had come for no other reason than to "accommodate" and held herself to be as "good as any of them." But the truth was, the Marvins were considered, even among their neighbors, as "a little above the common."

Mr. Marvin, although a poor farmer, had been a good Greek scholar. It was failing health that had driven him reluctantly to the fields, and he liked now to read in his Greek testament much better than to hoe his corn. Mrs. Marvin had been a teacher in her youth in a famous young ladies' institute, and they had kept Nannie in school long after some people said she ought to be doing something to help her poor father. For such a girl to become a common servant under Squire Hartwell's housekeeper was a matter for much comment. Almost without exception it had been thought that she might better have gone to the Elliotts' or some other well-to-do farmer's family where there was a mother to look after things, not a housekeeper to "set down on one."

But Nannie Marvin had a mind of her own. She could not have worked in the Elliotts' kitchen where Helen was her best friend, but she believed she could "wait on a housekeeper" who was a stranger and would know how to treat her only as a servant. So to the stone house she went. It was prophesied that she wouldn't stay a month, that if she got along with the housekeeper, she wouldn't be able to stand the old squire, who was said to be disagreeable to his help.

But all these prophecies came to naught. By degrees it began to be understood that Nannie Marvin was almost a fixture at the stone house. Squire Hartwell not only tolerated her presence, but, as the months passed, evidently liked to have her about. He ordered the housekeeper to let Nannie fix his books and papers, dust his room and bring his tea, gruel or whatever was wanted.

He also discovered she could read and had her read aloud to him by the hour. Then he found that she could write, and he dictated his business letters to her.

Almost before anybody realized what was going on, Nannie Marvin was established in the library as a sort of secretary to Squire Hartwell, who had heretofore scorned all such help. She and the housekeeper changed places, in a sense. From being summoned from her dusting or her egg beating with the word that the squire wanted her to read the news, she rose to the dignity of delivering messages to the housekeeper.

Mrs. Hodges was a sensible woman and did not resent the changes. On the contrary, a note of respect had crept into her voice, almost imperceptible to herself, whenever she spoke to Nannie, and she asked for her help more often than ordered it. She even bore in silence one morning the curt statement from the squire that she must "hunt up somebody else to trot around after her," because he wanted Nannie Marvin to himself.

When Squire Hartwell suddenly went abroad for an indefinite period, people were still wondering what Nannie would do when they heard with surprise that she was still to be in his employ. She was to have charge of the library, conservatory and garden, which were the squire's special pets. She was to write letters to him concerning such and such interests, and to receive and execute his orders. She was also to have a general oversight of the house during the absence of the housekeeper. For all these services she was to receive a regular salary with the privilege of staying at home.

Those who questioned closely enough to find out all these details were equally divided in opinion. Part were assured that Nannie Marvin was in luck and that they had never before known the squire to do a generous thing like that. The other part stated with equal assurance that no doubt he knew how to make the girl earn every cent of her money.

With the squire's homecoming, Nannie was promptly reestablished in the stone house. Indeed, she was there even when the housekeeper arrived and had an open letter in her hand from which she read directions for that good woman to follow. Everybody began to realize that Nannie Marvin was, as these country folk phrased it, "on the right side of the squire."

Yet many prophesied a different state of things as soon as it was discovered that the nephew took kindly to the quasi-secretary and treated her with the deference he would show to any lady. Surely the squire, when he got his eyes open, would have none of that. But they were mistaken again. The squire grumbled a little, it's true, when he saw that his nephew was unmistakably interested in Nannie Marvin. He said he didn't see why young people all had to be fools. Nevertheless, it became increasingly apparent that Nannie had won her place, if not in his heart, at least in his life. She had become necessary to him. Why should he complain if this was also the case with his nephew?

Once it was settled how matters stood, the old man carried things with a high hand. He dismissed without warning a stable boy who had dared to say "Nannie Marvin," and he told the housekeeper somewhat sternly that she must teach her servants to say "Miss Marvin," if she had any who did not know well enough to do so.

It took the good people of the neighborhood some months to get accustomed to this surprising state of things, and then, behold, a new surprise! One morning, all the neighborhood for miles around quivered with the news that Rex Hartwell and his uncle had quarreled, and the squire had changed his will and cut Rex off without a penny! The neighbors gathered in knots at the leading produce store in the village, or in one another's sitting rooms and kitchens, and discussed the details. The day after the quarrel, the squire's lawyer had been closeted with the squire for two hours and more. When he came out, he had halted on the wide piazza, swept his eyes in all directions over the rich fields and said, "Too bad! Too bad!"

By degrees, all the particulars were gathered in that mysterious way in which news scatters through country neighborhoods. It appeared that Squire Hartwell had set his heart upon his nephew's becoming a lawyer. He had said nothing about this during their stay abroad, nor indeed for the first five or six months after their return. When the young man tried to talk of his future, he had even put him off with a curt sentence to the effect that there was time enough to think of such things.

Then suddenly one morning when the summer was over, the squire began to talk about his plans for setting the young man as a student in the law office of an eminent friend of his. He talked about this quite as a matter of course, as though the decree had gone forth from Rex's birth that he was to become a lawyer. Then it was that these two strong wills had clashed. Rex Hartwell, never having heard one word from his uncle on the subject of his profession, and having excellent proof that it was not a matter of the slightest consequence to that gentleman what he did, had chosen for himself, and chosen early.

All his ideas of success in life were connected with the medical profession. He may have inherited this interest, as well as fostered it in his early boyhood. Many of his vacations had been spent with a friend in the family of an eminent physician, where his leisure hours had been passed in poring over such medical works as he could understand. When he went abroad with his uncle, having at certain hours leisure to do as he would, he had chosen to mark out for himself a course of study looking toward his chosen profession. He had made such good use of his time as to be eager, even impatient, for the hour to come when he could begin his medical studies in earnest.

It may be imagined what a blow it was to a young man of his temperament to be confronted with the announcement that now the time had come for him to begin his law studies. To give up his own plans and force his mind to a course of study that hadn't a single attraction for him was, he felt, utterly impossible, and he courteously but firmly said so.

His answer was met by a storm of wrath such as he had not supposed a gentleman could display. As the interview continued, the young man discovered that to have chosen the medical profession was evidently an even more heinous crime than to have refused the law. His uncle was absolutely bitter, not only against the profession itself, but also against those who he declared had warped his nephew's mind in that direction. Was not the utter failure of his father to earn even a decent living by his pills and powders sufficient reason why his mother would not have wanted her boy to follow in such foolish footsteps?

Oh, he knew very well that the mother had wanted him to become a doctor. All women were fools where business was concerned, and his sister Alice had been one of the most sentimental fools of them all. He should know her, he hoped, better than her boy who was five when she died. It was mere sentimental twaddle with her.

She wanted him to inherit his father's tastes! To inherit his father's failures, she might better have said, declared the squire, along with his skill in leaving his family penniless! He despised the whole race of pill vendors, and not a penny of his money would be turned into any such channel. He had himself intended from his babyhood to be a lawyer and had been thwarted, not by fault of his, but because of the meanness of a certain doctor. He would give his nephew thirty-six hours to decide whether he would carry out the plans that had been formed for him or go his own way — without a cent in the world.

Squire Hartwell did not understand human nature very well. Perhaps no course he could have taken could have more firmly settled the young man in his purposes. He replied with outward calmness that he did not need thirty-six hours to consider. He had planned as a baby to be a doctor, like his father, and as a boy and a young man he had kept that determination steadily in view.

He was sorry his uncle was disappointed, but not even for inherited millions would he sell himself to a life's work for which he was not fitted and in which he was sure he would make only failure. And then he had gone out from his uncle's presence, sure that the old man would keep his threat and cut him off without a penny.

CHAPTER IX

OVERTURNED PLANS

he public's opinion, as represented by the little world that knew these people, was two-sided as usual. There were those who were sure Rex Hartwell would live to regret his folly and obstinacy. The idea of throwing away millions just because his father had been a doctor! What was the promise of a *baby* to his mother? She must have been a silly mother to have thought so young a child could be influenced. In all this discussion, logic was no better attended to than it generally is in public opinion.

Others rejoiced in the spirit the young man showed. They said the squire had ruled people all his life, and for their part they were glad he had found his match.

But it was hard on Nannie. Everyone wondered if she would stay in the squire's employ. No, she did not. Squire Hartwell found it necessary to quarrel with her also, because he could not make her say that she thought his nephew was a simpleton and that unless he complied with his uncle's wishes she would have nothing more to do with him. Nannie was curtly dismissed from the house on the afternoon of the day that Rex had received his dismissal. The squire only relented sufficiently to say that if, in the course of a month, she got her common sense back and was able to reason "that addlepated follower" of hers into something like decency of behavior, he might be prevailed upon to change his mind. It angered him that Nannie made no reply to this beyond a very wise smile that said as plainly as words could have done, "I think you know your nephew, and me also, well enough to expect no such thing."

For days after that, Squire Hartwell was savage with everyone who had to be near him. The poor old man missed Nannie almost more than he did his nephew, and perhaps needed her more.

The separation was certainly hard upon the young people as well. All their well-laid plans had been overturned. They had held a tacit understanding between them that near Christmas there would be a wedding, and then Nannie would assume management of the old stone house. Her husband could easily go back and forth to town every night and morning while he was studying, and both of them agreed that since Squire Hartwell evidently took it for granted that such arrangements would be made, it would not be fair to him to plan otherwise. This habit of his taking things for granted was responsible for much of the trouble. Had there been a frank talk and a full understanding from the first, it's possible that much sorrow might have been avoided.

Squire Hartwell, however, had all his life been in the habit of assuming that people could read so much of his plans as it was necessary for them to know without any help from him. When he became reconciled to the marriage, he had, without any hint from the young people concerned, spoken of the holiday season as the time when most foolish deeds were done. He had then begun to refer in a casual way to matters that he and Nannie would attend to while that husband of hers was away at his books. How were they to know the older man meant law books?

No other two people in the world could have been as much together as were uncle and nephew in those days without a better understanding of each other's plans. But Squire Hartwell's lifelong habit of reticence, except in certain directions, was as strong upon him as ever, and the dislike he had to being questioned was well understood.

During one of his allusions to the future, Rex had remarked that it took money to make daily journeys to town to spend one's time in study. The squire had answered sharply that he did not see any occasion to worry about that. Hadn't there been money enough for him to spend his life in study thus far? It hadn't given out yet; when it did, he would be duly notified. These two unfortunate young people took it as a hint that they were not to worry about money, so they didn't. And now they had been duly notified!

Among Squire Hartwell's closing sarcasms to Nannie on that last afternoon had been the question of whether she supposed her excellent-brained Rex remembered that it took money to "spend one's days in study," to say nothing of supporting a wife!

During those trying days, Nannie Marvin took refuge, so far as Squire Hartwell was concerned, in almost total silence. She had begun to have a measure of affection for the lonely, crabbed old man, a feeling that was fast disappearing as a result of his persistent unkindness to his nephew. But her memory of what had been, as well as her sense of self-respect, kept her silent instead of allowing her to pour out the truth upon him as she felt at times a keen desire to do.

They had gone out from the stone house, then, those two, to reconstruct their plans as best they might. They were not crushed. Both had been brought up on too rigid an economic basis to feel keenly the loss of money — at least, they thought they had. Of course, it's one thing to be poor and have a father or uncle who is, after all, the responsible person and who will probably manage some way for one in his care. It's quite another to be responsible yourself, not only for your own expenditures, but also for the needs of others. This they were as yet too young and carefree to realize, however. They talked it all over cheerfully between bursts of righteous indignation.

"You don't blame me, do you, dear, for not trying to have myself ground into a lawyer at his dictation?" Rex would ask wistfully, having already asked the same question in every possible form. Nannie would reply, as she had a hundred times already, "Of course not, Rex! How can you ask such a question when I know that all your tastes and talents lie in another direction? I always hated their musty old law books, anyway, and it never seemed nice to me to make one's living by the quarrels of others. Your uncle is just the sort of man to like such a profession, though. I believe he enjoys quarrels. It's so much nobler to be planning to save lives. I dream of you, Rex, as coming to some home where they are all in a panic, where the attending physician has failed, and where, as a last resort, you, the great Dr. Hartwell, are called in to save a life! Just think of it, Rex, a life! Then compare that with the work of a lawyer!"

He always laughed merrily over the tone of contempt with which she exploded that word *lawyer*. Once he said lightly, "Oh, Nannie, you're not logical. You forget that as a lawyer I might make so eloquent a plea as to convince judge and jury to save a man from the gallows."

But she had logic for that. "No, it isn't in the least the same thing. No doubt he would be a miserable wretch who ought to be hanged, and you would have to twist and smirch the truth in order to save him. But a doctor is next to God in the way he holds life and death in his hand."

She grew grave and sweet with the close of her sentence. Whether logical or not, Rex Hartwell loved to hear her and to have her add, "Besides, a promise is a *promise*, even if it's made by a little child, and you know you promised your mother that you would be a physician."

So they replanned their lives and looked bravely down the long stretch of years wherein they must be separated. They told each other they were young and strong and could endure it and that it should not be so very long. They would both work so well and wisely that obstacles would be overcome almost before they knew it. And in spite of all they were happy, and at times they pitied the lonely, old man who had banished them.

The young man speedily found a position in a doctor's office in the city, where for certain services rendered he was to receive board, opportunity to study and the privilege of asking what questions he chose. It was not so easy for Nannie to find work. Rex Hartwell was willing to drudge, but he found that he shrank from the thought of drudgery for her. In the abstract, it was brave and beautiful of her to plan hard work. He liked to hear her speak of it. But when it came to a definite position, he shrank with such manifest pain from each one offered that Nannie hesitated and remained at home. Meantime, her friend Helen Elliott was making such a beautiful success of the country school where she had taught for two seasons that Nannie envied her and wished so much for a similar position.

They interested themselves somewhat in the new heir to the Hartwell estate. They knew the name was King and that a remote and almost forgotten family connection made a show of justice in the new will. It was said that at one time Squire Hartwell had seen the young man when he was a child of seven or eight and told him that if he grew up and became a lawyer, perhaps he would leave him some money to buy law books. The boy had grown up, but he was not a lawyer. Opinion was divided among the country folk about what he was.

Nannie heard somewhere that he was an author and asked Rex if he might possibly be connected with that Stuart King who wrote those articles in the *Review* that created such a sensation. Rex thought not, because he knew his uncle despised a mere writer of books — unless, indeed, they were law books. Then they wondered whether the heir would come soon to visit his fine acres, whether he would be an agreeable addition to the neighborhood, and, naturally, how he would treat them should they ever chance to meet. And both of them understood the uncle so well that they had not a thought of his relenting.

Matters were in this state — with Rex Hartwell studying hard in the physician's office in town and snatching a few minutes each day to write a line to Nannie, who had the harder lot of waiting at home for work to come to her — when a new excitement filled the neighborhood. Suddenly, unexpectedly — as he had done everything else in his long life — Squire Hartwell died. One morning, driving about his grounds, giving orders in his most caustic style; the next, lying in state in his parlor with the housekeeper wiping her eyes as she tried to give particulars.

Speculation ran high about whether the new heir would honor the funeral with his presence, and great was the disappointment when the report was circulated that he was abroad and would be represented by his lawyer.

The funeral was held, and all from the village and countryside, as well as many from the city who had known Squire Hartwell in a business way, honored his dust with their presence. But it was Rex Hartwell, disinherited, who followed him to the grave as chief and, indeed, only mourner. Nannie Marvin cried a little as, seated in the Elliotts' family carriage, she followed the body to the grave and tried to remember only the days in which he had been almost kind to her and had seemed to be planning for her and Rex.

Rex Hartwell had to be more than mourner. It had been so natural to associate him with his uncle in recent years that people fell into the habit of coming to him for directions about what should or should not be done. He gravely assumed the responsibility and did his best. Why not, since he was the only one left who bore the name? Even though the broad acres and bank stock had been left to someone else, he did not intend to forget that the dead man was his uncle and that during all these years he had clothed and fed and educated him. There was no omission of the slightest mark of respect offered in his uncle's memory. The people looking on said it was "real noble of the young man." Nannie Marvin, weeping and watching furtively his every movement, felt sure this was true.

Following hard upon these excitements came another, so great as to throw all others into the background. The new will that had been talked about, and the visible results of which had already been so disastrous to two lives, could not be found! The family lawyer affirmed that it had been made and witnessed and managed with all the forms of law, and then that the squire had taken it into his own keeping, rejecting almost haughtily his lawyer's offer to take care of it for him. He was by no means in his dotage, he had said, and was entirely capable of looking after his own papers. Apparently he had looked after his own so successfully that no human being could find it.

In vain they searched, and searched again, the squire's private room, his library, his writing desk and closets, and his large, old books, some of them not opened for years. It was not found. In vain the lawyer's young clerk, who had read many detective books and heard several detectives talk, searched the old house curiously for some secret drawer or panel like those in his books. No trace of such mysteries could be discovered, and all were at last obliged to give up the search.

The lawyer, who liked Rex Hartwell and Nannie

Marvin as well, but who liked better still to have everything connected with legal matters done decently and in order, was at first greatly disturbed. This seemed like playing with serious interests. Why should Squire Hartwell have taken hours of his valuable time and resisted all his attempts at advice if he meant simply to destroy the will when made? Or, supposing that he had, after so short a time, actually changed his mind, why had he not communicated the fact to his man of business so that he might have been prepared for the change?

Looked at from the standpoint of mere friendship, it had a gratifying side. The old lawyer was entirely willing — nay, glad — that Rex Hartwell should come into possession of what was rightly his own. But certainly the method of securing it was trying to a man of business such as himself.

However, after the lapse of weeks, during which no possible suggestion had been overlooked and the most skillful hands had assisted in the search, even the lawyer admitted there was no good cause for further delay. The proper legal steps were taken, therefore, and Rex Hartwell came into formal possession of his fortune.

Plans went forward briskly after that. Some people thought that under the circumstances the marriage might take place immediately. But Nannie and Rex determined to show every mark of respect possible, and it was therefore Christmas again to which they and their neighbors were looking forward with an almost equal degree of eagerness. It would be such a wonderful thing to have the handsome old stone house presided over by Nannie Marvin! Quite different, they decided, from having her there under Squire Hartwell's orders, even though she was his nephew's wife. Didn't everybody know that the old squire would have managed her and her husband as well? But now there was reasonable hope that the house would be thrown open to company as it had not been for nearly a quarter of a century. They knew that Nannie and Rex would be the most delightful people to visit.

In view of all these experiences, it was not strange that Mr. Elliott's new hired man, by keeping his ears open and occasionally asking a discreet question, came into possession of the whole story. He could even ask an inquisitive question without exciting any surprise. The various scenes in the drama lived out before them had such intense interest for many of the simple country folk that they could well appreciate the interest of even a stranger. John Stuart amused himself by wondering what they would have thought could they have discovered that the would-be heir was actually "Mr. Elliott's hired tramp."

Concerning this same heir, there had been much speculation about how he bore the news of the lost will and what he would do about it. The utmost he had done was to institute, through his lawyer, as thorough a search for the missing property as it seemed possible to make, and then to rest content. He had money enough, and his tastes did not lie in the direction of accumulation. Why should he care because the people who ought to have the old man's fortune had secured it? It had been easy for him to put away all personal desires with this reasoning. But when he found himself in the very neighborhood where these curious events had taken place, he discovered he had a keen personal interest in all the actors.

CHAPTER X

WHAT IS TRUTH?

ne could not long be a member of the Elliott household without discovering that Helen was not one of those teachers who work for the sake of salary and forget their scholars the moment the door closes upon them for the day, remembering them with reluctance the next morning when necessity compels. John Stuart, before he had been in the neighborhood a month, had heard enough about her school incidentally to want to visit it. Yet an opportunity for doing so seemed improbable.

Farmer Elliott, although his trust in his hired man grew daily, seemed to have formed the habit of himself looking after his daughter. He had been overheard to say with great satisfaction that his man was so entirely trustworthy that he could get away better than he had for years. The aspirant could only bide his time.

One evening, while the family was at supper — John and Susan, according to the fashion of the neighborhood, being seated with them — a discussion arose in which the former was deeply interested. "You ought not to go out again tonight, Roger," Mrs. Elliott said with an anxious glance. "You are hoarser than you were an hour ago. It would be a pity to get a cold fastened upon you for the winter perhaps."

"Oh, there's no danger of that!" the father said cheerily though hoarsely. "It is a nice night for a ride. The air is crisp but not disagreeable. It will be as clear as a bell this evening."

Then Helen added: "Father, Nannie and Rex would like to go out with us. Rex promised he would help me when he could this winter, and Nannie says this evening would be a good one to commence in, because it will be such a lovely moonlight that she would rather be useful than not, with a ride at the end."

They laughed over Nannie's characteristic way of putting things, and then the mother had a sudden relieved thought that involved a glance toward John and a significant look at her husband. She voiced it only with the tentative half-sentence "If Nannie and Rex are along, why not — ?" She spoke low for her husband's benefit, but loud enough for John's quick ear to catch and his quick brain to understand.

"All right," said the farmer. He raised his voice and continued, "John, I believe I'll let you drive the young people out to the schoolhouse this evening. Not that it would hurt me, but Mrs. Elliott seems to think I need a little coddling."

So John's opportunity had come. Not to visit the school, it's true; but one could tell a good deal by a visit to a schoolhouse. As for why it was to be visited that evening, he had no idea. No one seemed to remember that he was an entire stranger to the ways of the neighborhood. He must learn by watching and waiting.

The long, low, uninviting building known as the Hartwell schoolhouse was a revelation to him. All his experience of school life had been connected with great four-story buildings with fireproof walls and general massiveness. He told himself that he must certainly have known there were other styles of school buildings, but he found he had no associations with any other. He looked about with the deepest interest on the queer-shaped seats and wooden desks marred by more than one generation of jackknives.

Yet if he had but known it, the little schoolroom was by no means typical, being a palace in its way compared with many he had visited. The floor was beautifully clean and had a strip of cocoa matting down the main aisle. The lamps, set into home-made brackets fastened at regular intervals to the walls, shone with cleanliness and were numerous enough to make a fairly well-lighted room.

The teacher's platform was neatly covered with a square of cheerful red carpeting. On the desk was a fern growing in a pot and several other hardy plants that by dint of being carefully covered every night and removed on Friday nights to the sheltered closet, managed to flourish through the long, cold winter. There was also, besides the desk chair, a little red rocker.

The white walls were adorned with pictures in great variety — not only the charts and maps common to a schoolroom, but also several prints in colors, cheap copies of certain famous pictures, and an open Bible in blue and gilt, with the text large enough to be read distinctly. Altogether, however uninviting the building might be from the outside, it was cheerful enough within.

Nannie Marvin, especially, was charmed. "What a pretty place you have made of this little room!" she said. "I remember it used to be particularly ugly. I told Squire Hartwell once that I wouldn't think he would like such a horrid old building named for him. Isn't that wall pretty, Rex? The pictures are all so cheerful, and the coloring is in excellent taste. If there were only some comfortable seats for the scholars and a carpet on the floor, it would be quite a pretty parlor. I'll tell you, Rex, when — ," she stopped suddenly with a glance toward John Stuart, then laughed. He knew she had been about to indulge in a daydream of what would be done when her name became Hartwell.

Further talk was interrupted by the arrival of scholars, or guests, or audience; the most interested person there had not yet discovered what the evening's program was to be. It was an incongruous company, apparently, with sharp contrasts in age, although clearly confined to young people. There were little boys of an age that John supposed were always in bed at that hour; there were tall men of six feet and over; and there was every grade between.

Some of them he recognized as having seen at the club gathering but a short time before, and others were unmistakably of a lower grade than the club visitors. They shambled in awkwardly enough, seeming to be anxious chiefly to avoid observation. Yet there were distinctly two classes.

Quite a number came in briskly, eagerly, as though glad to be there. They greeted Miss Elliott with effusion, but politely, and bowed not ungracefully when she introduced her friends. This class, John soon discovered, was Miss Elliott's day pupils. The others were their brothers and sisters and friends, who knew her only through these evening gatherings.

The program he presently found to be unique. Helen Elliott came over to him with a kindly explanation. "John, I suppose you were never at quite such a gathering as this? I hardly know what name to give it myself. I have been in the habit of giving one evening a week to this neighborhood during the winter season ever since I've taught here. This is the first meeting of the season. We have two sessions, from seven to eight and from eight to nine. For the first hour we divide into classes, whenever we can find teachers or talkers, and take up some subject the classes ask to have talked over. Then at eight we have a social religious meeting. We sing a good deal, pray and talk on some theme we hope will help them.

"These are not all my scholars by any means. In this neighborhood are some — quite a number, indeed — who are not able to come to school. They work in the woolen factory and are busy all day. We use these evenings for helping them in any way we can. Tonight Mr. Hartwell is going to take the older boys and young men, and Miss Marvin and I will divide the girls between us for the first hour. But there are several boys here younger than have been in the habit of coming. They asked to come, and I couldn't deny them. Still, they can hardly be interested in what Mr. Hartwell will say. I've been wondering if — did you ever try to teach little boys anything or to talk to them for their good?"

Visions of a winter years ago, during which he taught in a mission Sunday school and became fascinated with certain outcast, homeless children, flashed before John. He answered with enthusiasm, "I did once, a good while ago."

"Then would you be willing to take those five little boys over in that corner near my desk and tell them something you think may interest or help them? Usually we have subjects chosen the week before, but as this is our first session, we decided to let them choose on the spot what they would like to learn about. I haven't the least idea what those little fellows will ask of you. Are you willing to attempt it?"

He was more than willing. The little boys, with their good, honest faces and remarkably grave behavior, were quite as new to him as anything in his strange surroundings. They didn't look or act in the least like street gamins, the type of boy to which his one experience in teaching had belonged. Yet they had intelligent and, in two or three instances, mischievous faces. He was eager to know what they thought and how they expressed their thoughts.

The alacrity with which he consented roused vague anxieties in the young manager's mind. She had expected him to demur, to be almost frightened over the idea, to feel sure that he was not competent to teach anybody. She had hoped to draw him out, to awaken his interest in something besides his daily routine of work, and perhaps to do him more good than he could do the boys. But he needed no drawing out. She moved away slowly, more than doubtful about the wisdom of her request.

The doubt increased as the hour passed, and she watched the intent, eager faces of the boys as they bent forward to catch every word that was being said to them. The new teacher apparently held their rapt attention. They had neither eyes nor ears for anything else going on in the room. Helen's own work suffered; she was so anxious. What mischief she might have done by giving that strange young man an hour with those pure-hearted boys! What could he be telling them that held their undivided attention?

She closed the hour abruptly ten minutes before its time, unable to do much herself except to regret her hasty attempt to benefit John, and she resolved to learn more about him at the first opportunity. It wasn't enough that a man be faithful in his daily work and conscientious in the performance of all his duties. His mind, despite this, might be filled with such poison that it gave him pleasure to impart it. She had read of such men.

Turning away from his boys with keen disappointment that he did not get the opportunity to add those last few words he had planned, the young man took a seat in the farthest corner of the room where he had an excellent view of all that transpired. The hour that followed was one of deep interest to him.

It had not been called a prayer meeting, and in some respects it was different from any prayer meeting John had ever attended. Yet that name fit it as well as any. Instead of reading a set portion from the Bible, Miss Elliott read from a collection of Bible verses she held in her hand. She announced at the opening of the reading that she had been asked by three of her pupils to take the words "What is truth?" for their talk that evening. The phase of the subject they wanted to have considered was: How far from the exact truth could one tread in the interest of himself or another without reaching the realm called falsehood?

"In other words," said Miss Elliott, "what is truth, and what does it demand of its adherents?" Then she read her Bible verses — keen, incisive words leaving no doubt in the mind of the listeners about the Bible's definition of truth. Still the question remained, What is meant by truth? Or, as one of Miss Elliott's girls put it, "How far can one keep a piece of knowledge to one's self without earning the name of being false?"

At that moment, John Stuart happened to be looking in the direction of Nannie Marvin and was interested by the sudden change in her expressive face. She flushed for an instant and then paled as she turned startled, half-frightened eyes first on the questioner, then on Helen, and listened to every word the latter spoke with an eagerness born of intense feeling of some sort. The student of human nature found himself wondering why she would be so keenly interested. He wondered if she might be troubled by her habit of running often to the "meadow lot" and having herself reported as "not at home."

Miss Elliott answered the question quickly. "That depends, Emma. In the first place, does the piece of knowledge concern ourselves only? Will no human being be injured by our silence? Is there no reasonable probability that our silence will be misinterpreted so that harm may come? Do we sincerely believe that good and not ill will result if we keep silence? If one can answer an unqualified yes to all these questions, I think one may keep his knowledge safely to himself."

Nannie Marvin, who was not given to much outspoken testimony, suddenly added her thought: "Sometimes great harm is done by speaking of what one may chance to have learned."

The leader turned troubled eyes upon her. "Yes," she said slowly, "that is undoubtedly true. I've known a number of instances in which the truth of the old proverb 'Silence is golden' was emphasized. But I think that Emma has in mind another phase of harm. Perhaps I'm mistaken, but it seems to me that the danger of the present time, at least in our neighborhood, is to belittle the truth by what are called trivial departures from it. I'm afraid that some persons are learning to pride themselves on the skill with which they can evade the truth without telling what they call falsehoods.

I read of a boy who boasted that when his father asked, 'My son, were you out late last night?' he answered boldly that on the contrary, he reached home very early. And he laughed as he explained to his companion that he told the truth for once. It *was* early — very early in the morning! Perhaps that story will illustrate my point as well as any. There are people who evade honesty in this way and yet make themselves believe they are speaking truth!

"It's difficult to understand how a person with ordinary common sense can so deceive himself," she observed, "but I believe it's done. The times in which we live seem to be especially fruitful in devices for tempting young people to falseness. I heard a few days ago of a respectable girl who had so far forgotten herself as to assume a false name and carry on a correspondence as another person! What can have become of a young woman's self-respect who will stoop to such an act?"

Quick, excited, half-frightened glances were exchanged between certain of her pupils as Miss Elliott said this. Their glances, interpreted, said, "Whom does she mean? How much does she know?"

As for John Stuart, he felt as if she were pointing straight at him. For the first time since he could remember, a sense of shame possessed him, against which he struggled angrily. Why should the opinions of this country girl, who in her proscribed circle thinks she understands the world, have power to disturb him? Did he not know that his motives were beyond reproach? And was he not sure that no possible harm could result from his act? Still, for a *girl* to pretend as he was doing would be, he slowly admitted, not quite in accordance with his ideas of —

He left the thought unfinished, for Jack Sterritt, Rob's younger brother, was asking a question.

"Miss Elliott, couldn't a girl do a thing of that kind just for fun and not mean anything by it?"

Miss Elliott regarded him with stern eyes. "I don't know, Jack," she said at last. "We will try not to judge her. Possibly she might if she were very young and very ignorant and had no one to guide her. But I would be sorry indeed to think that any of my girls could stoop so low."

Then those quick, questioning glances were exchanged again, and this time John Stuart studied them.

The talk went on in this way for some time — question, answer and comment. The young medical student took much higher ground on the question of truth than did most of those present. He seemed to be in hearty accord with Miss Elliott herself, affirming unhesitatingly that the infinite mischief that had been done in the world by gossiping tongues had been done chiefly because their love of talk led them to depart from the truth.

"Jack," said Miss Elliott suddenly, "will you

pray?"

And then it was discovered that Jack, the awkward, blundering country boy, knew how to pray. In very simple sentences, without polish but with the ring of unmistakable sincerity, he voiced his desires and aspirations. John Stuart, listening with bowed head, felt embarrassed again. This time it was caused by the thought, What would I have done had I been called upon to pray? He had been a member of the church for more than thirteen years, yet he had never heard the sound of his own voice in prayer.

CHAPTER XI

SEARCHLIGHTS

ther prayers followed in quick succession. John Stuart was surprised that so many of Miss Elliott's pupils seemed to know how to pray. None of the prayers was long, and all of them had a quality of directness, as though the petitioners believed the Person addressed was present and prepared to give them audience.

After a little while, Rex Hartwell prayed, and again John felt a thrill of something like astonishment. How easy it seemed to be for that man to pray! For himself, he felt that he could have spoken to an audience of thousands easier than he could have arisen in that little room and asked of God the simplest thing.

But all these experiences were as nothing compared with what soon followed. John Stuart had never heard a woman's voice in prayer. Miss Elliott bowed her head and, in as quiet a tone and simple a language as she would have spoken to any of the persons present, voiced not only her own needs but the needs of others. John was amazed, but no other person in the room evinced the slightest surprise. Evidently it was an ordinary occurrence. Yet the prayer was unusual. It had about it a searching quality that seemed to force one to look into his own heart and view it, for a moment at least, as it must look to God. More and more searching grew the sentences, more and more earnest the call for help — for light to see their temptations, for grace to overcome them.

Then the little schoolroom was treated to a sensation the like of which it had not known before. As soon as Miss Elliott's voice ceased, a young girl sprang to her feet. John Stuart had noticed her with interest several times during the evening. He had said to himself that she was probably the star pupil and the leader among her set. She wasn't pretty, but her clear, gray eyes and intelligent face were pleasant to look upon. She impressed him as a girl of marked character and of ability in whatever direction she had opportunity to exercise it. She was much excited, and her eyes showed plainly that she had been crying.

"Miss Elliott," she said quickly, "may I speak? There's something I ought to say. I knew I ought to before — at least I thought about it and felt that I must every time I looked at you. It seemed to me sometimes as though your face was just a looking glass in which I could see my own heart. All the time, though, I told myself that I couldn't do it. But after that prayer, I *must*."

She faced her classmates. "Girls and boys, you know how I won the prize in that last history contest? Every question in the list was to be answered correctly, you know, and I was the only one who did. Now I must tell you that there wasn't even one. That next-to-the-last question I — ," the girl hesitated and caught her breath hard.

It obviously required great courage to proceed. Suddenly she turned and looked at Miss Elliott, and it was as if she gathered strength from the look.

She went on quickly, "I stood very near to Miss Adams, who had the history cards in her hand, and that one was on top. I — I saw the first words, two or three of them, enough to start me. I don't believe I would have thought of the answer if not for that. I almost *know* I wouldn't — my mind seemed to be a perfect blank. But when I saw those words, it all flashed upon me. I didn't think about it then — about its being dishonest, I mean. Not as I have since. I thought at the time that I had earned the prize. But I know now that I didn't. Oh, I have known it ever so long, and I wanted to give the prize back, but I couldn't bear to tell you I had cheated! Oh, Miss Elliott, do you think you can ever forgive me?"

With an outburst of bitter weeping, she sat down.

Miss Elliott's face was sweet to see. "Satan has been outwitted tonight," she said, "and the truth has triumphed gloriously. I'm sure you all think so. I feel like closing this meeting with the doxology."

At the meeting's close she went swiftly over to the girl, who still sat with bowed head.

On the homeward ride, a lively discussion took place. On the trip out, the two ladies had occupied the back seat, and Rex Hartwell had sat with the driver. Now Miss Elliott, who had determined to take that opportunity to begin her better acquaintance with her father's hired man, changed the seating arrangements in one quick sentence. "Rex, you may take care of Nannie going home. I'm going to sit with John." Then she had sprung lightly to her seat and directed the driver to give her the reins while he looked after the comfort of the others.

However, her opportunity for growing acquainted was to be limited. Nannie Marvin was in full tide of talk, and it wasn't Rex Hartwell to whom she wanted chiefly to speak. Once the horses were underway, she began. "Helen, I think you were horrid tonight. I never heard you go on so, working up those ignorant young people to such a pitch of excitement that they didn't know what they were about. I was never more sorry for anybody in my life than I was for that poor girl. The idea of her getting up such a scene as that because she happened to see a word on a card! What did you say to her? I hope you told her that she was a simpleton and that her poor little copy of Tennyson, or whatever it was, was honestly hers."

"I did not," said Helen quietly. "Instead, I rejoiced with her that she was able to overcome the temptation to silence and be her own truthful self."

"Then I think you're cruel! I don't know how you can be so hard. It's enough to turn one away from religion entirely. Think what you've done for that girl! All those ignorant boys — and girls, too, for that matter — making fun of her, looking down on her and mouthing over her story until it's made into a public disgrace. And everthing would have been smoothed over with just a word from you to the effect that she was excited, that no harm had been done and that there was really nothing for her to confess. Jesus Christ would not crush a girl in the way you did tonight, I know."

"Why, Nannie, dear!" said Rex, in low and wondering tones. He had never seen her so excited about so slight a cause. Helen, too, turned in surprise and regarded her in the moonlight. "You are mistaken, Nannie," she said earnestly, "entirely mistaken. Those girls will rally about her, and the boys will stand up for her bravely, every one of them. Did you see how they waited for her tonight, each eager to say what he thought? They will all be proud of her. For myself, I glory in her. When we have a generation of young people true to their convictions of right and unswerving in their truth, the world will be a better place."

"Oh, 'truth'!" exclaimed the excited girl scornfully. "I'm growing to hate the word. It is narrowness, not truth. All you said there tonight was just as narrow and bigoted as it could be. Your very prayer was hard. Helen Elliott, you will drive people away from religion if you let it make you as severe and opinionated as that."

"My dear," said Rex, drawing a wrap carefully about his charge, who shivered as she spoke, "you have overwearied yourself tonight. I don't think you can be well."

Truly, it was a strange exhibition from the usually genial, winsome girl. Helen contemplated her obvious excitement in deep perplexity. Why was she so disturbed by what had occurred? Didn't she think the teacher knew her pupils better than an outsider could? Helen was sure that the avowal made that evening would work for good, not ill. She rejoiced in it as an evidence of growing depth of character. She tried to express her thought, repeating with more earnestness what she had already said.

But Nannie Marvin had subsided into almost total silence. Even Rex could secure only the briefest responses from her. To his tender inquiries she replied almost petulantly that her head ached, and she added in what she tried to make a playful tone that she believed she needed to be left alone. Helen did leave her alone after a while, turning her attention to John.

"How did you get on with the little boys?" she asked kindly. "Had they a question for you?"

"Oh, yes, indeed!" he said, smiling over the memory of their earnest faces. "Several questions. One of the little chaps has been puzzled about his shadow — sometimes long, sometimes short — sometimes racing ahead of him, and again lagging behind. He expressed his puzzle so well that the others became interested, and we were just getting from the actual shadows to their moral representatives when you called us to order. I'm afraid that I left their inquiring minds somewhat in a fog."

For the moment he had forgotten himself. Those grave little boys puzzling over their shadows had taken him into his past. It was as if he were John Stuart King reporting to Fletcher or some other of his intimate friends. He was recalled to the present by the realization that Helen Elliott was looking steadily at him with a wondering, pained look. What could she think of the hired man who addressed such language to her with a degree of familiarity his position did not warrant? How should he correct such a blunder? She didn't wait for him.

"John," she said earnestly, "it has occasionally seemed to me that — that there was something about you we did not understand. I wish you felt that we — that my father was sufficiently your friend to confide in him if there is anything you ought to tell."

In the circle to which John Stuart King belonged, he had never lacked for words. But on this occasion there was absolutely nothing that he felt willing to say. His chief thought was, How exactly her eyes in the moonlight were like those in his picture of Truth!

After a moment she began again. "That subject about which we talked tonight is so full of importance. I sometimes think if we could get all lives centered in absolute truthfulness, so that they would be true to their inner selves as well as to those with whom they come in contact, all moral problems would be solved. John, I hope you're not being false to anybody — to your mother least of all. Does she know where you are?"

"Yes," he said, "I write often to my mother." He hurried his answer. What if the question had been extended?

"Does she know what you're doing?"

He had almost expected that and answered in the affirmative.

"That's good," she said, relieved. Then she inquired, "Did you have a chance to go to school when you were a boy?"

This honors man of a distinguished university hesitated and felt glad that just then the moon was in shadow. It was growing almost as difficult for him to speak the exact truth as it had been for Anna when she was planning her secret outing to the club meeting. At last he said, "I was always kept in school when I was a boy."

"I have thought from the language you use that you must have had opportunities. I've wondered, too, whether you were one of those boys for whom father and mother have sacrificed a great deal, and to whose manhood they've looked forward as the time of their reward. I know your father is gone, but I hope, John, that you are doing your best not to disappoint your mother."

He had disappointed her in several ways. She was annoyed with him at this moment because he was not loitering through Europe with her and Elizabeth. She had been vexed with him for years because he chose to write for the press and for pay when he had money enough to be a gentleman of elegant leisure.

"You might as well be a day laborer," she had said to him once when he was insisting upon regular and uninterrupted hours for study. Suppose he should tell all this to Helen Elliott! How was he to continue this conversation? He must generalize.

"Mothers and sons don't always think alike," he said, trying to speak stolidly, "and everyone has to think for himself."

"Ah, but, John, mothers are so often right, and sons, at least occasionally, live long enough to find themselves mistaken. If I were an honest, well-intentioned young man, I would think very carefully before I took any steps contrary to my mother's wishes."

"That's true," he said meekly. It was the only reply that seemed allowable under the circumstances. Plainly his questioner wasn't satisfied. He felt she was trying to study his face in the moonlight, which had become uncertain and fitful.

At last she spoke again, hesitatingly. "John, I don't want to force your confidence, of course, but I would like to be your friend in the truest sense of the word. To that end I would like to help you to think of the One who is the best friend a man can have. If you knew Jesus Christ intimately, I feel sure that He would help you to a better life than you're living. I don't mean," she went on hurriedly, "that I have any reason to find fault with your life. But there have been times when I've thought that perhaps you've fallen from some place you once held and that you're not now filling the place God intended for you. Am I right?"

Was she? Had he fallen? How was he to answer her? He felt his face burn over the thought of what he must seem to her, and he could find no words at all. She didn't wait long for them but went on gently.

"Have you ever given thought to these things? I mean, have you thought that you would like to be a real, earnest Christian, such a one as perhaps your mother is? Is she a Christian?"

"I believe so," he said at last. He found, poor fellow, that he hesitated even over that question! His fashionable mother, with her days spent in indolent luxury and her evenings given to opera, theater or kindred amusements — how would her religion look to eyes like Helen Elliott's? Yet ever since he could remember, she had been a member of the church, and she had been careful to let neither engagement nor fatigue prevent her being present at church on communion Sundays. Was she not, after all, as much of a Christian as he was himself? Their tastes lay in different directions, but perhaps in the sight of God his were no more religious than hers. In the estimation of this girl, he apparently had no religious character. How sure she seemed to be that the whole matter was something he had yet to settle! Should he tell her he was a church member?

"Helen," said Rex, speaking hurriedly, "may I ask you to let John drive as rapidly as he can? Nannie is cold. She seems to be in a chill. I'm afraid she's going to be ill."

"No, I am not!" said Nannie in a petulant voice, very unlike her own. "Why do you persist in drawing attention to me? I don't know what's the matter with everyone tonight."

But attention had been effectually drawn to her. Thereafter, Helen exerted herself to make her friend more comfortable and gave the word that sent the horses skimming over the road with such speed that they were soon drawn up before Mr. Marvin's gate.

CHAPTER XII

INTERROGATION POINTS

he lamp in the woodhouse chamber of the Elliott farm burned late that night, although the sheets of carefully written manuscript spread over the table did not increase in number. The occupant of the room was busy with thoughts he did not care to commit to paper. He had made certain additions to the furniture since his occupancy. One was a strongbox that locked with a padlock, wherein he kept certain books and all his papers during the day, safe from Susan's inquiring eyes. Another was a lamp of fair size that he had bought with his first earnings, explaining carefully to Susan that he had some copying to do in the evenings that required a strong light.

"He's got a girl somewhere that he writes to," commented Susan after she had described the lamp. "I found sheets of paper throwed away the other day, filled full of stuff I couldn't make head nor tail of. I got at him about it. I said I should have thought he would have throwed them away, and if he couldn't write better sense than that to his girl, she'd throw them away for him." After that criticism, John Stuart was more careful of what he did with rejected pages of manuscript.

But on this particular evening, the story he was writing didn't grow. Instead, he established himself in the rocking chair and stared out his one window on the fields lying white in the moonlight. His face was grave and perplexed. Certain words heard that evening seemed to repeat themselves in his brain with the persistency of a phonograph set to make a single statement.

For instance, "What is truth?" repeated itself over and over again, always in Helen Elliott's voice, and with her searching eyes enforcing the words. If she understood his position fully, would she call him an embodied falsehood? Would he ever be able to explain to her his reasons for his false position? Would she consider the reasons adequate? Well, suppose she didn't. Was he bound to justify himself in her eyes?

As often as the round of questions reached this one, he moved uneasily in his chair and held his mind away from considering the answer. He would rather take up the other question that was growing almost as persistent — whether he was himself satisfied with his false position. It *was* a false position, of course.

He looked the moon boldly in the face and told it gloomily that there was no use in mincing words. He had forgotten himself for two minutes that evening and talked in a strain common to his ordinary life, and with what result? She had looked puzzled and pained. More than once that evening she had brought a flush of shame to his face by words she had not imagined applied to him. When had John Stuart King ever had occasion to blush for his behavior? This act of his was all questionable, a shading of the truth, an intent to deceive.

"I sometimes think if we could get all lives centered in absolute truthfulness...." He seemed to hear again her singularly penetrative voice saying those words. He went on, mentally finishing the sentence. Had he committed all words to memory? They seemed to cling to him. Would it be possible ever to make her understand? There he was, back again to that question about which he did not intend to think!

Why not give it all up at once? He wasn't accomplishing that for which he had set out. Rather, in a sense, that had been accomplished some time ago. Now he was simply — wasting time? No, he assured himself. After all, he was learning new things every day, securing material that would serve him well for the future. But he was clearly not satisfied.

I suppose, he said to himself, if I committed arson and was sent to prison, I would learn a new lesson of life. But I doubt the end would justify the means! But that is nonsense. Still, he knew he was growing every day more dissatisfied, though not with the humble life. That simply amused him. It was still a relief to feel no trammels of society upon him. To be bound by no engagements to call, dine or attend a friend's reception. The plain, homely food, so much more excellent than he had supposed people of that class enjoyed, far from being tiresome to him, had been eaten with a relish he had not known for years. Moreover, he no longer spent weary nights tossing on his bed trying to woo sleep. Even though his was now a hard, clean bed in a woodhouse chamber, he dropped to sleep the moment his head touched the pillow and knew nothing more until the morning.

Clearly there were blessings connected with this experience. What, then, was at fault? It couldn't be the social position that chafed him. He laughed when he thought of the patronizing tone in which Rex Hartwell said, "Well, John, you keep their horses in first-class order, I see. I wish I could find as careful a man as you to look after mine." Rex didn't mean to be patronizing, simply to be kind, and John was not in the least annoyed — only amused.

He laughed with even more relish when he thought of Susan Appleby's honest attempts to civilize him, for the times were innumerable when that outspoken woman "got at him" for his good. He was equally indifferent to Nannie Marvin's efforts to be friendly with him, after the manner in which she tried to be to all the employees of the farm, as he was to Anna's grown-up and superior airs.

He looked grave, however, when he thought of Corey Elliott. The boy interested him because he saw in him great possibilities. Stuart King, the scholar, might do much for him. John Stuart, his father's hired man, was powerless.

It was the same, in a measure at least, with the boys he had met that evening. The rudest and most ignorant among them, by reason of being a factory hand or a boy struggling at home on a worn-out farm, considered himself a grade above a hired man and would not be disposed to take help or hint from him. Yet it was not simply being somebody's hired man that limited John's ability to be helpful. He felt assured that had this been his legitimate position in life, he could have built up, by degrees, such a character as would have commanded the respect of every boy in the neighborhood.

It's because I'm a sham, he told himself gloomily. The boys only half believe in me. They eye me with suspicion and feel the difference between what I profess to be and what I really am. I'm a growing object of suspicion. I could see it tonight in her eyes. I wouldn't be surprised to hear someone say I am a fugitive from justice! It is as Fletcher said: I can't do it. No man can be successfully, for any length of time, what he is not.

Should he drop the whole thing? There was an easy way out. He could say to Mr. Elliott that he had decided to go home; take his month's wages that were due the next day; telegraph Fletcher to express his trunk to Bennettsville; stop with it at an obscure downtown hotel where none of his set ever penetrated; rent a room and change his clothes; and appear at his rooms on Chester Square as John Stuart King. He would again be the author, returned at last from his summer wanderings. Within forty-eight hours at the utmost he could take up his dropped life and make all things as they used to be.

Could he? His startled consciousness asked this question of him with a force he had not anticipated. What about that picture of Truth on his study table that had so interested him? Would he ever again be satisfied with the pictured eyes when he knew that, not far away, their counterpart looked with real, living gaze upon those of her world — yes, and read them, apparently, as she would an open book? In plain language did he care to go back to his cultured, refined, rich life and

leave Helen Elliott secure in her father's farmhouse — never to see her again, never to make her
understand that he was true and earnest and had a
purpose in life as assuredly as she did?

"If I don't," he said aloud at last, still dejected,
"then it would be better by all means to go tomorrow. Let me retain at least a semblance of manhood. But I couldn't go so soon. It wouldn't be
treating Mr. Elliott well. I ought to give him opportunity to find a replacement for me."

He was shamefaced over the pleasure this
thought gave him. The idea that an honest reason
for a week's delay could set his heart to beating
faster! It was high time he went. He rose abruptly
at last, refusing to think longer upon certain
themes that kept urging their right to be considered.

"I'll go to work, I believe," he said with a laugh,
"and see if I can forget myself in the troubles of
Reuben and Hannah. I wonder what that precious
couple intends doing with me next? The idea that
an author creates his situations is nonsense. Witness how these two wind me about their little fin-
gers, compelling me to allow them to do and say
what I had not the remotest intention of having
them say or do."

Then he went over to his table for the first time
that evening and found lying there a bulky package addressed to "John Stuart." It was from
Fletcher, of course, but where did it come from? He
had driven over to the post office at five o'clock
and found nothing. Some neighbor must have been
ahead of him and brought the mail. He looked
troubled at it. This thing had occurred once or
twice before, and each time he had received a sus-
piciously heavy packet. Susan, the outspoken, had

said on one occasion, "Seems to me you get an awful lot of letters. I would think it would take all you
could earn to pay the postage if you answer them
all." It was evidently one of the things about him
that looked suspicious. Perhaps it helped to create
the pained and puzzled look he had seen in
Helen's eyes that night.

Oh, to be able to look into those eyes with perfectly honest ones, with nothing to conceal or explain! How he wished he were back in his own
rooms tonight with his present knowledge and
could start out tomorrow morning as John Stuart
King, student and author!

He could come out to Bennettsville by train, and
thence to the Elliott farm by the public conveyance,
and boldly ask to be boarded for a few weeks while
he studied the conditions of country life with a
view to a certain portion of his next book. Then
someone else could investigate the tramp question
that had started him on this adventure — he
wouldn't care.

But in that case how would he have known of
such a being as Helen Elliott? No, his experience
had been too rich to give up easily. Besides, he
couldn't have come to the farmhouse and boarded
with any such ideas. Being a man of honor, this
could not have happened. What was he talking
about? And what was the matter with him tonight?
That remarkable meeting had upset him. No, it
was that remarkable talk during the drive home.
How troubled she had looked!

He turned to open his letter. It enclosed others
bearing foreign postmarks. Fletcher's was brief
and ran as follows:

See here, my boy, isn't it time you gave

up this folly and came home? If you
don't appear soon, I shall get up a search
party and come after you. Dr. Wells asks
all sorts of questions about what you're
doing. Even Dickson from your bank
stopped me on the street to ask if you
were ill; he had not been called upon to
cash any of your checks lately. I can't
promise to keep the peace much longer.
How many tramps can you study, staying forever in one place?

I looked up Bennettsville yesterday,
and it's an insignificant little place, not
even large enough for a money order office. Is it headquarters for tramps? Do
come home, John. I'm tired of this, even
if you're not.

John laid down the letter with a faint smile on
his face and turned the two foreign ones over, apparently to study their postmarks. Then he opened
one written in a delicate hand. It began:

My dear son,
I have delayed writing for several
days, hoping to hear of you as back in
town. What can you be doing in the
country so late? And why don't you give
me your correct address instead of my
having to send letters always to
Fletcher's care? Don't you stay long
enough in one place to receive any mail?
If not, I don't see why you might not as
well be with us. We've been in the same
place now for three weeks. A quieter
place, with better opportunities for you

to go on with your interminable writing,
I am sure you couldn't find.

I think Elizabeth is rather hurt by your
conduct, although she wouldn't say so
for the world. She is certainly happier
than she was. But that is not strange, for
a girl of her age must have some amusement. I told her yesterday that if you
were within a thousand miles of her, and
likely to hear about it the same season, I
would almost accuse her of flirting. Have
a care, Stuart. Elizabeth is young and
beautiful and accustomed to attention.
She won't endure patiently neglect of
any sort. And if you're not attentive now,
what can she expect for the future?

There was more of it in the same strain. The
reader's face gathered in a frown, and he soon
skipped to the next page and glanced hurriedly
down its contents. Then he took up the other letter
with a sigh. It was shorter than his mother's, and
the hand was even more feminine and difficult to
read.

My dear Stuart,
We are still to address you nowhere in
particular, it seems. Your friend Fletcher
is certainly very kind. Does he have the
privilege of reading the letters before he
forwards them, to pay him for his
trouble? It seems sometimes as though
you are nowhere. We wonder daily what
you can find to hold you to the country
so long. The utmost that I could ever endure of the country was a very few weeks

in the summer. But I believe you always raved over it. It's another illustration of how startlingly our tastes differ.

We are really quite domesticated at this point. There is talk of our remaining all winter, in which case it would have been a delightful place for you to indulge your scribbling propensities.

There is a certain Mr. Capen here, an English gentleman with a prospective title, I believe, who is very attentive, chiefly to your mother, though of course he has to let me share his courtesies for propriety's sake. How would you enjoy a step-papa, my dear boy? He is not old, but neither is your mother. I'm not sure but it would be a good idea. If you say so, I will encourage it to the best of my ability.

At this point the letter was tossed angrily down, and the frown on John Stuart's face had gathered in great cords. He could not have told what it was that irritated him so painfully. He had for years contemplated the possibility of his mother's marrying again. Not exactly with satisfaction, it's true. They were so totally different that they could never share close companionship. Still, the young man had been wont to say mournfully to himself that his mother was all he had, and at the same time he had tried to prepare himself for the possibility of her assuming closer ties than his.

It was not astonishment over the unexpected, therefore, that helped to deepen the frowns on his face. It was, rather, the utter absence of feeling of any sort, or of heart, in either letter, that struck home with a dull pain. Mother and Elizabeth — the two names had been associated in his life for years — always indeed. Elizabeth was a second cousin, left early in his mother's care.

For at least four years he had thought of her as his promised wife. This had seemed a natural and entirely reasonable outgrowth of their intimacy. His mother had desired it, and neither he nor Elizabeth had been in the least averse to the arrangement. He had been somewhat tried, of late, by her apathy with regard to his literary studies and her indifference to his success as an author, but he had told himself she was like all young women.

Now, as the frowns deepened on his face until it was positively scarred with them, he admitted to himself that all young women were not like her. "What is truth? What is truth?" repeated the wretched phonograph in his brain over and over and *over*.

He was angry even with that. He swept all the papers and letters — Reuben and Hannah, the creations of his brain; Fletcher with his light nothings; his mother and Elizabeth with their empty nothings — into his padlock box and turned the key. Then he went to bed. But it was late that night, or rather early in the morning, before his perplexities were shut away by the curtain of sleep.

CHAPTER XIII

TRUTH VERSUS FALSEHOOD

orey Elliott was tilted back in an easy chair in one of the small reading rooms connected with the college. His attitude was that of a lounger, and several other young fellows were sitting or standing about in positions suggesting leisure and recreation. Some topic of considerable interest, involving a difference of opinion, had been up for discussion between two of them. Corey had just drawn attention to himself by asking, "Why don't you two fellows ask me to settle that dispute for you?"

"How would you know anything about it?" one of them asked. "You don't even know the person we're talking about."

"Don't I, indeed! What makes you so sure of that?"

"Well, do you? He has only been in town for about a week. He hasn't been out to the college at all, despite the fact that he has a dear cousin in this neighborhood."

"It's never safe to jump to conclusions, Harry, my boy. I know the color of his hair and eyes as well as I do those of my own father, not to speak of several other important items of information I could give you concerning him."

Harry was about to enlist him for his side of the debate when the other, who had been gazing meditatively at Corey, suddenly turned their thoughts into a new channel. "I say, Elliott, you weren't — upon my word, I believe you were — one of those fellows the other night!"

The color instantly flamed Corey's face, but he answered with his easy laugh. "What a definite question! What a lawyer you will make, Alf! Fancy pitching such carefully planned and lucid queries as that at the head of a trembling witness! Let me see. I was a 'fellow' of some sort the other night? Undoubtedly. I was one of a lot of fellows, no doubt, but how shall it be determined which lot you refer to?"

"He wouldn't joke like that if he had been with them last night," volunteered Harry. "You've heard of the precious scrape they got into at the Belmont House, haven't you?"

"Oh, some more gossip? That's right, Hal. Lawyers have to be on the lookout for all such little things. What did we do at the Belmont House to create such a sensation?"

"So you were one of them?" chimed in the other.

"I wonder we never thought of you. We knew you were out somewhere last night. Tell us all about it, Cor. If you hadn't been out of town today, you would know that there's been quite an excitement over it. Lots of stories are afloat. One is that the Prex is going to expel every one of you. It isn't true, is it? We think it would be mean punishment

for a little fracas like that, and gotten up in honor
of a stranger, too. We'll stand by you, Cor, if that's
it, though we thought it was mean of Bliss not to
invite all our set. It was Bliss's spread, wasn't it?
And what did you break, anyhow? Those yarns are
always so awfully exaggerated."

All the young men in the room closed about him
in great eagerness. All talked at once, each asking a
question about the affair at the Belmont House.
They had been brought back to a subject that had
excited them much earlier in the day, and they
thought they had gleaned all possible information.
Now, behold! Here was a new and unexpected
vein to work.

"I'm sorry you were with them, Cor," said one of
the older boys. "It isn't simply that one evening's
performance, but that fellow Traverse has a bad
name. I wouldn't care to be associated with him.
How came you to know him so well?"

"Oh, hold on!" shouted another. "Dick is green
with envy, Cor, because he wasn't invited. Don't
listen to his preaching, but tell us about the scrape
and how you're going to get out of it. We heard
they couldn't find but three that they were sure of,
and those three wouldn't give so much as a hint
about the others. You weren't one of the three,
were you?"

"My dear fellows! How am I going to know unless you tell me who the three were?" This was
Corey's laughing rejoinder. Then he added, his
face suddenly growing grave, "It's a bad business,
boys. I'm glad you weren't in it, though we had no
end of fun and didn't mean any harm. What's that?
Traverse? Oh, he isn't so bad as his reputation.
Hardly anyone is. No, we haven't been expelled
yet, at least I haven't, but there's no telling what

will come. You fellows will stand by us, won't you, whatever happens?"

In this way he parried rather than answered their questions for several minutes. At the time they seemed to themselves to be acquiring a great deal of information. But after it was over, they reviewed the interview with a mortified realization that Corey had told them nothing about the famous Belmont House trouble. In the midst of one of his half-serious, half-comic responses, a click like that of a closing door sounded in the alcove just behind him. He was separated from it only by a hanging curtain. He stopped suddenly and turned toward it. "Is someone in there, boys?" he asked. "I glanced in when I sat down here and thought it was vacant."

One of the boys pushed back the curtain and looked in. "No," he said, "there's no one here. It's that old door that gives a click every now and then."

Corey drew a sigh of relief. "I was preparing to be scared," he said lightly. "It would have been hard on me to have had the Prex, for instance, hiding there to listen to my confessions." Then the questions and answers went eagerly forward.

In point of fact, President Chambers *had* been standing in the corner of the alcove, almost concealed by the heavy curtains, looking thoughtfully at a book whose leaves did not turn. It was he who had clicked the door after he had passed through it.

Fifteen minutes later, while Corey Elliott was still alternately astonishing and irritating his small audience, Jackson, the dignitary who managed all the important affairs of the college, appeared with his courtly bow to say that President Chambers would like to have Mr. Elliott come to his office immediately.

"Now you're in for it!" exclaimed the boys, while Corey suddenly and in silence tilted his chair forward and sprang to his feet.

"I'm glad I'm not in your shoes," said Harry sympathetically.

"But remember," added another voice, "we'll stand by you."

Then Corey Elliott moved away, wondering what in the world President Chambers could want with him.

The president gave no time for consideration. Glancing up as the young man entered, he began without other recognition than the slightest possible bend of his stately head. "Elliott, you doubtless remember that I gave you fifty dollars yesterday morning and asked you to step in at Wellington's as you passed and pay the bill."

"Certainly, sir," said Corey politely.

"Very well. What did you do with the money?"

"Paid the bill, of course." And now Corey's voice had taken on both a questioning and a haughty tone.

"And secured a receipt for it?"

"No, sir. The receiving clerk was very busy, and he remarked to me that I might leave the bill with the money and he would send up a receipt by mail. I knew the college had constant dealings at Wellington's and supposed it would be all right. Is there anything wrong?"

"Yes, many things are wrong. This is by no means the worst feature. Words would not express my astonishment and, I may say, dismay at learning that you were involved in the disgraceful scene that took place at the Belmont House last night.

Had my information come from any other source than the one it did, I would have denied it indignantly on the ground that your father's son could not have been guilty of such a lapse. To find that you were not only a participant, but that the remembrance of it simply amuses you and is even to be boasted of, almost staggers my belief in young men altogether. I had not imagined it of you. I've decided that you perhaps anticipated the result of the disgrace in dollars and cents and are now aware that your share will amount to something more than fifty dollars. Plate glass and decorated china are expensive articles to play with, young man."

By this time Corey Elliott's anger, which had been steadily rising since the first words were spoken to him, had reached white heat. Yet he kept his voice low as he said, "May I be allowed to ask what informant against me is so trustworthy that on the strength of his words you feel yourself at liberty not only to accuse me falsely, but also to insult me by insinuations that I would think were beneath you?"

President Chambers looked steadily and sternly at the young man, but his voice was sorrowful as he said, "Elliott, if you were innocent, I would pass over the impudence of your language. I believe I would even rejoice in it. But it's bitter to me to remember that my informant was no other than yourself. I was in the lower reading room this evening, in the alcove just back of where you sat, and I heard your remarkably genial, even merry, admissions to your classmates. I also heard your frank avowal of intimate acquaintance with a man whom I believe to be thoroughly bad in every sense of the word. After that, can you wonder at my suspicions?"

The young man caught his breath in a sudden gasp and stifled what sounded like a groan. For a moment he stared almost vacantly at the stern face before him, as though he felt unable to gather his thoughts into words. Then he burst forth, "President Chambers, there was not a word of truth in what I said! I was just kidding the fellows to show them how easy it was to fool them. I hadn't heard anything about the trouble at the Belmont House until they told me, and I don't know any of the particulars even now. I've been away all day by permission of the authorities. The boys were so excited and so gullible that I couldn't help having a little fun at their expense. Besides, I had reasons for wishing — "

Here he came to a sudden stop. It was clear his listener did not believe him. The stern look never left his face. Instead, it deepened as he said after a moment of impressive silence, "Can I believe that a self-respecting young man, deliberately and without other motive than fun, would tell as many lies as I heard you tell to your classmates? Elliott, is it possible you don't see that this way of trying to evade disgrace is but a deeper disgrace? Listen!"

He lifted his hand with an imperative gesture as the impetuous young voice was about to burst forth. "You have accused me of insulting you by an insinuation. I did speak words to you that nothing but your own language, as heard by me, could have wrung from me, but I ought to speak plainer. You should know that the fifty dollars you say you left with the receiving clerk at Wellington's, he says he has never received. I came home from there, firm in the belief that you could explain the matter as soon as you reached here. I thought the hour might have been later than you supposed, and you might have felt compelled to let the errand wait until another time. Or perhaps it had slipped your mind. But when I heard you tonight and learned that you were one of those who had, but the evening before, defied authority and disgraced yourself and the college, and then that you could laugh over it, I felt justified in believing you had been tempted into other lines of disgrace.

"I don't wish to be hard on you," he added in tones less stern as he saw the suddenly paling face. "I would be glad to help you and to shield you from all the public disgrace possible. With regard to this affair at the Belmont House, the trustees and faculty are agreed that public and decided examples must be made of those who, in so flagrant a manner, defied college rules. Every student knows the position we hold in regard to these matters. It's not possible for any of you to sin ignorantly. But as concerns this other, Elliott, I'm persuaded that you may have been led into sudden temptation. If you will be true to me and state everything exactly as it is, I will shield you and give you a chance to recover yourself."

"You're very kind," said Corey, "very kind indeed! But I want you to understand distinctly that I don't wish any shielding from you, nor any 'chances,' as you call them. It will go hard with me if I don't make you repent this night's work." And turning, he strode from the room.

Corey had never been so angry in his life. The veins in his temples seemed swelling into cords, and the blood beat against them as though determined to burst forth. Bareheaded and without overcoat as he was, he strode into the chill night air, uncertain which way he went and indifferent to what became of him. The idea that he, Corey Elliott, son of a father whose word was accounted as good as a bond, grandson of a man who had been noted for his unswerving fidelity to truth and honor, should have it hinted to him that he had spoken falsely, acted falsely, actually descended to the place of a common thief! It was almost beyond belief.

Thus far, no thought of the immediate consequences of this state of things had entered his mind. That people would hear of it, that he would be expelled from college in disgrace, that his mother's heart would break and his father's be wrung with agony, did not occur to him. All he could feel was a sense of personal outrage and the overwhelming desire to punish President Chambers for the insults he had heaped upon him.

In that state of mind he was incapable of continued thought, or even of connected thought of any sort. Twice he made the circuit of the grounds, raging inwardly so much that he wasn't conscious of the cold night air. When at last he came to himself sufficiently to ask what should be done under the extraordinary circumstances that now surrounded him, the strongest feeling he had was a desire to escape from college authority. Not that he feared it. Not he! Rather he scorned it. The very grounds had suddenly become hateful to him.

If he could only be at home this minute, in his mother's room, telling her the story of his wrongs with his hand slipped into both of hers! His father would be sitting opposite with his keen, searching, yet sympathetic eyes resting upon him, and Helen would be leaning over the back of his chair, listening intently while she planned even then how to help him!

In the distance he heard the whistle of an outbound train. He stopped before a friendly lamppost and looked at his watch. In less than an hour there would be another train, going westward, and in two hours more he could be at home. Why not? Not in that state, hatless and coatless! No, he would venture into the hateful building long enough to secure what he needed.

Should he go, without a word to anyone? What right had those who had so outraged his feelings to expect courtesy from him? He still had no thought of consequences for himself. To be sure, it was less than two days to Friday, when he would normally go home anyway, but two days under the circumstances seemed an eternity.

He rushed toward the building where he roomed. Jackson was carrying the mail to the various rooms and held out a letter for him. It was from Helen. He stopped under the hall lamp to read it.

Dear Corey,
Father says it's foolish, but he really is not so well this evening. He has been feverish and somewhat flighty all day, and he asked frequently for you. We think he might have a more restful night if you could come down and sit with him. Could you? He's not seriously ill, you know, but there's fever enough to make us anxious. We shall send John to the station in the hope that you can come. But Father says that if you can't, you're not to worry in the least, and he bids me tell you that he is only sending for you to please Mother and me.

Corey gave a kind of groan as he finished. He had forgotten his father was ill.

"No bad news, I hope, sir." It was Jackson speaking with respectful sympathy, but Corey didn't answer him. Professor Marchant was moving down the hall. Corey turned toward him, speaking hurriedly. "Professor Marchant, my father is ill. Can you excuse me from college for tomorrow? I want to take the eight o'clock train."

Professor Marchant was prompt with his sympathy. He hadn't heard the latest news, and he took it for granted that the father's illness was very serious. How else was he to account for the obvious distress of the son?

CHAPTER XIV

FOR HER
SAKE

ohn Stuart did not leave the Elliott farm the following week, nor did he give notice that he intended to do so. Before he had quite settled it that this must undeniably be the next step, an event occurred that put it in the background. Farmer Elliott fell ill. Not seriously so — at least the doctor spoke cheerily and hoped that the tendency toward a course of fever would be broken before it had a chance to get seated. But the fact that Farmer Elliott was ill at all was sufficient to awaken almost consternation in his family.

Never, since the children could remember, had there been a day in which Father had not been able to attend to his usual round of duties. That he was actually ill enough to call a physician, and later to be sat up with at night, was a startling innovation. Of course John Stuart wouldn't think of leaving under such circumstances. Instead, he assumed Mr. Elliott's outdoor duties entirely and made himself so steadily necessary in the house that even

Susan said she didn't see how they would ever get on without him when he took a notion to leave, as hired folks always did.

In addition to the duties of his position, John had other cares and burdens known only to himself. Quite unexpectedly, he found himself painfully associated with the affairs of the Elliott family. During her father's illness, Helen was dependent upon him for her trips to and from her schoolhouse for the weekly evening gathering. They were generally accompanied either by Rex Hartwell or Anna Elliott, sometimes by both, for Rex had given himself with great earnestness to the business of helping the young men and older boys who gathered there.

Nannie Marvin, however, much to Helen's disappointment, had steadily refused to make a second attempt. She had a dozen excuses: She didn't know how to teach girls, not girls of that stamp; it was much better for them all to be under Helen's lead. No, indeed, she would not take boys instead. Rex could do better for them than she could. She was very busy just now; perhaps later in the season, when she had settled down, she might be able to help.

Helen was puzzled. Could it be Nannie's approaching marriage that made her seem so unlike herself? Of course she was busy, but not to be able to give a single evening in a week to work in which Rex was not only engaged but absorbed seemed strange indeed.

As for Anna, she frankly stated that she went for the fun to be got out of the going and coming, and not for any interest in the gatherings. John Stuart had been accepted doubtfully and with many misgivings as the present leader of the five little boys who had first interested him, mainly because they begged to be under his care and showed the keenest interest, not only in the meeting, but also in studying to the best of their small abilities the subject upon which he had talked to them. Helen, watching anxiously, could find nothing objectionable. Evidently John had more general knowledge than she had supposed, but as yet he seemed to be doing no harm. As soon as her father was well enough to be talked to, she must ask his advice, and together they must arrange this thing differently. And there, for the time being, the matter rested.

The father did not get well, however. Instead, the slow fever took obstinate hold of him, and while he was not at any time seriously ill, he was in need of constant care and was the subject of much anxiety.

To one evening class Rex and John Stuart went alone, Rex taking Miss Elliott's place as well as he could and being helped in ways that surprised him by the watchful John. He commended John warmly on the way home and then cross-examined him in a manner that made it painfully difficult to answer with even the semblance of truth.

Rex was kind, assuring John that, with the degree of education he evidently had, he ought to be able to get work better suited to him than that which he was now doing. He said he could imagine a chain of circumstances that might have led, in a fit of desperation perhaps, to taking the first thing that was offered. The times had been very hard indeed, and he honored him for doing anything honest rather than to live upon others. But when Mr. Elliott recovered his health, they would talk it over together and see what could be done.

Mr. Elliott, he was sure, would be the last person to try to hold a man to a place lower than he was fitted to fill.

Under existing circumstances, what could a self-respecting young man do but mumble something that was intended to sound like gratitude and then maintain silence? After that conversation, Rex told Helen that there was some mystery about the man. He was afraid that all had not been quite right with John's past. He seemed so utterly averse to frankness and didn't respond kindly to sympathy. Of course, this made Helen even more anxious and more careful.

About a week later, on the same evening when the Belmont House fracas took place, John was driving rapidly home from town when he met one of the boys belonging to Helen's, or rather to Rex Hartwell's, evening class. This shock-headed, clumsy, dull-eyed boy had seemed to John to have no distinctive character of any sort.

"'Evening," the boy said, halting close to the wagon wheel with the intention of arresting its progress. "I was comin' to meet you."

"So I perceive. Is there anything I can do for you?"

"I dunno. Maybe you can try, and maybe you can't. I went to see Rex Hartwell, but he has gone into town and won't be back in time, I reckon."

"In time for what, Thomas? Jump in, and we can talk while we ride. I'm in a hurry to get home. If I can help you in any way, I'll be glad to do so."

"I dunno as it's helping me," said the boy, clambering into the wagon. "Only I feel as though anything that would help her would kind of help me, somehow. You're a friend of hers, ain't you?"

"I hope so. Who is she?"

"Well, it's that Anna Elliott I'm talking about. I ain't much of a friend to *her*. She's always laughing and poking fun at us, but bein' she's her sister, I thought something ought to be done."

"Thomas," said John Stuart sharply, "tell me, in as few words as you can, what you're talking about."

Thus admonished, Thomas told with some idea of brevity the piece of gossip that had stirred him to action. He had learned, through listening to the talk of others who considered him too dull to join them and too stupid to report their sayings where harm might result, of a company of "fellows and girls" who were to spend that very evening at the Wayside House. One of the boys had a brother who worked at Wayside, and he said that supper had been ordered at ten o'clock, and there was to be a dance before and afterward.

"They're a lot of college fellows," explained Thomas, "and as mean a lot as they can get up, even there, I guess." From that verdict it will be understood what estimate Thomas was getting of higher education. "And they're going to bring a lot of girls with them from the city. Some of them have been there before, and Dick says no sister of his would have anything to do with them girls. But one of them they're going to get here is Anna Elliott."

"Take care, Thomas!" said John Stuart sharply. "Miss Elliott would not like to hear you using her young sister's name in such connection. If you're a friend of hers, you should remember that."

"I *am* taking care," said the boy impatiently. "If I hadn't been, do you think I would have tramped out here to tell you about it? I thought maybe it could be stopped, that you could do something about it. If you can't, why, I'll find somebody else."

"Yes," said John Stuart soothingly, much ashamed of his unnecessary outburst. "I see your motive is good. Tell me all you know about it. Something must be done. Why do you think Miss Anna is connected with it?"

"Because two of the girls from our neighborhood go to her school, and they overhear talk. They know that Anna Elliott and one or two other girls have been writing letters to some of the college boys. They don't sign their own names, you know. They don't sign the names of anybody that really is, and they just do it for fun, only you know what Miss Elliott thinks of such fun. You heard her a few weeks ago, didn't you, talk about that in the meetin'? Some of the girls looked at one another then — they saw she didn't know her own sister was doin' it. Well, the college fellow she has been writin' to has made a plan to come out here, get her and go for a ride, and bring her up to the Wayside House. Then he'll introduce her to them other girls, and they're a set! Jack says there's not a decent one among 'em, and it seems awful, don't it, to have her sister among 'em?"

"Tell me how you learned this last, Thomas."

"Why, one of our girls that goes up there to school sits right behind Anna Elliott and that Holcombe girl, and she heard them talking it all over. Anna, she don't know about being taken to the Wayside House. She just thinks she's going to have a ride with him, you know, and I s'pose she don't see no great harm in it. But Jack says she's one of 'em, that he heard the two fellows who came out to order the supper and room and everything talking and laughing about it."

Thomas must have been satisfied with the close

attention his story received. John Stuart listened and questioned and went over the main points again, approaching them skillfully from another angle to be sure the narrator didn't contradict himself. He felt sure at the close that the story he had heard had some foundation, enough to make it important to give it immediate attention.

John looked at his watch and found that the hour was even later than he had supposed. What was to be done must be done quickly. Then he hurried his horses and got rid of Thomas with the assurance that he had done all that was necessary and that the matter would receive prompt attention. He also urged him not to mention to another human being what he had told him. This last was earnestly impressed.

"Remember, Thomas, Miss Elliott would be seriously injured if this story should get out. Since there are only a few of us who know it, and all of us are to be trusted, we may hope to save her sister from unpleasant consequences and at the same time protect her. I'm sure I can depend upon you to make the others feel the same."

Thomas went away with the belief that he was being depended upon to do an important work, and also with the vague feeling, which had come to him before, that John Stuart was a "real smart man."

Yet John Stuart, left to himself, had no such comfortable realization of his power. He drove rapidly under the impression that there was need for haste, but just what could be done had by no means occurred to him. Had he heard this remarkable story earlier, he might have proceeded with caution and accomplished results without frightening anybody. Then again, for the hundredth time, came that dreary second thought that, were he himself instead of a man masquerading under an assumed name and character, his way would be infinitely plainer.

However, the obvious first step was to learn whether Anna was at home and, if so, whether she had an appointment for the evening away from home. Susan could help him that far. "No, she ain't to home," said Susan, shaking her head and speaking in a crisp tone, "and it's my opinion that she ought to be. I think her pa is a good deal sicker than they tell about. He ain't no hand to lie abed for common things."

"Can you tell me where to find Miss Anna? I have an errand to do for her."

"Oh, you'll find her, I s'pose, down to that Holcombe girl's house. At least that's where she has gone to spend the night," she said, looking somewhat doubtful. "I told Helen I would keep her at home if I was her, but Helen said she was so kind of nervous, not like herself, that her mother thought she'd better go. They think she's worryin' about her pa, but it's a queer kind of worryin' that'll be willing to go off and leave him all night. I don't see, for my part, what she finds in that Holcombe girl to be so fond of. They ain't a mite alike."

John left her still moralizing and went out in haste to consider. He had been gone all day on business that Mr. Elliott had felt to be important. He had heard nothing about plans, but Anna often walked home in pleasant weather. Now it appeared that she must have left in the morning with the intention of spending the night with Laura Holcombe. John didn't like "that Holcombe girl" any better than Susan did.

Without any clear idea of what he should do next, he went to Mrs. Elliott for permission to drive to the village on important business. It distressed him to remember that she gave a reluctant consent and evidently wondered, as well she might, what business of importance could call him back to the village, leaving work that had been long waiting for him. She was, however, too preoccupied to ask close questions.

Not so Helen. She came out to the wagon with a troubled face. "John, must you really go back to town tonight? There are so many things to be done to get ready for the night. Why didn't you stop and attend to the business when you came through?"

"This is something I thought of since," said John lamely enough. He went away angry with himself that he seemed to be living a life that made it necessary to give every sentence he spoke a double meaning.

The way of the dissembler is hard, at least, he told himself bitterly as he drove away. What did he mean to do next? He would drive at once to the Holcombes' and learn if Anna was there. And then what? He drove on hurriedly, entirely uncertain of his next move.

Would it have been better to have told Helen what he had heard? No, he answered himself emphatically, he would shield her as long as he could from any added anxiety.

He wondered how it would do to tell Anna he had a message for her and then take her home, telling her on the way the story that had come to his ears. Even if there was not a word of truth in it, it might open her eyes to the importance of taking the utmost care of her movements, lest they be construed as evil. This was the only course he had

thought of when he reached the Holcombes', only
to be informed that Miss Anna had gone to take a
short drive with a friend.

"Did Miss Laura go with her?" he ventured to
ask.

"Oh, no!" Mrs. Holcombe said. Laura was not
well enough to go out evenings. Didn't he know
she had been sick again? It was an old friend of
Anna's who had called for her, a college friend of
her brother, she believed. Then she, too, questioned closely in return and hoped Mr. Elliott was
not worse. Laura would be dreadfully disappointed if Anna had to go home.

He got away as soon as he could, taking the direct road to the Wayside House and making all
speed, but he overtook no one. There was a lively
company at the Wayside House, and among them
undoubtedly several forward young women and
some college men. So much of the story was true.
But Anna Elliott, so far as he could learn, was not
present.

He told the host he had called with a message
for a person whom he had expected to meet there.
Declining to leave any word, he was departing
when he caught a glimpse of Corey Elliott in the
small room opening from the main reception room,
leaning against a mantel and looking moodily into
the fire. He went out with a new trouble knocking
at his heart. Was sorrow coming to Helen through
this young man also? And was there nothing he
could do? Did the young man know his sister was
to be in the questionable company in that questionable house that night?

Busy with these thoughts, he drove slowly, all
the time on the watch. The long lane down which
he was driving was the private entrance to the

Wayside House. At the gateway he was stopped by a handsome coach. The driver, apparently a gentleman, was having some trouble with spirited horses who resented the appearance of the gatepost. The light from the gate lamp shone full on the carriage. Anna Elliott shrank back from the glare of light.

In an instant, John was at her side, speaking distinctly.

"Miss Anna, you are needed at home immediately. I came here in search of you."

"Oh, John!" she said, her lips pale with apprehension, "Father is worse!"

He had made no sort of reply. He helped her, frightened and weeping, from one carriage to the other, while her companion tried to express his polite regrets, looking all the time excessively annoyed. But John Stuart held himself to utter silence. He would have enough to say, under these peculiar circumstances not knowing in the least how to say it, when he had driven away with his charge.

CHAPTER XV

Tangles

J ohn," said Corey Elliott as he took his seat in the sleigh the following evening, "how ill is my father?" His voice shook with strong feeling of some sort, and even by the dim light of the station lamp, his face showed pale and drawn. John Stuart felt a keen pity for him, and as they rode swiftly along he talked as cheerily as he could.

"I don't think there's cause for serious anxiety. He has a slow fever, which is, of course, exhausting. But the doctor speaks confidently of the outcome. His inability to sleep has been the most trying feature of the trouble for a day or two, and in his semi-wakeful feverish thoughts there seemed to have been troubled fancies about you. That's why your mother and sister thought that if you could be beside him in health and strength, these might be dispelled, and he might be able to rest."

John was forgetting himself again in the interest

of the present moment. Had Corey not been too self-occupied to have noticed, he would have stared at hearing this form of address from the hired man.

Part of the sentence caused Corey pain. He drew a deep, quivering sigh that went to John's heart as he said tremulously, "He is troubled about me, is he? That seems almost prophetic, poor Father! I don't know how I'm to get along without his advice. I never needed it more." Then, after a moment's silence, he added, "John, I must manage in some way to see Helen alone tonight. Can you think how it can be done?"

He was in trouble, certainly, else he would never have appealed to the hired man in this way. He had always been more or less interested in this experiment of his father's and was uniformly kind to John. But it had been the kindness of condescension, as though he would always say, "I am Corey Elliott, a college student, and you are my father's hired tramp." The tremble in his voice, and his appeal, had in them a note of equality. He went on eagerly.

"The truth is, I'm in very great trouble. Of course I can't talk to my father, and equally my mother must not be disturbed now. But Helen has always time and courage for everybody's trouble. If I can talk it all over with her, I know I'll feel better at once. But I don't know how to manage it without worrying my mother and perhaps my father."

"Oh, I think we can arrange that," was John's cheerful reply. "I help in taking care of your father at night, and when he has enjoyed you for a while and is resting, we can plan to have you and your sister disappear together for a few minutes."

He did plan it successfully. No sooner was the father lying back with quiet eyes, resting from the pleased excitement of seeing his boy, than John, who had meantime been moving quietly about, arranging fire and lights and a dozen other small things to add to the comfort of all, came over to Mrs. Elliott, speaking low. "Could I remain here now on guard while Miss Elliott goes out with her brother for a breath of fresh air? I heard you urging it earlier in the evening."

Mrs. Elliott responded promptly. Helen, who had a week's vacation from school and was spending it all in her father's room, was a source of anxiety to her mother. "Go, Helen," she said earnestly, "and take a brisk walk with Corey out in the moonlight. It will do you good. Corey, carry her off. She hasn't been out of this room today, and there's really no need. John" — with a grateful glance toward him — "is as good as a trained nurse."

The father added feebly his desire for the same thing, and the two slipped away, only one being aware how eager Corey was to go. John, at his post near the window, ready for anything that might be wanted, watched the two pacing back and forth in the moonlight with a great ache in his heart. The boy was in trouble, and John, by reason of his own folly, was powerless to help him. If he were occupying his proper position in this household, how easily and naturally he could say to Corey, "Tell me all about it, my friend. It's but a few years since I was as young as you are. I can understand most things without being told and stand ready to help you in whatever direction help is needed." As matters stood, what could he say?

He puzzled over the possible trouble. If it was a question of money, and careless boys like Corey were always getting into money scrapes, how easily could John Stuart King have drawn a check for any reasonable amount! What could John Stuart, hired farmhand, consistently do? Yet what was there that he would not do for this merry-eyed, kind-hearted, free and easy boy? Not alone for his sake, nor for the sake of his father and mother, both of whom John Stuart loved, but because nothing this world contained would be better for him than to be able to bring a happy light into Helen Elliott's solemn and, in these days, anxious eyes. He told himself gloomily that at least to himself he would speak the truth.

Out in the clear, cold air, pacing briskly back and forth, never going out of sight of the windows where the watcher stood, were Corey and Helen. Corey was pouring out his eager, passionate story, almost too rapidly at times for coherence. Helen was alert, keen, questioning, yet alive with tender sympathy.

"Oh, Corey!" she said once, her voice full of sadness.

He hastened to answer the unspoken reproach. "Yes, I know. It all comes from my intolerable habit of joking, playing with the truth. You said it would get me into trouble some day, and it has. I didn't think it could. I thought you were overparticular, but I've learned a lesson! I don't do it half as much as I used to, Helen — I really don't. It's as though I can see your eyes looking right into mine and stopping the words. I wish I had seen them that night, but I was excited and anxious, you know, that the fellows — no, you don't know that, either."

"What is it that I don't know, Corey? Let me have all the truth this time."

The boy looked annoyed and hesitated a moment. Then he said, "It has to do with a matter that I wasn't going to mention for fear of causing you needless anxiety, but I shall have to tell it now, and it doesn't matter since it came to nothing. You know the Wayside House, at the junction, what a bad name it has? Well, there are three or four fellows in college who are about as bad as they can be. Two of them, it seems, have been holding correspondence with some girls in this neighborhood. I don't know who the girls are. They have assumed names, or at least names I never heard of before.

"One of the boys, named Hooper, is the worst scamp in college or out of it. He has been writing letters by the volume to this girl, whoever she is, and making fun of her to all the boys in his set. I don't hear much about their proceedings, for, as you may naturally suppose, I don't belong. But I overheard enough one night to interest me, and I went in where they were just as he was exhibiting a picture. The girl actually committed the folly of sending her photograph to him!

"Helen, if you could have heard those fellows talk as they bent over it, I think your eyes would have blazed! I caught only a glimpse of the face, and it was taken in a fancy headdress of some sort that shaded the features, but I was almost certain it was Nell Marvin! You don't think it possible that Nell could have sent him her picture, do you? I tried in every possible way to get another look at it, but the fellow didn't intend for me to see it at all, so I failed.

"After that I tried to find out what their next scheme might be. They always have something on hand, and I found that two or three of them had appointments with so-called ladies at that same Wayside House on Tuesday evening of this week. I

also learned that rascal Hooper had an appointment to meet the girl with whom he had been corresponding at the same place!

"The only thing I could think of was to rush off
down here and spend the evening at the Wayside
House. What a charming evening I had of it! Think
of being so near home as that, Helen, and not being
able to come home! Those precious scamps and
their so-called ladies were on hand, but there was
no girl among them that I had ever seen before.
The chief scamp, Hooper, wasn't there at all. He
was expected, however. I overheard all sorts of
conjectures about his nonappearance, and the fear
that he would come later held me there until the
party broke up.

"They had a lovely row, some of them, before
that time — drank too much, you know. Well, there
was nothing for me to do but to get back to college.
And, meantime, trouble had been brewing there
for me. This fracas at the Belmont House also occurred, you understand, last night. It would be
easy enough for me to prove an alibi, but how
much better off would I be in proving myself to
have spent the evening, and away into the night,
with questionable company at the Wayside House?
For that matter, only questionable companies
gather there, while respectable people do frequent
the Belmont.

"You can see why I was anxious to throw those
boys off the track in regard to where I was that
evening. I hadn't heard any particulars about the
trouble at the Belmont, and I don't know anything
about it yet save that some costly dishes and furniture were smashed. I suppose there will be a big
bill to pay, but of course I can get out of that. As to
the fifty dollars, I'm in awful trouble. I paid the bill

with that money as certainly as my name is Elliott, and I paid it to the assistant bookkeeper, who stands very high. How is it possible for him to say I didn't, and what has become of it?

"You see how it is, Helen. Circumstances are all against me. If I had been at home that night in my room, at work, as I should have been but for that notion I got that some of our young people were in danger, why, I could prove it in two minutes. In fact, there would be nothing to prove. The boys wouldn't have thought of such a thing as my being among that crowd if I hadn't pretended to know that wretch of a Traverse, whom I haven't even seen. It all comes back to this, Helen: I've been playing with falsehoods, and they have gotten me into a scrape, as you said they would. I don't see any way out.

"When I started for home tonight, I was too angry to think. I am yet, for that matter," he admitted. "What business had President Chambers to charge me with being a thief? Suppose the fifty dollars can't be found. What is that to me when I know I laid it down before the bookkeeper's eyes, and he acknowledged it? Helen, I've been treated meanly. I am sure Father would say so. But just how to manage it, I don't know. I suppose I'll have to pay it again. Do you think it would be possible for us to raise that amount extra, Helen, while Father is sick? And why should I pay it, anyway? Wouldn't that look like a confession of crookedness on my part? I can't think clearly. If there was only someone who could give me advice."

"How would it do to talk with Rex Hartwell?"

The young man shrank and shivered. "Helen, I couldn't! He would think I wanted to borrow the money from him, and I would rather work it out on the road than do that. Must people hear about it, do you think? There will be so many details to explain, and all sorts of false stories will get afloat. But then, if I'm expelled from college, it will be all out anyhow. What a miserable business it is, and I always prided myself so much on our good name. To think that I should be the one to stain it!"

The poor fellow's voice quivered with pain, and his sister arose at once to the situation. "Never mind, Corey. We shall find our way out. It's not as though you had really done any of the things with which you're charged. If that were so, it almost seems as though I couldn't bear it. As it is, we shall be shown a way to make the truth plain. Let me think it over tonight, and in the morning I'm sure some light on how to act will have come to us."

The boy's grasp on her arm tightened, and his voice had a husky note as he said, "You trust me, Helen, don't you? You don't believe for a moment that I'm guilty of any of those horrid things?"

Her reply was prompt and reassuring. "Why, of course, Corey. How can you ask such a question? I know you do nothing but play with falseness. If you would only give that up."

"I will, Helen; I give you my word on it. If I get safely out of this scrape, see if hereafter I don't make my communications 'yea' and 'nay.' "

They were opposite the window again, and Corey caught sight of John standing framed in it. This reminded him of something he had meant to say, and he broke in with it abruptly. "Helen, does John frequent the Wayside House? Last night, when I was hanging around, watching for what might develop, I saw him walk into the reception room and look around, as if he were in search of someone. I slipped into the small room, for, as you may well suppose, I didn't care to be recognized there. But I couldn't help wondering what had brought him. Do you suppose he can be of that stamp?"

Helen drew a weary sigh. "I don't know," she said mournfully. "I confess I don't know what to think of him. I would like to believe in him in every way; he's so kind to Father, so thoughtful of us all, and so entirely faithful in his work. But there are suspicious circumstances connected with him, and sometimes I'm afraid that — "

She broke off abruptly. Was it fair to speak any of her suspicions so long as it wasn't necessary? Memories of his talk during that ride home from her evening meeting came to her. John's language had been so unfitted to his position. Then she remembered the haste with which he had turned his horses and gone back to town but the evening before, though he knew there were pressing duties awaiting him at the farm.

What could possibly have called him to the Wayside House? He had an errand, he told her, at the Holcombes', and Anna had returned with him. Of course, this must have taken place after he left the Wayside House. He would not have dared to take her little sister there! Her face grew dark over the thought of this possibility — not that Anna would have allowed him to do so. That, of course, was folly.

It had not surprised Helen that the child had suddenly melted upon returning home. She had fits of nervousness over her father's state that could only be accounted for by supposing that she heard talk outside that made her believe he was more seriously ill than his own family thought. The child had cried a dozen times that day, and

Helen had not questioned, believing this to be the cause. Probably the Holcombes had questioned her with such serious faces and such foreboding sighs that the poor girl had been seized with a panic and welcomed John's appearance with joy. The utmost Helen had said to Anna had been in the form of a gentle rebuke for coming back with John. She had been reminded that he was still a comparative stranger and that their father had been careful not to trust him too fully.

And Anna had said, "Oh, you need not be afraid of John. He's a good man." And then had followed another burst of tears.

What this much-enduring sister said aloud, after all these reflections, was, "Oh, Corey, if everybody would just be frank and sincere in all their words and ways, how much easier living would be! I can't get away from the fear that John has something to conceal."

The protective instinct came over the boy. "Poor little woman!" he said with his arm around her. "So many of us to worry over and to help. You have helped me, Helen. Looking into your true face has been a tonic. I've made lots of fun of your truth-telling propensities, I know; but that wasn't being honest. All the time I admired you for it. I would like to have my face reflect my soul, as yours does. What do you think Wayland says? He's our star boy in college, you know — never does anything wrong. He says that when he looks at your photograph he thinks of every mean thing he ever did and is ashamed of it! Helen, I feel better. You've cheered me up somehow. I knew you would. Let's go in to Father."

CHAPTER XVI

REVELATIONS

orey Elliott's courage lasted well into the next morning, when he bade his father a cheery good-bye and assured him he would get away as early as possible on the following day. He would not go back at all, he said, were it not for some important matters at college needing his attention.

Helen, too, was cheerful. "Keep up a good heart, Corey," was her admonition. "The truth must conquer, you know. It always does. And, Corey, if you find that money is needed — I mean, if you decide it will be right to pay that money over again — we can raise it. Don't worry about that, either."

This she said in the face of the fact that money was scarce and that she had not the remotest idea how to raise the extra sum. Although Mr. Elliott was counted a successful farmer, he was by no means a wealthy man. To raise even fifty additional dollars, at that season of the year, would be no small matter.

When Corey was gone, some of the brightness that had been worn for his sake faded from Helen's face. She was haunted now with a nameless anxiety concerning Anna. The child was at home, having begged permission to remain there. She was well, she said, but she didn't feel like going to school. It seemed to her that she was simply unable to study just now.

"She's worried about her father," was Mrs. Elliott's conclusion. "She certainly must have heard some grave doubts expressed about his recovery. She cried last night whenever I mentioned his name, although I assured her that the doctor, when he came last evening, pronounced the symptoms to be better in every way. Do you think exaggerated accounts of his illness can have gotten around?"

"Possibly," said Helen, more reticent than usual with her mother. She resolved to have a quiet talk with Anna at the first opportunity.

It was late in the day before the opportunity presented itself. In fact, she finally had to make it. She grew the more resolved to do so as it became evident that Anna distinctly avoided a moment's private conversation with her. There was a stronger or rather a different disturbing force than their father's illness. The child was certainly nervous and had been, her sister reflected, for several days. Since her nerves were naturally in a healthy and well-managed state, it became important to learn what had unsettled them.

Just how Helen associated the girl's unrest with what Corey had told her about the Wayside House and the mysterious photograph, she could not have told. Indeed, she assured herself indignantly that she did *not* associate them for a moment. Yet the two anxieties persisted in floating through her mind. Nevertheless, whenever she recalled Corey's words about anonymous letters written by someone in their neighborhood, a strange shiver ran through her frame.

About the middle of the afternoon Anna came downstairs dressed for walking and announced to Susan that she was going for a long walk. Susan, who had been sorely tried with the girl's unusual nervousness, replied tartly that she hoped she would "walk off her tantrums" and come back acting like herself.

Helen was on duty in her father's room at the time, but as soon as she was released for a brief rest she made ready to follow, having taken note of the direction Anna had chosen. She understood her habits and met her on her return trip, just as she had planned, about half a mile from home.

"I've been sent out to take the air," she said cheerily to Anna, who had been walking with eyes on the ground and who started like a frightened creature at first sight of her.

"Is that so?" was the eager reply. "Then go on to the rocks. There will be a lovely sunset view tonight. I thought of waiting for it myself."

"No, I haven't time for watching the sunset today. I must get back and help Mother. Besides, I came this way on purpose to meet you. I want to have a little visit with you. We've hardly seen each other for a week or two." She linked her arm within her sister's as she spoke, and the two moved on together. Anna, however, had made no response, and as Helen stole a glance at her, she saw that she was crying softly. Her misery struck to the elder sister's heart.

"What is it, dear?" she asked in tones such as a

mother might have used. "You can't be worried about Father. At least, you needn't be. We're more hopeful of his speedy recovery than we have been for nearly two weeks. The doctor spoke positively this morning, you know, and Father feels and looks better in every way. Everything is going all right, Anna. What is it that troubles you? Has someone been telling you that Father was very ill and not going to recover?"

Anna shook her head and began to cry harder.

"Then it must be some trouble of your own, dear. I've seen for several days that something was wrong. Can't you confide in me, Annie? I thought I was your best and dearest friend next to Mother, and she is so busy with Father. Can't I take her place for a little while?"

"I don't know how to tell it," said poor Anna. Her tone was so full of abject misery that her sister was sure something was gravely wrong.

They walked on for some seconds in silence, the elder sister trying to determine how best to approach a girl who had suddenly become a bundle of sore nerves. She had meant to question her closely about why John was at the Holcombes' and how it was that she changed all her plans and came home with him. But the girl was too excited now, and too miserable, to talk about personalities. She determined to try to interest her in something that she had forced herself to believe was entirely outside her sister's knowledge. Perhaps through that story Anna would get control of herself and start to realize there was real trouble in the world.

"Corey told me a strange thing last night," she began quietly. "He's troubled about some of the college boys, wild fellows — not at all of his set, of course. There's one in particular, named Hooper, about whom he is especially anxious. At least, he's the one for whom he has the least hope of any young man in college. He says there is hardly any evil that boy is not capable of planning. He overheard through some of that set that certain very bad or very foolish girls had been corresponding with them — strangers, you know, Annie, never having so much as met them!

"What especially worried Corey was that this Hooper has a correspondent in *this* neighborhood. Can you imagine who it can be? They use assumed names, he thinks, and she has even sent him her photograph! Would you suppose that a girl who had intelligence enough to write a letter could be guilty of such an act of folly as that? Corey came upon the fellow when he was exhibiting it, laughing and making simply terrible speeches over it. Corey caught just a glimpse of the picture and has been haunted ever since with the idea that it bore a resemblance to Nell Marvin!

"Of course, it was a mere resemblance," Helen pointed out, "but think how dreadful! It makes me angry for all pure-hearted girls to think there are others who can bring their class into disrepute in this way. Then, worse than all the rest, those fellows had planned to bring a party of so-called ladies out to the Wayside House night before last for supper and a dance. This Hooper was to come out here and take his correspondent to the Wayside to join them. Corey was so troubled about it all — for fear, you know, that some poor, ignorant girl in our neighborhood would get into trouble — that he secured leave of absence and came out to the Wayside House."

"Corey came to the Wayside House!" interrupted Anna, her voice indicating intense excitement. She trembled so violently that the hand resting on Helen's arm shook as if with an acute chill.

"Yes," said Helen gravely, and with sinking heart. Something very serious must be the matter. Her hope was, poor sister, that Anna must have become aware in some way of the correspondence and knew who was carrying it on and that her conscience was troubling her because she had kept it secret. She tried to finish her story without visible agitation.

"He spent the entire evening at the Wayside House — in such company, he says, as he was never in before and desires never to be in again. But he knew none of the people, at least none of the girls. And this Hooper didn't appear at all. He doesn't know now whether Hooper learned in some way that he was there and feared he would recognize the girl, or what detained him. Corey is still worried. He talked with me this morning about it and suggested that perhaps you could help us to get at the truth. It touches home, you see, coming right into our neighborhood. Do the schoolgirls ever talk up any such ideas, Anna? None of them would go to the Wayside House, of course, but there is no girl among your classmates who would write an anonymous letter, is there?"

Anna gave no answer, and Helen, suppressing an anxious sigh, after a moment went on. "There's another thing. Corey says that, while he was waiting there that evening, he saw John moving about in the large room as though he, too, were waiting for somebody. Corey didn't speak to him because, of course, he didn't care to be recognized in that place if it could be avoided. But he couldn't help wondering if John were in the habit of going to the Wayside. I can't think that he is, and yet I don't know. There's something suspicious about him, and I've been disappointed in a good many people of late, so I can't help wondering about his character, too."

"Is the Wayside House such a perfectly dreadful place, Helen?"

Anna's voice had asked the question, but it was so hoarse and constrained that her sister felt she wouldn't have recognized it under other circumstances. She looked anxiously at the tear-filled face and spoke gently: "Why, Anna, dear, it's hardly necessary for you to ask that question. You know the reputation of the house. Our father, you remember, would not think for a moment of sending one of us there on an errand, even in broad daylight. Why do you ask? Do you think John goes there often? Had he an errand he felt was important? He must have gone early in the evening, before he went to the Holcombes', of course.

"I confess that all his movements on that evening looked suspicious to me. The fact that he had to drive back to town at all, when there were so many duties awaiting him at home, seemed strange. I don't like to suspect someone of wrongdoing, but we ought to be careful about John. We're responsible for his being in this neighborhood, I suppose.

"And as to this other matter, we simply can't put it away from us. One can't help fearing that some poor girl who has no mother and has had no bringing up has been led into evil right here in our midst. If it were one of my scholars, Anna, it seems it would almost break my heart. But I can't think of any of them who would be tempted in this way."

"It isn't one of them!" exclaimed Anna, bursting into a perfect passion of tears and speaking words so choked with sobs that Helen could scarcely understand them. "It isn't one of your girls. It's just me, your own sister. I have done it all! I didn't mean any harm. It was just for fun. They dared me to do it, the girls did. Laura Holcombe said I wouldn't dare to write a letter to anybody because of you. She said that if I had a grandfather and wrote to him, I would have to show all my letters to you before they were sent, and a lot more stuff like that. So I thought I would show them I wasn't afraid. I thought, too, that it was real fun, and I didn't think for a minute that any harm could come of it. Oh, Helen! Have I disgraced you all? And will Father and Mother have to be told? Oh, I wish I could die!"

She turned suddenly and threw herself down on an old log by the path. Burying her face in her hands, she sobbed as though her heart would break. Helen stood still, regarding her with an expression of mingled pain and wonder. She had hardly even taken in the thought that the poor, ignorant, misguided girl she had been alternately blaming and feeling sorry for ever since she had heard of her could possibly be their Annie! Solicitude for her sister finally overmastered other feelings.

"Get up, dear," she said, bending down and reaching for the child's arm. She tried to make her voice very kind. "You mustn't sit there or you'll take cold. We must hurry home as fast as we can. Mother will be needing me. We mustn't trouble Mother and Father with this now," she continued as Anna allowed herself to be helped up from the log. "We must do the best we can until Father is well. But, Annie, I must know all about it from the beginning, every word, if I'm to be of real help to

you. Those people who came to the Wayside
House that evening, had you anything to do with
them?"

"I didn't know I had," said poor Anna. "I'll tell
you every bit of it, Helen. We picked out the name
from the catalogue because we liked the sound of it
— Augustus Sayre Hooper. Laura said it had a
very aristocratic sound, and she wouldn't be surprised if he were a connection of the Sayres of Bos-
ton. All I thought was that he would be a nice,
smart young man like Corey, you know, and that it
would be great fun to get letters from him and
make him think all sorts of nice things about me. I
didn't mean ever to see him or to let him know
who I really was. But, Helen, he wrote real beautiful letters. I thought, after a while, that he was
everything that was good and noble and that it
would be an honor to be a friend of his. I'll show
you his letters, and you'll see how truly noble he
makes himself out to be — I mean, without prais-
ing himself in the least. It does seem as though
Corey must be mistaken about him."

"Go on," said Helen. Despite her effort to the
contrary, her voice was cold. This sister of hers
was both younger and older than she had thought.

"There isn't much more," said the poor girl
meekly. "He kept wanting to come and call upon
me. He said that a matter begun in jest had developed into earnest, and he felt sure that we would
be good friends for life and that he needed my influence and letters to help him through the temptations of college life. You know it's a life of
temptations, Helen. I've often heard Mother and
Father say so. He said I had done him good already; that I would never know, in this world, how
my writing had helped him over some hard places.

"I wanted to do a little good, Helen — I really did. I can never be like you, helping everybody and interested in everybody, no matter how common and uninteresting they are. But I thought I could help him, and I can't bear to think that what Corey says of him is true."

Another burst of tears. Helen felt the strangest mixture of emotions. She could have shaken the trembling girl leaning on her arm for being such an arrant simpleton, and she could have gathered her to her heart and wept over her as the innocent dupe of a villain. And she was still such a child! They had thought her too young to be troubled by temptations of this sort.

"Please, Annie, try to control yourself and tell me all about it," she said at last. It was the most she could bring herself to say. "Does the Wayside House meeting come in?"

"Why, he said he wanted me to go and take a ride with him. He was to meet me at Laura Holcombe's and — oh, Helen, there's something more that I'm afraid you'll think is dreadful. He wanted my picture a good while before this, and I wouldn't send it to him — not my own, of course. I hunted through the photographs in Corey's collection for a fancy one, and I came upon that one of Nell Marvin's that she had taken in her wedding finery when she was her Aunt Kate's maid of honor. You remember. You can hardly see her face in it because there's such a cloud of drapery. Well, I sent him that and let him think it was me."

"Oh, Annie!" The listener could not repress this single outcry of indignant pain.

"Was it awful, Helen? I can feel how terrible it all was now. It is strange how dreadful things sound, told over to you, that seemed nothing but fun when Laura and I planned them! I hadn't the least idea that he would ever learn whose picture it was. Then, when I began to know him better and enjoy his letters, and really like him, I thought it would be such fun to let him come and call on Laura and me and show him that the picture he had been raving over was not mine at all. I thought we would have a good laugh over it, and that would end the matter.

"So that night he came. Laura and I were to go for a drive with him, but Laura wasn't well enough to go, and he insisted on my going without her. He said I had promised. He didn't mind about the picture in the least. In fact, he said he liked my face much better than he did the pictured one. I thought he was everything that was good and noble. I didn't know we were going to the Wayside until just as he was turning in at the gate. Then he said he had an appointment with a college friend. When I told him I didn't want to go there, he asked if I would just step in with him for a moment or two while he spoke to his friends, and then we would come right out. He said he had no idea that the house was any different from other country hotels and that he must warn his college friends of its local reputation."

"Did you go with him to the Wayside House?" interrupted Helen.

CHAPTER XVII

UNDER SUSPICION

er poor sister! She was all but stunned over the magnitude of the discoveries she was making. It seemed to her that every sentence Anna spoke revealed a new horror. The idea of her pure-hearted young sister, whom they had looked upon as hardly yet out of her babyhood, descending to such depths as these!

To a nature like Helen Elliott's, an anonymous letter was in itself a poisonous thing. And an anonymous letter addressed by a young girl to a man, and that man a stranger, was to her a form of disgrace from which she shrank with all the force of her strong, pure nature. Yet she must meet and face disgrace such as this and help her sister to overcome it if she could. Therefore, she controlled all exhibition of her feelings as much as possible and asked that probing question, "Did you go with him to the Wayside House?"

"No," said Anna. "I didn't. Just as we were driving into the gateway, we met John with the car-

riage. He told me I was wanted at home immediately. I was frightened half to death, for, of course,
I thought that Father must be worse. He took me
out of the carriage, put me into ours and drove
away quickly without saying a word until we were
on the road. Then he frightened me more by telling
me what a dreadful thing it was for me to go to the
Wayside House.

"You needn't worry about John, Helen. He is
good. He made me promise I would tell you all
about it. He had heard it somewhere, the whole
story — about the letters, I mean, and all — and I
promised I would tell you every word, and I have.
It wasn't just because you came out to meet me that
I told you. I've been planning all day how to do it,
and I meant to do it before I slept. Oh, Helen, do
speak to me or I shall die! Have I disgraced Father
and Mother and you and everybody, and have I
injured Nell? Oh, dear me! If I *could* just die and be
forgotten!"

It was a childish wail and for the moment did
not appeal to Helen's heart. Somehow she felt
more humiliated still under the force of this new
truth. John, the hired man, her father's tramp,
taken in out of charity in the first place, had to be
the one to come to the rescue of her sister! And the
burning question was, how did he come by the
knowledge he possessed?

If only he were a simple, honest hired man, earning his honest living by daily toil! If he had been
one of the roughest and most uncouth of their
back-country neighbors come to the rescue, she
could have blessed him. But what was John? Possibly, for all she knew, a worse man even than
Augustus Sayre Hooper, having knowledge of evil
because he was himself of that same evil world.

But then again, in light of what he had done for Anna and the whole family, perhaps she should view him more kindly.

Then came the thought of the humiliation in store for her because of the necessity of talking the whole wretched business over with John, discovering just how much he knew and, if possible, from what source he had gathered it. Her face burned at the mere idea and then paled at the memory of Nell Marvin and the disgrace that had been carelessly brought upon her. What would Nannie say if she heard of it, or *when* she heard of it? Must it not, as a matter of honor, all be told?

The poor girl found herself bewildered over these questions of right and wrong, uncertain which way to turn. If she could only have appealed to her clear-headed father or her quiet, far-seeing mother, but she was firm in the conviction that neither of them must be told at the present time. Of course, it was out of the question for her father, and she couldn't feel that it would be right, under present circumstances, to add to her mother's burdens.

Meantime, what was to be said to Anna? Not one word of comfort had she yet spoken, for she had not reached the point where she could sincerely speak comfort. She struggled with the sense of disappointment and angry irritation she felt against Anna. How could a girl who had grown up in such a home as hers, with such a father and mother, have gone so far astray? If this was what the wicked, outside world did for a sheltered and carefully guarded one, how could girls who came up without the environment of a Christian home ever escape? It was thoughts like these that made her answer the child's last appeal so coldly.

"People can't die, Annie, at a moment's notice and leave the consequences of their...mistakes to others." She had hesitated for a word and had almost said "sins," but a glance at the woebegone face beside her restrained her tongue. "It's much more noble to live and do one's utmost to set right anything that may have gone wrong through fault of ours."

There was one more probing question she wanted to ask. "Annie, you say you did not at any time realize you were doing wrong. It was just a bit of fun from which no serious consequences were expected. Will you tell me, then, why you didn't explain the whole scheme to Mother and me and let us share the fun with you? It seems to me that we're both capable of enjoying fun and quite ready to sympathize with it. Had you thought of that, dear?"

Anna's eyes drooped, and there was silence for several seconds. Then she said, speaking low, "Helen, Laura Holcombe thinks you're overparticular about some things, and I'm afraid she has made me feel so sometimes. I told myself that that was the reason I said nothing to you about it. But I'm going to speak exactly the truth after this, to myself as well as to other people, and I know now that I didn't tell you because I felt that you and Mother would be sure to put a stop to the whole thing. At first I didn't want it stopped because it was such fun. He wrote such merry letters, and after that I liked him so well that I wanted you to meet and like him, too, before I told you anything about it. Then I thought he would be a friend to all of us. He said he was going to take pains to get acquainted with Corey, and that, being older than he, there were perhaps ways in which he could help him."

Helen's lip curled derisively. Such a creature as he help Corey!

It was probably well for both girls that home duties held their attention closely for the remainder of that day. Certainly the older sister was not yet ready with either advice or comfort beyond the few words she had compelled herself to speak.

When at last she was at liberty to go over the whole trying business in the privacy of her own room, she tried to shoulder calmly her perplexities and responsibilities and determine what should be done. But she found quietness of spirit very hard to assume. She had hoped to give this first hour of leisure and solitude to Corey and his serious troubles, and, behold, here was a much more serious matter pressing upon her, claiming immediate and absorbing attention.

It's true that Corey had brought his troubles upon himself by the merest folly, but there was a bright side to that trouble — it was folly and not deliberate sin. What if he had been one of the company at the Belmont House on the evening in question and had been forever associated with the disgraceful scene, minute particulars of which were spread out in the evening paper for the wondering country people to read? No names were mentioned, but such matters always got abroad, especially in the country. What if one could not indignantly deny that Corey had had the remotest connection with it? Or what if he had been goaded by poverty into the appropriation of that fifty-dollar note? Certainly there was a bright side! What a rest of soul it was to her to realize that not so much as a passing doubt about his honesty had disturbed her.

When it came to a matter that Corey chose to consider important, his word could be implicitly believed. What an infinite pity it was that he found his amusement in exaggerations or, as in this case, in positive untruthfulness. But there was a way out for him, and that a speedy one. Or if not — if it came to public embarrassment and disgrace to endure — there was always that central brightness flashing out from the thought that she could be sure he was bearing disgrace unjustly.

But Anna's trouble was on another plane. The poor child had undoubtedly gone astray. Not so far as she might have gone, for she had been mercifully shielded from an introduction to a world outside of and far below her such as an evening at the Wayside House would have given her. Would it perhaps have been a revelation that she actually needed in order to open her eyes to the dangers awaiting foolish feet in that cruel world? Not that Helen would have had the experiment tried for the world! And to think, they had John to thank that it was not!

Then she thought again of the interview she must have with him and the careful questioning there must be to find how much or how little he knew. What did that mysterious and, at times, suspicious John know of the world? How conversant was he with the Wayside House and places of like reputation? How much of what he would tell her would be truth, and how much invented to suit the occasion? It was very bitter, but it seemed to her then that, because of the habit of falsifying that had taken hold of people, there was almost nobody whom she could trust. Then again, everything he had done so far had been to the benefit of the family.

Never mind; she must shoulder the burden and do the best she could. Perhaps she ought not to have waited until morning. Her young sister's name might even now be tossing about among the low and the coarse. Also, there was Nell Marvin's photograph. How were they to get possession of it again or to explain to Nellie and her father and mother Anna's share in the wretched transaction?

At last she gave up trying to think, reminding herself that she was simply taking counsel of her own overwrought brain. And then this sorely tried young disciple of Truth, who had been bitterly stung by falsehood, remembered her refuge and knelt to pray.

Corey Elliott, as he was being driven to the train station that morning, certainly had cares enough of his own to think about. Nevertheless, he gave some attention to John. In some ways he anticipated Helen's train of thought. Why had John been at the Wayside House? Who was John, anyway? And to what extent were they justified in trusting him as they had?

With his young eyes having recently been opened to certain temptations and dangers that waited for the unwary, he wondered if it had been wise to leave his sisters, especially Anna, so much in the care of this unknown man upon whom they must be more or less dependent now that their father was ill. Yet the fellow had a good face and had done good for the family, and Corey couldn't help being interested in him.

Perhaps John was weak and had been led into evil surroundings since coming to their neighborhood! He wondered if there was some word of warning he might speak, even though he was so much younger than John. Certainly Corey had changed much in a single night. There was no inclination now to appeal to John for sympathy. Instead, he was putting his own affairs in the background and trying to plan in a manly way for others. The thought occurred to him that it might possibly be his duty to get leave of absence from college and remain at home until his father was able to be about again. Then came the stinging thought that circumstances might make this unnecessary. He might be, even now, suspended or expelled from college!

The thoughts of the two young men had crossed without their realizing it. John spoke first, breaking a silence that had lasted for several minutes. "Mr. Corey, you told me last night that you were in trouble. I've thought about it a good deal. I wish I could help in some way. Your father has been very kind to me. If it's anything about money, perhaps I could — I've got a little money laid up. I know young men in college sometimes need more money than they think they will."

Corey turned and regarded him with a suspicious look. So he had money laid up! That was very strange. Not that an honest working man, who was getting fair wages and had only himself to care for, might not be able to lay up a little money. But John had been with them so short a time and had come in the regular tramp fashion, asking for food, supposedly to be paid for in work. Did that look like a man who had money laid up? It must be money he had secured in some way since he had come to them. Was he a professional gambler, or was he simply a bungling gambler, trying his hand at it from time to time and occasionally winning by a sort of accident? In that case, was it the Wayside House and its frequenters who had led him astray? Meanwhile, some reply must be made to his offer.

"That's very good of you, I'm sure!" With an attempt at a good-natured laugh, he continued, "College fellows are always in need of money, I believe, but I hadn't thought of appealing to you. Suppose I should be in need of, say, fifty dollars? I fancy that would be a larger figure than you could compass?"

"No," said John, falling unsuspiciously, even eagerly, into the trap, "I could lend you fifty dollars as well as not. I could raise it in an hour's time. I could telegraph you a money order, you know. I'll be very glad to do it if you'll let me, and you needn't be troubled about paying me. Any time in the future when you can do it as well as not will be all right."

Every word he spoke increased the suspicion against him. Corey, who had not the slightest idea of borrowing money from him and had mentioned the sum merely to learn, if possible, the extent of John's resources, was for the moment in doubt about what reply to make.

"It's certainly very generous of you to offer to help me," he said at last. "And, of course, I'm obliged to you. But at present at least, I won't borrow. I have to confess that you've given me a surprise. I didn't imagine you had a bank account. The circumstances under which you came to my father had not led me to suppose you were a moneyed man."

John's face grew red from the taunt and the realization of his own folly. He had made another mistake. He drove on for some seconds in silence, then said coldly, "A man can earn money, Mr.

Corey, by working with his hands and be honest about it."

"Of course he can," said Corey heartily. "I don't want you to imagine for a minute that I look down upon any working man or feel superior to him. But, John, an honest working man who has money laid up doesn't, as a rule, turn tramp and come into a neighborhood where he is an entire stranger in search of a meal. However, that's none of our business, I suppose, so long as you do your work well. You look as though you would like to say something of that kind to me, so I'll say it for you. I'll tell you something that may surprise you.

"I had occasion to go to the Wayside House on business night before last, and I was very sorry to catch a glimpse of you in the same place. You may be so much of a stranger in the neighborhood as not to understand the character of that house. If that's so, the sooner you can be put on guard, the better. So far as I know, no respectable person frequents it, and it's the regular resort of some of the worst characters in this part of the country. If you're a good, honest fellow, John, as I want to think you are, you won't mind my plain speaking. I'm quite sure that my father would not like to continue in his employ a man who is in the habit of going to such places."

"I was never at the Wayside House before in my life," said John quickly. "It was very important business that took me there that evening. I saw you there, Mr. Corey, and wondered at it. I have heard about the house. Your father himself told me of some things that have taken place there. You've been good enough to tell me you were sorry to see me in such place. Now perhaps you'll excuse me if I say that I had much the same feeling about seeing Mr. Elliott's son there."

Corey laughed. "There are two of us, are there? I believe it was also my first visit to the renowned spot. Strange that we chose the same night, isn't it? Do you know what I would advise? That neither of us go again. The business that I thought called me didn't amount to anything. It would have been better in every way if I hadn't gone. I daresay the same could be said of yours."

John made no audible reply to this tentative question. In his heart he said, Indeed it could not! If you knew what took me there, my lofty young man, you would go down upon your knees in gratitude for my effort and its success.

They were nearing the station, and as the horses were restless from the passing of a freight train, the driver had a good excuse for giving undivided attention to them.

After his passenger had alighted and bowed his good morning, he turned back to say kindly, "I don't know whether I thanked you for your kind intentions. I really am very grateful. If I ever need your help in any way, I shall be sure to remember. And if you should need my help at any time, I shall be glad to give it."

Then he ran for his train.

CHAPTER XVIII

ACTS 9:11

ohn Stuart drove home from the station in a mixed frame of mind. There was undoubtedly a ludicrous side to the interview just closed. He had been thinking more or less about Corey Elliott for several weeks, partly because he seemed such a merry-hearted, easily led fellow, and John knew the peculiar temptations of life in certain colleges for such as he. John also knew by reputation certain students at this particular college who he fancied were friends of Corey. But mainly — this he told himself with that stern resolve to *think* just the truth — because he was Helen Elliott's brother and evidently peculiarly precious to her. And her interests — John never allowed himself to carry his trains of thought in this direction an inch farther.

But he laughed, in spite of the undertone of gloom, over the ludicrous side of the interview. He had been troubled for Corey, and Corey had been troubled for him. He was suspicious that Corey had gotten into trouble that would bring sorrow to his sister, and Corey was suspicious of him in a dozen different ways. Both of them had been guests, at least once, at a disreputable house, and each deeply regretted it for the other!

After the laugh his face gloomed. He had failed in his attempt at helpfulness, and reasonably so. He had to admit that all he had done was to make his own position more suspicious.

"That's what I am," he said irritably, "simply an object of suspicion. The boy frankly tells me of it! I'm a fool, and I continue to get myself more deeply involved each day. Yet what can I do? It would be the vilest ingratitude to leave them just now, in their trouble, but until I do leave them, I fear there's nothing I can do to help them. I've certainly put myself into a strange position."

He sighed heavily and then gave the horses an irritable flick with the tassels of his whip, as though they were to blame. As they quickened their steps and hurried him homeward, he continued to make himself miserable over the various efforts he could now make for the Elliott family, if he were in their eyes what he was in reality.

Seated in the train, speeding toward college and trouble, Corey Elliott went over his recent interview with a half-smile on his face. It was so ridiculous to think of *John* offering him money! But it was kind of him and showed warmheartedness. The fellow ought to be helped. Why wasn't Helen at work trying to do it?

He was obliged to smile again over the folly of that thought. Poor Helen seemed to be the one who always had to shoulder the family burdens. Had he not himself just laid a heavy one upon her? Doubtless, too, she was doing what she could for

John. She would not be his sister Helen if she weren't.

This thought reminded him of a little note that had been thrust into his vest pocket. Helen had handed it to him as she bade him good-bye. "Read that when you're quite alone," she had said. It was doubtless some added word of sympathy for him in his trouble, or a suggestion regarding the way out. Dear Helen! She had probably lain awake half the night thinking of him, while he, after sitting with his father until midnight, had been so thoroughly tired over the excitements of the day that he had put everything from him and gone to sleep like a veritable schoolboy.

He glanced about him at his fellow passengers. The train was full enough, but nevertheless, he felt quite alone. Not a face there invited his attention. He would read the little note and see what suggestion Helen had to offer. She was levelheaded, this sister of his, and anything she had thought out was worthy of consideration.

> Dear Corey,
>
> I turned your affairs over and over in my mind a hundred times, I think, last night and found no light or comfort until I suddenly remembered a direction I had once resolved to follow: "Casting all your care upon him, for he careth for you." I proved it once more, taking the whole matter, with all its possible entanglements, to Jesus Christ.
>
> When I arose from my knees, of course not a circumstance was in any way changed. Yet my weight of anxiety was gone! I felt sure you would be brought

safely through and that the experience
would work for your good.

Do you know what I thought next?
"Oh, if Corey only *prayed!*" It does seem
strange, Corey dear, that you're not willing to try that simple remedy for all ills
that has never been known to fail. Won't
you let me ask you once more, more earnestly, if possible, than I ever did before,
to take it all to Christ?

Now I can almost hear your old refrain
about being a goat and having therefore
no right to the sheep's pasturage. But
you know that's simply a merry way of
begging a serious question. Suppose a
sheep persisted in remaining outside
with the goats, though offered all the
protection and privileges of the sheep-
fold? But I don't mean to preach. I only
want to ask you most earnestly if, in this
crisis in your life, you will not test Jesus
Christ.

The young man slowly folded the little note and
laid it away. Its contents had been very different
from what he had expected. He couldn't tell why
the simple words appealed to him so forcefully. It
wasn't the first, nor indeed perhaps the hundredth
time, that Helen had, in one form or another, put in
an earnest plea for him to become a man of prayer.

He had put her petitions aside with lighthearted
courtesy, always with the mental resolution to
give attention to this matter sometime. And with
this concession he had always been able to turn his
thoughts quickly into another channel. This morning he was not. In vain he tried to concentrate his

thoughts on his present perplexities; to arrange an interview with President Chambers; to apologize for some of the rude words he had spoken on the evening before; to plan ways of making plain his absence from the city on the Tuesday evening in question, without confessing he had spent it at the notorious Wayside House, where several of the college men had already encountered disgrace. Above all things, he wanted to plan some feasible theory concerning the disappearance of that fifty-dollar note.

He could not concentrate on any of these matters. Instead, his brain kept constantly repeating to him that last sentence: "I only want to ask you most earnestly if, in this crisis in your life, you will not test Jesus Christ." That was a startling way of putting it! Almost irreverent if it had come from any other pen than Helen's. Had one a right to talk about testing God? Straightway came to mind an old verse learned in childhood: "Bring ye all the tithes into the storehouse...and prove me now herewith, saith the Lord." What was that but a challenge to be tested?

It was true, as Helen had intimated, that he and Anna had actually jested about their being goats while all the rest of the family were of the best sheep in the fold. But on this particular morning it didn't seem like a jest. He didn't want to be left out, homeless. He wanted to claim utmost and eternal kinship with that blessed father and mother of his.

Then he thought of how pale his father had looked after the fever went down and how the hand he had held out to grasp his had trembled. That kind hand that had never failed him in any need! If God really were like a father, how much he needed Him now! To be able to tell the whole story to that blessed earthly father of his would be such a relief! If one only knew how to go in that way to God! Certainly that was the way Helen understood religion. There was no sham to her, not the merest shadow of hypocrisy. He tried to determine just what his own belief was.

At given times in his life, he had experienced moments of what might be called sentimentalism. That is, his emotional nature had been reached by some powerful appeal to it in the name of religion. But he had never been moved deeply enough for action. The impression being made this morning was different. There was nothing in Helen's note to excite him or to awaken emotion, yet he felt himself arraigned, as before an invisible judge, to account for his position.

He believed in prayer, of course — his father's son could not have done less. But just what did he believe in regard to it? Why this, beyond question: that it was possible for a human being to secure audience with One, known in history as Jesus Christ, a divine being, infinite in wisdom and power and love — therefore, a being both able and willing to befriend him. Why, then, if he were a person of average common sense, did he persist in holding himself aloof from the help that such a belief undoubtedly afforded? Why shouldn't this powerful Friend be his friend? Why shouldn't the promise on which his parents and his sister leaned, the promise of divine guidance for the asking, be his also?

He confessed to himself that, very often indeed, as he had looked into his sister's pure face and earnest eyes, he had been reminded of a Bible verse, learned in his early boyhood. It spoke of certain persons who marvelled at the boldness of two disciples, Peter and John, and recognized that they had been with Jesus. He admitted that had he been inclined to be skeptical, his sister's singularly consecrated life would have been an unanswerable argument to him.

But he wasn't skeptical. Nothing he had studied in school seemed clearer or more certain to him than did the fundamental verities of the Christian religion. Only a few days before, in a free-and-easy conversation with some of the students, certain skeptical sentiments had been advanced, and he had assured the speaker that he had three volumes of the evidences of Christianity in the persons of his father and mother and sister. And that any fellow who had opportunity to study them, he said, would as soon think of doubting the daily sunrise as of questioning the foundations on which such living as theirs was built.

He recalled the promptness with which he had made that response. And he told himself he was an inconsistent fellow, unworthy of credence. How was his life proving that he had benefitted from living with such godly persons? He knew certain boys whose home life might be thus described. If he honestly believed what he professed to when he talked with the boys, why not avail himself of the offered help? He certainly was in trouble. He might put it aside for the time with the assurance that there was a way out, yet all the while he was conscious of an undertone of grave anxiety.

"That's an awfully selfish motive," a voice inside chided. "You ought to be ashamed to go to God for the first time for any such reason." He didn't recognize the speaker as the enemy of souls, but his good sense gave an immediate answer.

"What of that?" It would be a selfish motive that would prompt him to seek human help. Yet if there were an available human friend at this moment, one who had both ability and desire to help him, it wouldn't take him two minutes to decide to seek him at the first opportunity and lay the case before him. He could conceive of a man who would be great enough to overlook past indifference on his part, even slights, and come forward to his aid. There were such people — undoubtedly there were such fathers. Didn't he know that if he were the worthless creature President Chambers evidently considered him, and yet he had gone frankly to his father with the story of his trouble, his father would have met him more than halfway and helped to the extent of his ability? Why should it seem such an incredible thing that God, who had chosen to name Himself Father, would do as much?

Yet let him be sincere in this matter. He would not go even to his earthly father without being ready to say to him, "Father, I have done wrong. I've gone contrary to what you would have advised and have brought this trouble upon myself by my folly. I want you to understand that I don't mean to get into this sort of scrape again. I intend to follow your footsteps after this as well as I can." Was he ready to make such a statement to a Father in heaven?

Had he counted the cost? Yet, after all, what was the cost? What obligations were required to become a member of this family and claim the privileges of sonship? It seemed wonderful to him afterward to remember how frequently during that morning's conference with himself there appeared before him words that he had learned in childhood, ready to answer his questions authoritatively. One such came now: "What doth the Lord thy God require of thee, but to fear the Lord thy God, to walk in all his ways, and to love him, and to serve the Lord thy God with all thy heart, and with all thy soul?"

These were tremendous obligations, certainly. Yet he knew they were entirely reasonable, considering who he was and what he knew of God. Had he not always intended to give this subject serious attention at some time? Did he not believe that it was everyone's duty to use his common sense in this, as in all other matters, and act in accordance with his best judgment?

Those fellows who had bad habits to give up and who didn't dare to make the best they could of their lives certainly had excuses for delay that he had not. He believed he had been simply a fool to put off settling such important questions as these. He didn't know why he had done so. It seemed strange that they persisted in his mind so much now. It was vain to try to push them aside with the excuse that he had affairs requiring immediate attention. They pushed relentlessly to the forefront of his mind.

Instead of going in search of President Chambers, as he had intended to do as soon as he reached the college grounds, he went directly to his own room and closed and locked the door.

For more than an hour he sat with folded arms staring straight into nothingness, thinking as he had never thought before in his life. Recalling it afterward, he realized that all thoughts of what was awaiting him at college had left him for the time being. This one other subject pressed its claims in a singularly assertive manner. At the close of the time he arose with the air of one who had settled something; then he crossed over to the window, drew down the shade and dropped upon his knees.

"Jackson," said President Chambers that afternoon, "did Elliott return by the morning train?"

"Yes, sir. He came in at eleven o'clock."

"Do you know where he is?"

"He went directly to his room, sir, and I haven't seen him since. I noticed particularly that he didn't come out at the twelve o'clock hour."

"Jackson, go to his room and say that I would like to see him immediately."

Jackson bowed himself away and in a brief space of time returned alone.

"Well," said President Chambers, "did you find him?"

"Yes, sir, he is in his room, but — "

"Did you give him my message?"

"No, sir, I didn't, because he is — he is very much engaged, sir, and I didn't think you would like to have him disturbed. I didn't even knock at the door."

"Indeed! What's the nature of an engagement that is so important in your eyes that you can't deliver a message from me? Is it visible from the keyhole?"

"No, sir, I didn't see him, but I heard him. To tell you the truth, sir, he is praying."

A sudden softened look overspread the handsome face of the president. He had not known that Corey Elliott ever had engagements of that kind.

"Very well," he said to the waiting Jackson, "you did quite right. Watch your opportunity, and send Elliott to me as soon as he is disengaged."

CHAPTER XIX

"BEFORE THEY CALL,
I WILL ANSWER"

orey Elliott waited for no word from the president but, as soon as he was permitted to enter, went straight toward him and spoke rapidly: "President Chambers, I was just coming to ask if I might speak with you, when Jackson told me you had sent for me. I want to beg your pardon, sir, for the very disrespectful words I spoke last night. I was so excited and angry that I didn't realize what I was saying. I told you the truth, sir, in every particular, but I can see, upon reflection, that under the circumstances you are perhaps justified in not believing me. In any case, I ought not to have said what I did."

"Sit down, Elliott," said President Chambers, motioning the young man to a seat. "I want to have a little talk with you. There are two of us repenting, it seems. I sent for you in order to tell you that I spoke last night without due consideration. Within an hour after my words with you, information came to me that proved the truth of your statements with regard to the Belmont House disgrace. I am more glad than I can tell you to learn that you weren't present that evening and aren't in any way associated with the affair. At the same time, I learned another thing that caused me pain. Are you willing to tell me where you were on Tuesday evening?"

Corey's face flushed, but he answered quickly: "I'll tell you, sir, although I can't say I like to do so. I spent the evening and the greater part of the night at a country hotel called the Wayside House, about five miles from my own home. It's a disreputable place, and my father has never approved of my stopping there, even on business. Nevertheless, I thought I had business that evening that would justify my going."

"Are you willing to tell me the nature of the business?"

"In part, yes. I had reason to fear that a young person in our own neighborhood had been led into trouble and was in danger of being led further. So, on the impulse of the moment, I went out there to learn the truth, if possible. It came to nothing, and I'm sorry I went. But that's where I was on Tuesday night."

The president's grave face lighted with the semblance of a smile. "I'm very glad to hear it," he said heartily. "For one thing, I am glad to have an authentic witness to what occurred at the Wayside House that evening. I'm aware that some of our students were the planners of that choice entertainment, and I need hardly tell you that all the circumstances connected with it will be most carefully inquired into. You may be able to do the college good service by helping us to put down this form of iniquity. I congratulate you on having learned that none of the girls of your own neighborhood was implicated in the disgraceful affair.

"And now, with regard to the fifty-dollar bank note you left at Wellington's, no light has been thrown upon its mysterious disappearance. But, in view of the light that has come to me from other sources, I'm prepared to ask your pardon for my last night's insinuations and to assure you that I have no hesitancy now in taking your word that you did with it just as you said."

For the first time since his troubles had come upon him Corey Elliott felt a choking sensation in his throat and knew that, if he had been more emotional, he would have burst into tears.

"Thank you," he said with difficulty. "It's very good of you, indeed, after all the lies you overheard me tell in fun. But I assure you, President Chambers, I never told a lie in earnest in my life. I could hardly belong to my father's family and not be truthful."

"I can well believe that," said the president heartily. "I know your family well, and I knew your grandfather. But I wonder if I may remind you that, when you get your sport in such ways, you are playing with edged tools?"

Poor Corey's face flushed deeply. "I would think myself an idiot," he said, "if I had not learned that lesson. But, President Chambers, what can have become of the fifty-dollar note?"

The president shook his head. "I don't know, Elliott. We won't go into that. It's one of the mysteries that may never be explained. Suffice it to say that I entirely exonerate you from all blame in the matter."

"But I cannot have it left so, sir. It *must* be found! There are two of us who will suffer unjustly all our lives if it's not."

"You gave it to young Esterbrook, Elliott?"

"I laid it down before his eyes, and he said he would attend to it in a moment and then send up a receipt."

"And you have entire confidence in Esterbrook?"

"I would as soon think of *my* appropriating the money as of *his* doing it!"

"I'm glad to hear you say so, Elliott. I, too, have strong confidence in that young man. Therefore, as I say, it must for the present remain a mystery. But let me repeat my assurance — "

Just at that moment came a knock at the door, and Jackson's head appeared.

"A note for you, sir, marked 'Haste!' "

The president held out his hand, broke the seal and glanced through the contents with a smile on his face that grew as he read. Then, rising, he went over to Elliott, held out his hand and said, "Let me congratulate you, my boy. I'm glad I assured you of my perfect faith in your word. The missing note has been found. There isn't even the dignity of a thief in the matter. Esterbrook was humiliated to the dust to find it with some refuse paper in his own wastebasket!"

That afternoon John Stuart made the Elliott horses travel faster than they had ever been known to do in their short and easy lives. He left them uncared for at the gate while he hurried into the kitchen and intercepted Helen on her way to her father's room with a tray of tea and toast.

"A telegram for you, Miss Elliott." As he spoke, he took the tray from hands that trembled and waited while they tore open the fateful yellow messenger. Mrs. Elliott, coming at that moment from the sickroom, waited, her face pale, only for a second. Then Helen laughed, and her mother's heart went on beating again.

"What is it, dear?"

"It's from Corey, Mother. It says, 'Okay. Hallelujah!' and not another word beside. Corey was having some trouble in college that he did not want you worried with, and he's safely out of it."

"Trouble in college!" repeated Mrs. Elliott wonderingly. "About his studies, do you mean? Helen, your father is calling." And Helen was spared the duty of replying.

Her way through difficulties was less bright than Corey's had been. She found it hard to determine just what ought to be done. The interview with John was not as trying as she had expected. She had said that, if it were only one of her scholars to whom she was indebted for shielding Anna, she could be grateful. And, behold, it was Thomas, the dullard and blunderer! John kept his share of the proceedings in the background. From his standpoint, what he did was the merest commonplace that would have been done, as a matter of course, by any employee of Mr. Elliott.

Helen felt soothed by his manner. But no sooner had she left him than she began to reflect that it was very unlike the manner of the average working man. Once or twice he had appeared strangely embarrassed, beginning a sentence that seemed to have a suggestion of helpfulness in it and then suddenly ceasing before it was completed. Did he know more than he had chosen to tell her? No, that couldn't be, for his story had been direct and explicit. He hadn't hesitated or compelled her to question him for particulars. Yet there was something strange about him.

She dismissed him from her mind and took up Anna's problem. Could she wait until her father was better and ask his advice? No, she couldn't. Circumstances settled that point all too promptly. Despite vigorous exertions on the part of John Stuart that she knew nothing about, a painful publicity was given to the affair. A scandal, such as gossips love to feed upon, had arisen in connection with that evening at the Wayside House. Reporters traveled everywhere, hungry for every particular that could in the remotest degree be connected with it, being skillful in putting together particulars that needed a microscope to make them fit the central story.

Under such circumstances it became impossible to keep hints about Anna out of the daily papers. Her name was mercifully and by great effort suppressed, but a certain class of reporters know how to prepare a dish so marked in its flavor that, though even its initials be not given, those who pass may recognize it.

They found an efficient helper in Laura Holcombe, who, having been sharply reprimanded by her parents for her share in the disgrace, was sulky and took revenge by telling freely all she knew about the correspondence between Anna Elliott and the unknown college boy, as well as the engagement to drive with him without the knowledge or consent of her own family. Laura had even discovered, in some way, John's share in that evening's program, and this made a most tasty morsel for the reporters.

It wasn't that Laura Holcombe was malicious to that extent. She even cried when she found that some of her talk had gotten into the papers and was plain enough for all acquainted with the locality to understand. She hadn't meant to brew deep mischief for her friend, but simply to talk while she was angry and could find interested listeners who weren't too scrupulous in repeating what they heard. It was a salutary and much-needed lesson for Laura.

They had selected two names from the college catalogue and each written a letter. Laura fully understood that it was only because the name she happened to choose belonged to a gentleman who took no notice of it that she was not in a like plight with her friend. Actually, it's doubtful if she would have gotten herself into such a plight under any circumstances. She understood this wicked world much better than Anna and belonged to that wretched class of human beings who can urge another on to depths that they themselves are too wise to descend. The one had sinned ignorantly, as a child. The other had held back like a girl who knew too much about the world of sin.

Helen, weeping and praying, realized what the sisters and mothers of today are so slow to learn — that ignorance is not a shield. If she had only talked more plainly with Annie instead of trying to shelter her and keep her in ignorance of the dangers that lie in wait for the unwary!

Meantime, she thought as well as prayed. That photograph, which ought never to have been sent, must be recovered. After careful deliberation she resolved to write for it herself. Indeed, there was no one else to do it. She considered the wisdom of putting the matter into Corey's hands and decided she musn't. Corey was young and not too discreet where his feelings were engaged, and he was in the same building with the offender. A serious quarrel might result if he undertook to have an interview with Augustus Sayre Hooper.

So Helen wrote the letter, such a one as Helen Elliott could write on occasion. Augustus Sayre Hooper arose from its perusal with, for once, a true opinion of himself. He wrote a reply that made Helen's indignation burn, but he returned the photograph. The sarcasms in his letter may have been increased by the fact that he wasn't finding the way of the trangressor easy. The wrath of President Chambers had been poured out upon him, and prompt expulsion from college had followed investigation. His only solace was that he didn't suffer alone. His two boon companions who had also spent the evening at the Wayside House faced even greater disgrace.

It had been impossible, of course, to save Corey from the knowledge of Anna's share in the disgrace. Indeed, the evening papers would have enlightened him had he heard from no other source. His pain and shame, when the astounding facts first revealed themselves to him, were impossible to describe. He told Helen afterward that, but for the thoughtful sympathy and unfailing kindness of President Chambers, it seemed to him that he would have died. To think that the ignorant country girl he had rushed away to try to warn and save had been his own beautiful sister, his playmate and darling!

"It's a factory town, sir," he had explained to the president before he knew this terrible fact. "There are girls by the dozen who are densely ignorant of the common proprieties of life. My sister is trying to help them in every way she can, and I thought it might possibly be one in whom she was interested."

"I understand," President Chambers had said. "It was noble in you, Elliott," but his voice had a curious, almost a pitying, note in it. Corey had wondered at the time, and his face had burned over it later. Even then, probably, President Chambers had known who the girl was!

Smarting under the shame of it all, Corey had written such a scathing letter to his young sister that he regretted it afterward. And she cried over it as nothing up to that time had made her cry.

In truth, she was having a lesson that might well be sufficient for a lifetime. It wasn't enough that she had all but broken the heart of her father and mother, for the day came when they, too, had to know the whole affair. She had also made the faces of brother and sister burn with shame for her.

And the neighborhood, that portion of it that was least to be respected, got hold of scraps of her story and imagined more, tossing it back and forth on rude and careless tongues until there were many who began to look askance at her and speak of her as "that Elliott girl."

"No wonder her father is so ill," they said. "It's a wonder he didn't die." They added that they had always thought Anna Elliott a bold-acting girl, and they guessed Helen's pride would be taken down a little now. Other such words came back to Anna, by one source and another, until she fairly shunned the daylight and was in such a deplorably nervous state that it was judged wise to keep her out of school. Helen regretted this for her bitterly, knowing what an ordeal it would be for her when the time came that she must return.

The time came speedily to this watchful sister when she felt only pity for the poor flower whose brightness had been crushed before it was really ready to bloom. Undoubtedly she had done wrong, and of course she ought to have known better. But she had sinned so ignorantly and so childishly. She had honestly believed in all the fine theories that Augustus Sayre Hooper had spun for her on paper. She had thought that, through her, a friend rich and wise and powerful had been introduced to the family, one who would do vaguely wonderful things for Corey and all the rest of them.

Helen, as she went carefully over the letters, anxious to know just how much poison had been scattered through them, could not but admit that the young man had a talent for writing. Most of the letters were sparkling with fun. And the compliments, though lavish, were so gracefully worded that it wasn't surprising that one as young as Anna had been pleased with them. To Helen's older eyes, there was an offensive undertone that led her to see distinctly from what depths of shame and pain their darling had probably been rescued.

If the child had only shown her the letters! Why had this not been done? Why weren't she and Anna so intimate that nothing of this kind could have been carried on without her knowledge? There wasn't so great a difference in their ages that confidential relations between them should be unreasonable — she was only a trifle over four years the elder. Had she been too much absorbed in her more mature and cultivated tastes so that the child had instinctively drawn away from her as unsympathetic? Couldn't she have interested herself more heartily in the merry schoolgirl's pursuits and plans if she had tried, and so been able to shield her?

Such searching thoughts were hers during the reading of those letters, and some strong resolves were born of them. Those resolutions were nearly broken within the hour, however, for it tried her so to see Anna weeping bitterly over the burning of those same letters.

"I can't help it," sobbed the child. "He may not be good, but his letters were lovely. Nobody will ever write such nice things to me again. People look at me as though I weren't fit to speak to, and I didn't mean any harm. I don't believe he knows he has done wrong. He wouldn't do anything to hurt me for the world."

And then Helen knew she must be very wise and very patient. More than mere fun was involved in this dangerous escapade of her sister's. The young villain had reached and awakened her girlish heart.

CHAPTER XX

THORNS

he most bewildering of Helen's experiences during this trying time was connected with Nannie Marvin, her childhood playmate and the closest friend of her young womanhood.

She went over one afternoon to the Marvin farm, armed with Nell's returned photograph and the resolution to tell Mr. and Mrs. Marvin exactly what had occurred. She would also have to make what excuse she could for her young sister.

Nevertheless, she admitted to her own heart a strong sense of relief upon learning that Mr. and Mrs. Marvin were away for the day. Therefore, the first talk could be had with Nannie alone. It ought not to be hard to talk to Nannie, Helen thought. The main features of the story she knew already — everybody in the neighborhood did. The trouble was, they knew much more about it than the facts would justify.

Helen, therefore, began at the beginning and told every detail as briefly as she could, shielding

212 ISABELLA MACDONALD ALDEN

Anna as much as downright honesty would admit.
She was troubled over Nannie's persistent silence
during this recital. She had expected to find the
Marvins in a thoroughly indignant frame of mind,
and she realized they might find it hard to forgive
Anna for placing their daughter in such a questionable position. Of course Nannie would share this
feeling, yet Helen had hoped that Nannie, being
herself so young and merry, would understand
how childishly and ignorantly it had all been done.
Even now, Anna didn't quite comprehend what a
gross wrong she had done her friend.

She had expected Nannie to interrupt her with
some such suggestion and with possibly a word of
sympathy. She did nothing of the kind. No sphinx
could have sat more silently and immovably
through the entire story. When at last she spoke,
her words were entirely different from those her
friend had expected or hoped for.

"After all, Helen," she said, "what was the use in
telling me this? It doesn't do Nell or anybody else
any good so far as I can see. You have the photograph back, and it belongs to Corey's collection.
Why didn't you put it up with the others and let it
go? The beloved public hasn't gotten hold of the
photograph part of the story so far. Probably they
won't. Why need anybody have been wise for
that?"

Helen gave her a surprised, pained look and
was unable to keep reproach from her voice: "Why,
Nannie! How could I do such a thing as that?"

"Why couldn't you? That's what I'm asking. You
wouldn't harm anybody by silence, and there's a
sense in which it would have shielded Anna. Nell
can't help but be angry when she hears of it, and as
for Father and Mother, I don't know what they'll

say. Father is so terribly particular about such things, in the same way you are. If I had been you, I would have just kept it quiet. But I know you well enough to be sure your dreadful conscience will give you no rest until you've told Father and Mother every turn of the story. You ought to have lived in the days of the martyrs, Helen. Did you really have no temptation to a different course?"

"Temptation?" said Helen hesitatingly. "I didn't think of it as a temptation, but perhaps it was. The thought came to me that, if the story of the photograph wasn't known at all, it might cause less pain to others to have nothing said about it. But you're quite right, Nannie. I couldn't get consent from my conscience to take such a course, as it savored too strongly of deception.

Besides, such things always get out," she added. "I've been expecting every hour to hear fearfully exaggerated accounts of it all, and to have had to come to you then with the truth would have been much more humiliating than to do it now. It was that thought which made the right course plain to me, because I realized I would have been ashamed to have it known that I had possessed the truth from the beginning.

"No, I've thought it all over, Nannie," Helen said, "trying to learn just what would be the right thing to do. And the more I've thought and prayed, the more firm has become the conviction that in this case, as in most others, entire frankness was the safer and wiser course. I've now told you all that there is to tell. No stories, however garbled, need add in the least to your anxiety or annoyance. Suppose I had kept back portions of the truth and had been obliged to confess them by piecemeal afterward. Don't you see how instantly you would be troubled with the thought, 'Perhaps there's more of it still that she doesn't choose to tell.' As it is, I believe you will trust me."

"Oh, trust you!" said Nannie impatiently. "No one ever had any doubts about being able to do that! You are fearfully frank, Helen. I think that if it's possible to carry sincerity into fanaticism and almost into sin, you do it.

"I tell you," she said, with a resolute air, "if I had been you, I would have kept entirely still about the photograph. Poor Anna has had enough to bear because of her silly little venture into a hateful world. I don't believe Nell will make life any easier for her on account of it. Nell is older than I am, Helen. She's inclined to be prudish, or overparticular, like some other people I could mention." This last was an attempt at merriment.

"Not that I'm sorry, of course, that she's growing up to be such a discreet young woman. But still, I confess to a feeling of sympathy with the giddy ones who play with edged tools while they're children and cry about it afterward. If Anna had come to me with her escapades, I would have shielded and coaxed her into common sense again, and neither you nor anybody else would have been the wiser."

Helen rose to go. No good could result from prolonging such an interview. "I have helped Anna as well as I knew how," she said sadly, "and have shielded her in every way that seemed right. But I can't go contrary to my ideas of right to shield anybody. One must have 'a conscience void of offense' in the sight of God if one is to have any comfort in life. Poor Anna is having a bitter lesson, but my hope is that when her eyes are fully opened to the realization of her wrongdoing she won't shield herself at the expense of truth.

"I don't think I'm fanatical, Nannie. I wouldn't go up and down the streets blazoning any story. I hope this one may be kept from the public as much as possible. Certainly I shall speak of it to none but your own family, as they're the only ones who have a right to know the facts. What I said was that things always get out in mysterious ways. Perhaps the way may not be so mysterious this time. Laura Holcombe is earnestly trying to put all the wrong upon Anna and leave herself blameless. She, of course, knows about the photograph. I presume she'll tell it. I don't know why she hasn't already.

"That is Anna's misfortune. I would gladly shield her from it if I could. But I saw no honorable way except to tell you the whole story. She herself did not want me to tell you, though she quite agreed with me that Nell and your father and mother must be told. I don't think she could ever have been happy again if it had been managed in any other way."

"She has caught the disease from you," said Nannie, still trying to speak lightly. "I'm glad I'm not your sister! You may be sure I won't speak of the photograph. If I had my way, even now Mother and Father would not be troubled with it. But I can see there's no use in arguing with you."

"My father doesn't think that any other than the exact truth would be honorable treatment of your father," said Helen coldly. Then she went away without trusting herself to say more than a muffled good-bye.

As she walked slowly homeward, she went over the interview in sorrowful detail. She hadn't realized before how much she had counted on a word of real sympathy from her one intimate friend. She couldn't understand the change that had taken place in Nannie.

Nannie's standard of right and wrong had not always been so low. As unlike as possible in general appearance and phrases of speech, Helen had supposed that on all vital points they thought much alike. Only lately had Nannie seemed to be drifting away from all her old standpoints.

It couldn't be Rex Hartwell's influence, for he hadn't changed unless he stood on *higher* ground than he had once occupied. Helen recalled the faithful work he was doing at the schoolhouse among her boys, giving up one of his cherished evenings for the purpose. She also remembered the stand that certain of the boys had taken lately, impelled by the influence of Rex. No, she exonerated him from all blame. But it was bitter to lose in this way the friend of her girlhood.

Could she have seen Nannie within ten minutes after her departure, her bewilderment and anxiety would have deepened. That young woman, as soon as the door closed after her friend, locked it and even slipped the bolt, as though that would make her more entirely alone. Then she flung herself on the bed and buried her face in the pillows with bitter weeping. Not quiet tears, but a passionate outburst such as an excited child might indulge. She knew she was alone in the house and perhaps for that reason gave fuller vent to her emotions.

"Oh, what shall I do? What *shall* I do?" Again and again this wailing cry filled the silent room. There followed an interval of comparative quiet, then excited exclamations.

"I never can! I never will! She need not talk at

me in this way. What are Anna Elliott's babyish pranks and Nell's old photograph compared with this? She as good as told me to my face that I could never be happy again. Oh, me! I know it! I know it! I can never respect myself again, never. Respect! I hate myself. And Rex would hate me if he knew. There would be plenty to point the finger of shame at me. I can never do it, and I don't believe that it's the only right way.

"Helen is hard, hard! She is insane over that word *truth*. I *hate* the word. I wish I had never heard it. As if there were no other virtue in the world except hard, cold truth. And the more mischief it could work, the more virtuous an act she considers it to speak! I won't believe any such thing! What mischief the truth could work in this case! And silence could work no real harm to anybody. To think that in a few weeks is to come my wedding day, and I have such burdens as these to bear! It is too cruel!

"If anybody but me had discovered the truth, I could have borne it. Or if it had been as we thought in the first place, I wouldn't have cared. I had grown used to it, and I didn't feel so badly about it. But to think of it now, after Rex has planned so and arranged everything, drives me wild. I'm not going to think anymore about it.

"Helen Elliott may preach all the rest of her days and look at me out of those eyes of hers, as if they were made of plate glass and she would show me my real self through them! I wish I need never see her again. I'm doing right — I know I am — and I'm not to be turned from it by a sentimental girl who doesn't know anything about life and has never been tried for herself. It's easy enough to confess the faults of others. Why didn't she make poor little Anna come and tell us? She has forgotten that there are other considerations in this world besides what she calls Truth.

"What about the fifth commandment? I must think of my poor father, who has struggled all his life under a burden of debt, and my mother, who is growing old far too fast under her weight of care. Can I force back the burdens that Rex is ready to lift from them both? Oh! What *shall* I do? I'm so wretched, *so wretched!* And I thought I would be so happy! I'd like to die and get away from it all. But I don't suppose I'm ready to die.

"I can't even pray anymore. As soon as I kneel down, this hateful thing comes and stares at me and insists upon being thought about. It's a wonder that I haven't gone insane. Perhaps I shall. I know exactly how people feel who are tormented day and night with a single thought that won't go away for a moment.

"I'm growing cross and hateful under the strain. I never used to treat Helen as I have lately. I treat everybody badly. I've seen Mother look sorrowfully at me sometimes, as though she couldn't understand me. I'm even cross at Rex occasionally, and he's so persistently good. What's to become of me if this state of things continues? Am I never to have any happiness, any peace, again?" The outburst was followed by another bout of tears.

She did not overrate the change in herself. Interested friends had been watching her with anxiety for some time and commenting on her steadily failing health. Some of them thought Rex Hartwell really ought to hasten the marriage and give Nannie the rest she evidently needed. She was probably trying to save her mother in all possible ways and so was overdoing it. Others had it that she was

undoubtedly killing herself trying to buy a wardrobe that would be in keeping with her future position. So foolish of her! Why didn't she wait and let
Rex supply the wardrobe afterward? Still another
group felt sure that Rex ought to have sense
enough to manage the money question beforehand
in some way. It was ridiculous for a man who had
thousands of dollars in the bank to let his wife kill
herself in getting ready to marry him.

The Marvins and the few friends who were intimate enough to know that Nannie's bridal preparations were very simple indeed and that Rex had
exhausted his ingenuity in efforts to assist her with
money were at an entire loss to understand. Why
would a girl for whom life was about to bloom in
all its beauty, apparently without a thorn to disturb, have dark rings gathering under her eyes and
admit the fact of almost sleepless nights, growing
daily more nervous and irritable? Her mother,
who, when the trials of poverty were heaviest, had
been prone to say she took fresh heart whenever
she came in contact with Nannie's sunny face, carried about with her a daily anxiety such as poverty
had never forced upon her. But she could only
wonder and wait and pray.

Helen's call that day marked a crisis in her
friend's life. The girl lay prone on her bed for an
hour or more, breaking the silence only by occasional exclamations. Then for another hour she lay
wide awake but was so entirely quiet that intense
work of some sort must have been done. After that
she arose, bathed from face and eyes as much of
the traces of tears as she could, rearranged her dis-
ordered dress and hair, sat down to her writing
table, and prepared the following brief, imperative
message:

Dear Rex,

I know it's not your evening to come, but you must come nevertheless. Don't let anything hinder you. I must see you tonight without fail, and as early as it's possible for you to come. I have something very important to tell you, something that can't wait for another day.

Nannie

This letter she gave to John Stuart as he drove by on his way to town, instructing him to place on it a special delivery stamp and be sure to have it go in that afternoon's mail.

Thus summoned, Rex Hartwell excused himself from an evening class at the medical college and took the six o'clock train out, arriving at the Marvin farm just before eight.

Nannie was still alone. Her father and mother were in town for a weary day of shopping and errands. The younger portion of the family had gone merrily forth in the farm wagon to meet them at the station, not so sadly disappointed as they might have been, under other circumstances, to have Nannie refuse to accompany them. They hadn't known, until the last moment, that Rex was expected that evening. They discussed the situation as they rode along.

"I wonder what Rex is coming for tonight? I thought he had a class. He had better take care of himself. Nan is doing high tragedy tonight of some sort. She looks as though she might shoot him on occasion." This came from Kate, the family hoyden, who always excused any unladylike conduct on her part with the statement that she ought to have been a boy and was trying to atone to her father and mother for the disappointment.

"I wonder what can be the matter with Nannie?" added Lillian, her next in age and most intimate sister. "She hasn't been her real self for weeks, it seems to me. If getting ready to be married has such an effect on everybody's nerves as it does on hers, I hope I never have to go through the ordeal!"

Then Alice, more staid and thoughtful than either of her older sisters: "Mother is afraid Nannie isn't well. I can see she's very anxious about her, and Nan certainly hasn't acted like herself for a long time. But I suppose when she's married and settled down she'll feel differently."

"Isn't it fun," said Kate, "to think of Nan as a rich woman, able to go where she likes and buy what she likes? But she doesn't seem to see much fun in it. I got off a lot of stuff to her this morning about how I looked forward to talking with the girls about 'my sister Mrs. Hartwell,' who is abroad this winter or spending the summer at Bar Harbor, Niagara or some other grand place. But she didn't laugh a bit. I believe it even vexed her. Her face grew so red, and that strange look she has sometimes lately came into her eyes. All she said was, 'Don't be a simpleton if you can help it. There's more to getting married than going abroad and having a good time.'"

"She does act strange," said Nell, the youngest Marvin, thoughtfully. "I read a story about a girl who acted very much as she does but she was going to be married to a man she didn't like. She hated him, in fact. That can't be the way with Nannie, can it? She just idolizes Rex. I believe that if anything should happen so that she couldn't be married to him, it would kill her."

CHAPTER XXI

How Good
He Is!

hile her sisters freely discussed her affairs, Nannie Marvin waited alone for the coming of her intended husband. It would have taken only a casual observer to discover that she was in a state of intense though suppressed excitement. She was carefully dressed and had never looked prettier than on that evening which she felt was such a fateful one for her.

She was relieved at the thought of being alone in the house. For days the good-natured comments of her sisters and the anxious surveillance of her mother had been all but torture to her. Yet she started nervously at every sound, and when at last she heard Rex's well-known footsteps on the walk, she alternately flushed and paled as a girl might have done who was watching for her beloved after an absence of months instead of waiting for one with whom she had parted but the day before.

She sat quite still. It seemed to her that she hadn't strength enough left to step into the hall and open to him the old-fashioned farmhouse door. As it happened, he didn't wait for her. He had met the merry group of girls at the station and learned from them that Nannie was alone, so he let himself in to the hospitable door that, after the fashion of the neighborhood, was rarely locked. Pausing for only a tap at the parlor door, he opened that also and went toward her.

Rex recognized at once the unusual excitement that was upon her. Indeed, he had read it in her hurried note. More than one perplexed hour he had spent of late in trying to determine what was troubling Nannie. Could it be that she was breaking in health just now, when the long struggle with poverty was over and he was about to place her in that position she was fitted to grace?

Long before this he had made it unnecessary for her to worry about the future of her parents or sisters. He had insisted upon utmost frankness in regard to these matters, reminding Nannie that she would be in a position to give practical help to the young people. He rejoiced to remember that schools, musical advantages and those mysterious perplexities that come under the head of clothes were largely within the power of money. He had taken much pleasure in impressing upon Nannie that it was simply her duty to plan for her sisters just what she would like for them.

As for the mortgage that had rested heavily for years on her father's weary shoulder, it was already a thing of the past, the prospective son-in-law having flatly refused to wait until he was formally admitted into the family before disposing of it. He had looked forward with satisfaction to the pleasure he would give Nannie in presenting to her father the cancelled papers, but it had not been a happy time. Instead of smiles and gratitude, the bewildering girl had given herself up to what were evidently very bitter tears.

The next morning, she confessed to her mother that her night had been almost sleepless, and she had gone about more heavy-eyed and far more nervous than before. All things considered, Rex was beginning to count the days when he could take Nannie away from surroundings that seemed to be wearing her out.

On this particular evening, she didn't rise to meet him but sat erect in the straightest and most uncompromising chair the room contained. A strange pallor was on her face, and her eyes shone like stars.

"What is it, Nannie dear?" he asked, bending over her. "I'm afraid you're not well tonight. I made all possible haste after receiving your summons and was relieved to hear from the girls, whom I met at the station, that you were much as usual. But I think they're mistaken. You're not so well."

"Sit down!" commanded Nannie. "No, I don't want that," she snapped, as he drew an easy chair forward and prepared to place her in it. "I want to sit right here where I am, and you take that seat opposite me. I have something to tell you. I don't want you close beside me, Rex. I can't talk so well then. I told you in my note that I had something very important to tell you. I want you to sit where I can see every change on your face, and I want you to help me if you can. Oh, I need help! It's very hard!

"Rex, we cannot be married at Christmas. We can *never* be married! You won't want me to be your wife when you've heard my story. Don't interrupt me, please," she said with an imperative gesture when he endeavored to speak. "Wait till you hear what I have to say. I thought I couldn't tell it, but I've determined that I must and will. I will if it kills me. Oh, Rex!" She stopped suddenly and placed both hands over her heart, as if to steady its beating. But when he sprang toward her, she motioned him back.

"Never mind. It's nothing. I'm not sick. Don't come, please. Sit there where I told you. It's true, as I said — we can't be married. I can't decide what you'll think when you hear what I've done — or haven't done. Yes, I can. I know you'll think it's terrible, and it is. I can see it plainly now, yet I made myself believe it wasn't so very bad — that, in fact, it was the right thing to do.

"Perhaps I would have kept on thinking so but for Helen Elliott. She is awful, Rex, *awful*! Don't interrupt me. I'm going to tell you the whole story, just as that girl did at the schoolhouse that night. Do you remember? It seems as though I ought to have as much courage as she, doesn't it?

"Rex, *I have found the will!* The lost one — you understand? I found it a long time ago and have kept it a secret. Oh! I didn't hide it away. Don't think that. I found it by the merest accident when I wasn't looking for or even remembering it. And I made myself believe, for a time, that because I happened upon it in that way, so long after everything was settled and everybody satisfied, there could be no harm in just keeping still. Oh, Rex, don't look at me that way! Can't you look — some other way?"

"My poor little girl!" Rex Hartwell's voice, though grave, was full of tenderness. Once more he arose, but she waved him back.

"No, hear the rest. I must tell it all now. I would

die if I had to keep it to myself another hour. That old secretary in your uncle's room — you know how many times we went through it together, as well as the lawyer, the lawyer's clerk, the detective, and I don't know how many more, and found nothing? Well, I wasn't even hunting, remember. I had given up all idea of ever finding that will. I believed your uncle had destroyed it and that he meant you to have his money.

"Do you remember when the housekeeper wrote asking me to go up to the house and look under the rug in your uncle's room for that lost ring of hers? It was the only place she could think of where she hadn't looked, and she remembered pushing it back and forth on her finger the last time she talked with him. Do you remember that you couldn't get away from the office to go with me and that I went alone? It was then that I found it. Now you know how long I've waited!

"I had to push the old secretary out of its corner, and as I pushed it and slipped in behind it to take up the corner of the rug — I knew that poor woman's ring wasn't there, but I meant to be as thorough as possible in the search for it. Then I saw a bit of paper sticking out from the back of the secretary. Do you know that board that was put across to strengthen the back? That's where it was.

"I don't know how I happened to pay so much attention to it. I had no thought of the will, but I pulled at it and thought it was strange that a paper should have worked itself in there. I wondered if it came from the drawer or had slipped down from the top. I saw that it had probably not shown at all until I caught my dress on a little corner sliver and loosened the board, or at least shook it. I pulled at the paper until I began to see writing, your uncle's

hand — 'Last Will and Testament' — then I knew! I
don't think I fainted quite away, but I know the
room began to whirl around, and everything grew
dark.

"When I came to my senses, I pushed the paper
back where it was before. It slid in so that no corner
of it showed. Rex, I know you'll believe me when I
tell you that I did this mechanically, without a
thought of hiding it. Then the thought came to me
that no one would find it there, so I got a knife,
slipped it in and worked at the paper until I had
made a little corner of it show, just as it did before.
Then I pushed the secretary into place and came
away. I meant to tell you everything, of course. But
the next time I saw you, those plans about your
office, the case of instruments and the expensive
books had all come up, and it seemed to me that I
couldn't.

"It wasn't for me — indeed, it wasn't. You know
I'm not afraid of poverty. What else have I known
all my life? But for me to be the one to crush all
your plans and ambitions and set you back dozens
of years perhaps — I couldn't bear it. If the property had been left to some poor person, I think I
would have felt differently about it. But that Mr.
King has enough without it. See how indifferent he
acted when he believed it was his, never even coming to see it.

"It was thinking over all this that made me decide to let things go. I wasn't to blame for its not
being found in the first place, and how could I be
to blame now? Why need I go and blazon it to the
world, spoiling all your beautiful plans? I saw the
date, Rex, just that horrid date! I *couldn't* do it, and
I haven't.

"All these weeks I've struggled with my horrible

secret, part of the time feeling I had a perfect right
to keep still and let others find the will if they
could, and part of the time feeling as though I must
go out on the street and shout it to everybody who
passed. I can truly say I haven't had a happy moment since that hour, but it was only this very day
that I reached a decision. Helen came to see me this
afternoon, and her eyes seemed to burn me. They
were to me like the eyes of God. If I couldn't endure her eyes, how could I meet His? I determined
that before I slept again, or tried to sleep, and before I tried to pray, I would tell the truth.

"I knew *at last* that I was doing wrong, and I
called upon God to be my witness that not another
night should pass before I told you the whole and
left it for you to decide what must be done next. I
know, without your telling me, that I have for-
feited your love and trust. I have been mean and
false, and I know they're traits you hate. You're
like Helen: Nothing would tempt you to falsehood
or silence where truth was at stake.

"You can't marry me now, Rex; you can't want
to. I despise myself, and I know you can't help but
despise me. I want you to understand that I free
you entirely from our engagement and, if you
never speak to me again, exonerate you from all
blame. I know only too well that you could never
be happy with one whom you couldn't trust. Now
I want to ask of you a favor. Will you go away at
once, without speaking any words, and leave me
alone?"

"My poor little Nannie!" said Rex Hartwell, and
with one stride he was beside her and had gathered her into his strong arms. "I'm so sorry," he
said, stroking back the hair from her forehead and
speaking soothingly, as he might have done to a

trembling child. "I'm so sorry you bore this burden all alone instead of letting me share it with you. No wonder you've torn my heart by growing thin and pale. Hush, dear! I will hear no more self-accusing words from your lips," and he stopped the words she would have spoken.

"I've let you talk long enough. It's my turn now. I won't have you say you've fallen. You've been tempted of the devil these many days, but the truth in your soul has triumphed. It was a heavy temptation. I, who know you so well, can understand better than any other how infinitely greater it was to you because it involved me. Don't you know, Nannie, that it's never you of whom you think? I'm sure you never would have carried your silence through to the end. The Lord takes better care of His children than that."

She needed those words of soothing and trust, needed them more than she realized. Her poor brain reeled, and for a second time during this strain, the world grew dark before her. But this time, strong arms held her.

The interview, begun in this startling manner, lasted well into the night. Many questions pressed forward for consideration. In the dining room the family lingered over a late tea, the younger portion chatting lightly, and the weary mother exerting herself to give them every possible item of news, interrupting herself once to ask anxiously, "How has Nannie been today?"

They recognized the note of anxiety in her voice. Kate, who had opened her lips to reply that Nannie had been "as cross as two sticks," checked herself and only said, "Oh, she has been much as usual. What did you do about the velvet, Mother? Could you match it?"

The mother sighed and glanced toward the closed parlor door, wondering that Nannie didn't come out for a minute to welcome them. Then, motherlike, she put herself aside and gave careful attention to the details of the day. It grew late, and still Nannie did not appear.

At last Mrs. Marvin expressed her surprise. Rex was so much at home with them now that he rarely passed an evening with Nannie without coming for a few minutes' chat with them all. She and Nannie's father had been gone all day, an event unusual in itself. She felt as though she had been gone for a week. Then it occurred to her to wonder at Rex being there at all. She thought he had an engagement for Thursday evening.

"He has," said Kate, "but he was ordered out here tonight for some special reason. I don't know what it was, but I know Nan sent a special delivery note to him. She was in the fidgets when we went away because he hadn't arrived, although she knew the train he would have to come on wasn't due yet. Let Nan alone, Mother, and don't worry over her. She'll fume herself into good humor after a while. It's all because she's getting ready to be married, I suppose."

They had family worship presently, and the family group separated. Mrs. Marvin was the last to go upstairs. She looked hesitatingly toward the parlor door and took one step in that direction, then retreated. Ordinarily, or at least before this strange new mood had come upon Nannie, nothing would have been simpler or more natural than for her to have gone in for a little visit and a good night to Nannie and Rex. But as it was, the mother hesitated, then decided Nannie might not like being interrupted. There were so many things nowadays that she didn't like.

The house grew still, but the mother lay awake for a long time, vaguely troubled. Rex was not in the habit of keeping late hours. He was too earnest a student for that. Something unusual must have occurred.

In truth, such unusual things as would have amazed the mother were taking place behind that closed door. Well was it for Nannie Marvin that she had given her confidence to a strong character. Rex was tender and patient, entirely unexcited, and sure from the first moment about what was to be done next.

"It will be all right, Nannie," he said, and his voice was not only soothing, but even cheery. "Don't worry about it anymore. Tomorrow you shall go yourself, if you wish, or I will go for you and get the paper. We'll place it in the hands of my uncle's lawyer with the simple statement that it has at last been found, and we'll ask him to take at once the proper steps to place the rightful owner in possession.

"As for what money has been spent already, I anticipate no trouble on that ground. The prospective heir has not shown himself a man eager for money, and a mistake of this kind he will be willing to wait for a man to rectify. There hasn't been a great deal spent, Nannie, not as men of wealth count. I've been economical. The habit of my life asserted itself and helped me in that.

"Then," he concluded gently, "for you and me, there is simply the waiting that we planned before — not so long a waiting. I've done good work the past year and feel much more assured of what I can do than I did a year ago. I don't think it will be for very long, Nannie, and I know you'll be brave, as you were before, and put fresh heart into me every time I see you."

He wouldn't let her speak many words. He assured her cheerfully that she had said quite enough for her good. Especially he would not permit another word of self-condemnation, declaring that he had already borne from her more than he had believed possible in that line, and he was not to be tried any further. The only time he grew positively stern was when she tried to repeat her assurance that she could not hold him to his engagement with her.

"Hush, Nannie!" he said, and his face was very grave. "You must not speak such words. In the sight of God you are to me as my wife, never more tenderly beloved than at this hour, when by His grace you have overcome a great temptation and stood bravely for truth and purity. Only God Himself shall separate us, dear, and I believe He will let us do our work for Him together."

How good he is! Like an angel of God! This was her thought of him.

CHAPTER XXII

WHAT OUGHT I TO DO?

t the end of an hour, during which time Rex had made an earnest effort to bring peace to Nannie's troubled heart, flattering himself that he was succeeding, she rose up from the easy chair on which he had placed her and stood before him resolute.

"No, Rex, listen," she said. "I must speak. You're like — you're almost exactly like — what I can imagine Jesus Christ would be like if He were here on earth again. But I have suffered enough to know, now that I can think connectedly, that there's something more for me to do. I must be honest *now* at any cost. I've been honest to you, and that was the hardest of all, but there are others, Father and Mother and, oh — everybody! Must I not, in order to be true, let everyone know the truth? It seems so to me. I wish I could do it right away. If there were a great meeting tonight, in the church or somewhere, where all the people were gathered who have ever known me, I would like to go down and tell them I found that will many weeks ago and hid it again. I would like to describe just how it was done so that there would not be one least little thing omitted."

Her excitement had increased, and her misery was pitiful to see. In vain the young man talked low, soothing words, trying to reason with her, to persuade her to trust him, and to let him manage the entire matter in the way that would be right and best. She shook her head. "No, I can't trust you. You aren't God, you know, although you can forgive as He does. You're just human, and you might make a mistake. You want to shield me, you see. You're so pitiful for me, so eager to comfort me. I bless you for it, Rex. You have saved my reason, I think, but I can't trust your judgment — not in this."

Suddenly a new thought came to her. "Rex, if I could see Helen Elliott tonight — I mean now. I *must* see her. Her love for me isn't great enough to blind her judgment, and she will tell me just what I ought to do. She knows, Rex, and she doesn't spare even her own sister from humiliation. Besides, I've treated her shamefully. Only today I spoke cruel words to her. I feel as though I must tell her the reason for them right away. Couldn't you go across the meadow and bring her? It would not take but a moment, and she would come at once if she knew I needed her. Will you?"

He hesitated for only a moment. He shrank from the ordeal, but if Helen could quiet her friend, she was certainly needed at this moment, and he hoped she could be trusted. At least there seemed no other way but to try. He let himself quietly out the front door while the tide of talk was highest in the dining room, and he sped across lots to the

Elliott farm. With much wondering Helen obeyed the summons promptly, and she and Rex walked almost in silence across the fields.

"Nannie is in very great excitement," he said as they neared the house. "She has something to tell you that will doubtless surprise and pain you. I wish she had not thought it necessary, or at least that she had let me talk for her, but I know I can trust your good judgment. Such a terrible strain as she has put upon herself is dangerous in the extreme. At almost any cost, her excitement must be allayed. She seems to think, among other crimes of which she accuses herself, that she has ill-treated you, but I am sure she exaggerates that."

"Why, the poor child!" said Helen. "What an idea! I can easily dispossess her mind of any such feeling. I know she has been in some sort of trouble for a good while. My only wish is to help her."

Nannie was standing at the window watching for them. She came toward them eagerly, her excitement in no wise abated. "I knew you would come," she said, holding out her hand to Helen. "You never fail me, no matter how hateful I am. Oh, Helen, you've been a good friend to poor little Annie, but a worse than Annie is here! The child's escapade is as nothing compared with my deliberate sin. I want you to know the whole story."

She told it briefly with almost painful frankness, making not even so much of an attempt to shield herself as she had done to Rex. Helen was startled; there was no question about that. The temptation was in a form so foreign to any that she had felt. She held herself, of course, from any such expression and spoke only the tenderest of sympathetic words.

But Nannie scarcely heeded them. She hurried

on, "There was a reason for my wanting to see you tonight, right away. I cannot trust it to Rex — not in this. He is too anxious to shield me. He can't bear to give me any more pain. But at the expense of pain and humiliation, no matter how extreme, I feel I must do right. And somehow I felt that you, with your calm, quiet eyes, would see just what right is. Helen, must I not tell everybody about it as I have told you? Father and Mother and all the world? Isn't that the only way to be true?"

Rex Hartwell turned anxious eyes upon Helen. Was she to be depended upon, or had her ideas about truth become fanaticism such as would demand further martyrdom of poor Nannie?

Her reply came without an instant's hesitation. "Oh, Nannie, no, indeed! I think you did just right to tell Rex everything; I don't think you could have respected yourself otherwise. In regard to your father and mother, it seems to me that you have a right to exercise your own judgment. If you want to tell them — if you would feel better to do so — I can understand that feeling. But as for the lawyer and all the others, what is it to them? Justice is to be done in every particular, and, as I look at it, that's enough. Am I not right, Rex?"

He gave her a grateful glance as he said that he had offered the same advice, but that Nannie had been afraid his feeling for her biased his judgment.

By nightfall of the following day, the neighboring countryside and the little village near at hand, and even the large town a few miles farther away, were in a buzz of excitement over the latest developments in Squire Hartwell's affairs. The missing will had come to light! Nannie Marvin herself had found it and given it to Rex, who had taken instant steps toward having the property pass into the hands of the rightful heir! Many and varied were the circumstances said to be connected with this discovery. The story as it traveled grew so rapidly that both Rex and Nannie might have been excused from recognizing their share in it. Never had anything occurred in the neighborhood that was so thoroughly exciting.

Poor Anna Elliott reaped some benefit from this sudden outburst of interest — her own affairs were forgotten for the time being. All tongues were busy trying to glean, as well as to give, information about how Nannie "bore it," what the Marvins said and did, what Rex would do now, and whether, after all, he would still be married.

The Marvin girls came in also for their share of attention. Somebody said it was to be hoped that Kate Marvin would now be cured of her habit of boasting what her sister was going to do and to wear and how her rooms were to be furnished. Some said that "pride must have a fall" and that the Marvins had always been rather too lofty for their good.

But for the most part, the country was sympathetic and regretful. It certainly was hard for poor Nannie — so much harder, all agreed, than if the matter had stayed settled in the first place. Also they agreed that it was undoubtedly an added drop of bitterness for Nannie to have found the will herself. None of them knew, either then or afterward, through what depths of terrible temptation Nannie waded before that will was really found.

Neither did those beyond their immediate family circle ever learn just how the Marvins "bore it." Soon after the astounding announcement of the discovery had been made to the family, Mrs.

Marvin was closeted with Nannie for an hour or more. When she came out, her other curious daughters could see she had been crying. Yet they couldn't resist the temptation to question her. There were so many particulars they wanted to know. Where had the will been found? How had it been found?

Kate, the inquisitive one, said in response to one item, "Why, Mother, Nan hasn't been at the stone house in ever so long! How does it happen that she did not find it until now? Oh, I believe I know just how it was! It must have been hidden away among those old papers Rex brought for Nannie to look over at her leisure, and she has just gotten to it! Was that the way, Mother?"

And then Mrs. Marvin resolved that she would answer no more questions but would issue her mandate. "Girls," she said impressively, "you're all old enough to feel deep sympathy for your sister in this trial, which is to her, of course, a very sore one. Our own share in it is heavy enough, yet after all, what is it compared with Nannie's? You can readily understand that questioning and cross questioning and surmising, keeping the matter constantly before her, will simply be so much torture. She has found the will, and it is to be placed today in the hands of the proper authorities. That's all that is really necessary for any of us to know, and I want it distinctly understood that there must be no more talk about it.

"Don't mention the subject to Nannie except, of course, in the way of a word of sympathy. And even that I hope you'll make as brief as possible. The poor child is not well, remember, and this strain upon her is very heavy. It becomes us to help her in every way we can. I look to my girls to be considerate and patient.

"You'll come in contact with hundreds of people hungry for details about matters that are none of their business. All you need say to them is that Nannie came across the will in an unthought-of place and that it had dropped there at some time and secreted itself, so there's no mystery about it. If you can truly say you have decided not to annoy your sister with questions, you may be able to suggest a line of common propriety to others."

They saw the force of their mother's words, although they grumbled a little at her disinclination to discuss the matter with them.

"You might tell us all about it," said Kate. "Then we wouldn't be so likely to bother Nannie. There are a dozen things I'd like to know. It's too horrid mean, anyway! Rex ought to have the property. It's his by every law of common sense and decency. I declare, if I had been Nan, I believe I should have pitched the old will into the grate and said nothing."

"Katherine," said Mrs. Marvin, her face pale, "I am astonished and shocked! How can you allow yourself to repeat such terrible words! Do not for the world say anything of that kind to Nannie."

"Why, Mother!" said Kate, astonishment in every line of her face, "I don't understand you in the least! What possible harm could it do to repeat such utter nonsense as that, even to Nannie? She's not so far beside herself that she wouldn't recognize the folly of it."

Mrs. Marvin turned away hastily, glad that some household matter called at that moment for her attention. How could she have explained to her daughters the thrill of horror that the mere suggestion of such a course had given her?

Rex Hartwell didn't go to his office that day. He had other duties pressing upon him. The plans for his entire future had been overturned in a moment of time, and he must at once set about planning a new future. His first duty was at his old home.

He came for Nannie by appointment, and they went together to the stone house where they had both spent many pleasant hours. Nannie herself led the way to his uncle's room and pointed silently to the secretary while she seated herself on his uncle's study chair close at hand. She had resolved to be where she could study every change on his expressive face during this trying scene.

Neither spoke while he wheeled out the old-fashioned piece of furniture, placing it at an angle for Nannie to see. There was the corner of the fateful paper peeping out just as she had said. Had it not been peeping out, it was reasonable to suppose it would never have been found. And had Nannie's dress not caught in the rough edge, it would not have peeped out. On such trivial accidents as these do great events sometimes hang. Rex pulled at the paper as Nannie had done and drew it out, studying the characters as he did so.

"It's my uncle's handwriting without a doubt," he said gravely, "and that's the correct date. It certainly hid itself away securely. Well, Nannie," with a rare smile for her, "I'm glad we found it before we complicated matters more than they are." He opened the writing desk as he spoke and took therefrom a large envelope such as lawyers use. Then he slipped the important paper inside it and sealed it carefully.

"Aren't you going to look at it?" asked Nannie faintly.

"No. Why should I? We practically know its contents, and I would rather the lawyer should be the first to examine it." He drew out his pen and supplied the proper address.

"There," he said cheerfully, "that matter is out of our hands. I will go to town this afternoon and place it myself in our friend's keeping, with the request that he make all speed toward the proper adjustment. And now, Nannie, let's have a talk."

As he spoke, he thrust the envelope into his pocket and, going over to the south windows, threw open the blind to let in a glow of sunshine. For the first time, Nannie noticed that a cheery fire was burning in the grate. She had been too preoccupied to think of it before. She looked at it wonderingly.

"Yes," he said, answering her look, "I've been here before this morning. You didn't think I was going to let you come to a closed and chilly room, I hope! Are you quite comfortable? Let us take these two chairs that you and I have used so often before and draw up to the grate and have a visit."

In utter silence she obeyed his directions, dropping herself into the capacious leather chair he wheeled forward. He took its counterpart and settled it close beside her. Then, as if by mutual consent, they looked about the great room furnished with lavish hand. It had been a favorite room with both of them. It was here that Nannie had written those numberless letters for Squire Hartwell, and it was here that she and Rex had held those long talks while his uncle was taking his afternoon nap. It was here that they had expected to spend much of their time as husband and wife.

"You shall write business letters for me," Rex had told her whimsically. "No, I have it: You'll write out my lecture notes for me. I'll see if you can throw as much light into them as you used to do for some of my uncle's obscure sentences." What plans they had had in connection with this room! Now they were here to bid it good-bye.

"I would like to have these chairs," said Rex reflectively. "We've had such good times in them. I wonder if the owner would sell them to us sometime? I wouldn't if I were he. They're splendid, old-fashioned chairs. You can't buy such these days."

Nannie had thought she had no more tears to shed, but her eyes grew dim as she listened. How could he talk about it so quietly, so cheerfully? Her heart was breaking for him. He turned toward her presently with a cheerful smile. Suddenly he moved his chair a little in front of her and, leaning forward, took possession of both her hands.

"Nannie, dear," he said with a kind of cheerful gravity, "I'm glad of a quiet talk with you in this old room where we learned to love each other. There's something I want to tell you. It involves the reason why this thing doesn't break me down as once it might have done. Of course I'm sorry not to have immediate comfort for you and your father and mother — our father and mother, dear. They're all I have. But even that is only a matter of waiting a little longer. We're young and strong, you and I, and it will be strange if we can't carry out eventually the best of our plans.

"Meantime, I have come into the knowledge of an inheritance beyond computation. Do you know, I wonder, that the Lord Jesus Christ has in these last few weeks become more to me than I had realized He could ever be to a human creature? I've begun to have a dim realization of what it means to 'put on Christ.' I've wanted to talk it over quietly

with you, dear, and above all things to have you
share my experience. It's not that I've just begun
the Christian life, you know. I realize I've been a
member of the family for years and an heir to the
wealth stored up for me. It's simply that I have just
begun to claim my rights. By and by, when we
have time, I would like to tell you just how I came
into this knowledge and experience, as well as
why I think I've been content with a starved life for
so long.

"But what I want now is that you and I should
kneel down here together in the room that we supposed was to be ours and consecrate ourselves
anew to His service. I had thought we could use
wealth for Him, but since He plans it otherwise, let
us gladly accept the direction as His best for us.

"And, Nannie, one thing more: I don't want you,
dear, ever to speak again as though there was a
possibility of our life, yours and mine, being two.
God has joined us, and through the blessing of
Him who has overcome the power of death, even
that shall not separate us. You have been for weeks
the subject of a fierce temptation, and God has carried you safely through it. Your life and mine will
be the stronger forever because of this exhibition of
His grace. Shall we kneel together, thank Him for
this, and begin life all over again from this hour?"

Nannie Marvin never forgot that prayer. In some
respects it was unlike any she had ever heard before. She arose from it feeling certain that God had
set His seal to her forgiveness and that He had
been very tender and gracious both to Rex and to
her.

CHAPTER XXIII

THE NAKED TRUTH

mong those who were counted as outsiders, the most astonished and disturbed person over the news of the recovered will was John Stuart.

Notwithstanding the fact that both Rex and Nannie seemed eager to have the news spread as far and as fast as possible, it happened that John, who had been sent ten miles into the country on business connected with the farm, didn't hear of it until that evening, when he brought Helen from the station. She had been in town doing errands for her father, and John, as soon as he reached home, had been sent to meet her at the train.

She began by eager questions. Had he seen Mr. Hartwell that afternoon? She had expected him to be on the train, but he must have taken an earlier one. Did he know whether Mr. Hartwell waited for the lawyer? John had not seen Mr. Hartwell nor heard of a lawyer, and his face expressed so much surprise that she was constrained to ask if he had not heard the news.

"I remember you've been away today," she said with a smile, "but our little neighborhood is in such a ferment that I didn't suppose you could be at home for fifteen minutes without hearing about the recent excitement. But I forget that you don't belong in this neighborhood. Perhaps you didn't hear about the second will Squire Hartwell made?"

He had heard people talk about a second will that had been lost, and from all accounts he had thought it a good thing that it was.

"It certainly seemed so to us," Helen said with a little sigh. "But now that it's found again, I suppose we must change our opinions and at least hope that good will result."

"What!" said John Stuart. He reined in his horses with such suddenness that they resented it nervously. "Miss Elliott, you cannot mean that that ridiculous will has been found!"

Helen was a trifle annoyed at his exceeding interest. Why should it be a matter of deep importance to him? This was carrying curiosity to the verge of impudence. She replied with cold caution. The will had been found, she believed. Miss Marvin herself had discovered it and had notified Mr. Hartwell.

"When did this happen, Miss Elliott? Are you sure the paper has already passed into the lawyer's hands?"

There was no mistaking John Stuart's interest, even eagerness and anxiety. Helen was more and more annoyed. "Probably it has," she answered with exceeding coldness. Mr. Hartwell was not the sort of man to delay when he had important matters to look after. He had gone into town on the same train with her for that purpose, and she had

no doubt but that it was attended to by this time.
Why did John care to know?

For once John Stuart wasn't even aware of Miss
Elliott's coldness and annoyance. He was still
eager and anxious.

"But you spoke of his waiting for the lawyer.
May he not possibly have failed in seeing him? Excuse me, but it's important for me to know the
facts."

"I can't imagine why! Judge Barnard was not at
home early in the afternoon. I met him at the west
end of the city, but I presume he returned in time
for Mr. Hartwell to see him. Whether he did or not
doesn't concern even me, and it's impossible for
me to conceive why it should interest you in the
remotest degree."

"It is because I won't permit any such absurdity,
and I might possibly be able to avoid this offensive
publicity."

He had forgotten himself entirely and for the
moment had spoken the very thought of John Stuart King in that person's voice and manner. He was
recalled to his second self by feeling, rather than
seeing, Helen Elliott's stare of unbounded
astonishment, mingled with a touch of terror.
Could the man who was driving her father's
horses have suddenly become insane? How else
could such remarkable words be accounted for?

Instantly he knew he had blundered irreparably,
but he was excited and annoyed. What of it? he
asked himself recklessly. She'll have to know the
truth. That ridiculous will has spoiled everything!
Yet what is the truth? Or, rather, what portion of it
must she know at once, and what must yet be concealed? He thought rapidly and spoke again without perceptible delay.

"I beg your pardon, Miss Elliott. I was much excited and forgot to whom I was speaking. I have reasons for being interested in this will. When you hear them, I think you'll admit the reasons are sufficient. If I may see you alone this evening for a few minutes, I can explain."

"I don't wish any explanation," she said with grave dignity. "I have nothing to do with your views of this subject, unless you mean there's something you feel you ought to tell me."

That last was an afterthought pressed into words by her conscience. Ought she to turn away from a man who perhaps needed to follow out his sudden impulse to tell something he had concealed? He felt her exceeding coldness and evident shrinking from an interview with him, but his reckless mood continued. She should see him and talk with him, his real self, at least once.

"There is something I think I ought to tell you," he said, speaking with as much dignity as she had.

"Very well. I shall be in the sitting room tonight after seven o'clock, and I don't know of anything that will prevent your seeing me alone for a few minutes if that amount of caution is necessary."

A much-disturbed man occupied the woodhouse chamber that evening. As soon as his horses were cared for, he went directly there and locked himself in. He touched a match to the carefully laid fire in the small Franklin stove that Farmer Elliott had suggested he set up for his comfort. Then he sat back and stared gloomily at it, feeling as though comfort had gone out of his life.

When he had laid the fire in the morning, he had looked forward to a long evening spent in this quiet retreat. The evening was meant to do much to further the interests of Reuben and Hannah, those creatures of his brain whose daily living he had the privilege of fashioning and directing.

Now he felt he wanted none of them, that he hated them both and would, perhaps, put them both out of existence with the next stroke of his pen. What was the use in playing with fiction when real life stalked before him in such dreary shape? What had he done by a few reckless words? Made it impossible for this part he had been playing to be acted any longer, and therefore made it impossible for him to see again the one for whom he had long been playing it.

For this one time he let the truth appear to him unrebuked. It was for Helen Elliott's sake that he had carried on this deception week after week, month after month. It wasn't because he was studying human nature in a new guise, nor because he wanted to try the effect of plain living and very regular hours, nor because he was sleeping so well and had such a fine appetite. It wasn't even because he took to heart the unkindness of depriving Farmer Elliott of his valuable services at a time when he most needed them.

All these things would do to say on occasions when his conscience would admit them, but to-night it demanded straightforwardness. He was lingering here that he might sit opposite Helen Elliott at table and watch her expressive face and hear her voice — to be near her. This was the plain truth. And these things were possible only because he was her father's hired man.

Given that other truth he had offered to explain to her, he instinctively felt that, for a time at least, he could not hope for her friendship. Could he ever hope for it? As he answered this question to his conscience, the blood mounted and spread over his face until his very forehead was red. Was it possible that John Stuart King had put himself into a position of which he was ashamed? What did he want of Helen Elliott's friendship? Suppose she were willing to laugh with him over the part he had played, admire his cleverness, approve his motives and agree that they should be good friends hereafter. Would he be satisfied?

It humiliated him to realize how far removed from satisfaction his feeling would be. What, then, did he expect? He kicked an unoffending stick of wood at his feet as he told it angrily that one who had made an utter fool of himself had no right to expect anything.

Suppose he had a chance to tell her every detail of the truth. Would he do it? What would she think of Elizabeth, his intended? And then he drew himself up sharply. He was insulting her by intruding Elizabeth into the interview. Nay, was he not even insulting Elizabeth? The important point was, what did he think of her?

If there were directions in which John Stuart King was not strong, he certainly was not a weak man. His friends attributed to him unusual strength of character. While they may have mistaken a certain form of obstinacy for strength, as is often done where people are not intimate, still the word *weak* would not apply to him. Anyone who understands his own nature would have pitied John Stuart King that night as the extent of his moral degradation slowly revealed itself to him.

He was engaged to be married to one woman, yet every fiber of his being was athrob with the thought of another! He had permitted himself to linger in this place of temptation long after he had admitted to his heart that he was tempted. He had

put the thought aside, laughed at his conscience —
or rather placed a stern seal of silence upon it —
and deliberately — yes, that was the proper word
— yielded to the desire to be near Helen Elliott.
Studying her for a character in fiction indeed!

Long before, he had admitted that was not his
purpose. He had let her into his heart, and she
must forever, whatever else happened, be a part of
him. She was too sacred for fiction, and he felt the
glow on his face deepen as he recalled certain
words of hers.

He had been driving them from the station, Rex
Hartwell, Nannie Marvin and Helen, and they had
been discussing his work — John Stuart King's —
as it had appeared in a current issue of a popular
magazine. Helen was sitting beside him with her
face turned slightly toward those in the back seat,
and every line of it was visible to him. "I don't
think I like him," she had said, "not wholly. Oh, he
has undoubted talent. I think he will be recognized
as one whom we call a great writer. Perhaps he
deserves the name better than most of them.
They're all disappointing."

"In what sense does he disappoint you?" Rex
had asked, and John Stuart had blessed him for it,
since it was the very question he desired to ask.

"Why, he ignores — they all do — the greatest
thing in the world," she had replied with a slight
laugh. "In his great character, his 'Reuben' that one
can see he desires to be great, one is sensibly reminded of his omissions. For all that the story indi-
cates, he might have been born and reared among
a class of beings who have no religion, if there
were any such, so utterly does he ignore it. A great
fact in the world, swaying lives all about us —
more than any other single idea ever has — how is

it being great to write a history of any life and leave out all reference to it?"

How distinctly he remembered every word of her clear-cut sentences! They had cut deeply.

"Probably he has no religion," Rex Hartwell had replied, "and therefore cannot be expected to produce any in fiction."

"Then ought he to profess to describe life?" Helen had asked. "Do you believe that in our present civilization there is any life, or at least any with which ordinary fiction deals, that isn't distinctly affected by what we call religion?"

The talk had drifted away after that, from definite authors to a general discussion of fiction and its legitimate realm. John Stuart had listened closely, with a degree of interest that would have amazed the talkers, and had carried home some sword thrusts to consider. He had worked way into the night over his chief characters, Reuben and Hannah, trying to reconstruct their lives on a basis that he felt might interest Helen, and he had failed. He could do nothing with them.

Like many another writer of fiction, he learned that his characters were not plastic clay in his hand to be molded as he would. He had created them, but they had wills of their own and would insist upon carrying out their own ideas of destiny. No, it was more humiliating than that. He had failed in creating them. They weren't like the great Creator's work, "made in God's image." He had brought them thus far, dwarfed and misshapen, and they refused to be re-created.

He remembered vividly his experience and his disappointment on this evening when he told himself that such a life as Helen Elliott's was too sacred for his kind of fiction. Must he descend yet lower in the moral scale and admit he couldn't even retain Helen Elliott as a friend?

He sat long, staring into the glowing fire until it grew disheartened and died out and a chill began to creep over the room. He utterly ignored Susan Appleby's repeated calls to "come this minute if you want any supper at all." He felt sure that to sit down opposite Helen Elliott just then and try to eat would choke him.

Just what was he to say to her in that interview for which he had asked? Why had he been such a fool? Yet what else could he have done? If that intolerable will that ought never to have been made could have stayed hidden, he might have planned his way out less painfully than this. But at all hazards he must put a stop to that folly.

He sprang up at last with a sudden realization that it was nearly seven o'clock. He must make ready for that interview, and the making ready required time. In an obscure corner of the woodhouse chamber stood a trunk that he had himself brought from the express office a few days before. It had been sent for under the vague impression that there might come a crisis in his life before long that would demand an appeal to its resources. He strode over to it and unlocked it. Fletcher and his city tailor had done his bidding, and all the belongings of a gentleman's dress were soon being tossed about the room.

When he was dressed completely, even to the fine handkerchief with its faintest possible suggestion of the breath of violets, he looked in his twelve-inch mirror and laughed. The short, dry laugh had no touch of pleasure in it. What a humiliating thing it was that there should be such a transformation by the aid of mere clothes!

CHAPTER XXIV

"I HAVE STARTED OUT NOW FOR TRUTH"

elen was in the sitting room, waiting for her caller. To say she was annoyed does not express the situation. Yet her face, besides being grave, was somewhat disturbed. If she had spoken her innermost thoughts, she would have said she was tired of it all, almost tired of everybody connected with her world. It had been such a trying world to her lately, so full of petty intrigues that had, like most intrigues, their serious and dangerous sides. It was also full of twists and quibbles and prevarications when the truth would have served every purpose better and shielded its adherents royally.

Corey's trouble, for instance, was born entirely of his propensity to toy with words and let others gain what impressions they would therefrom. But her face cleared for a moment at the thought of Corey. The watching Father in heaven had been true to His word, and even Corey's follies had been made to work together for his good. His feet were securely settled at last on the Rock.

But there was poor Annie, led astray in the first place by her love of mystery to have a secret to whisper over with Laura Holcombe. What would be the outcome of the "fun" she had pursued? Would she ever recover from the shock she had received upon discovering what the great censorious world thought of such things?

She had had her lesson, poor darling! She had learned it wasn't father, mother and sister alone who were "overparticular." When it came to experiences like hers, the very people who had hinted at "strait-laced notions," "overstrained ideas" and "fanatical theories" were among the first to hold up hands of horror and cry, "Who would have believed she could do such a thing?"

Oh, yes, the child had learned a lesson she would remember, but who could be sure that the sweetest flowers of innocence had not been crushed in the learning? Certainly it had been a bitter experience for them all. And Helen, who knew how fond the gossips were of talking, felt that the end was not yet in sight.

Then, too, there was Nannie, her friend since childhood, beloved as few girlfriends are. Yet, as Helen grew old enough to realize and understand it, how constantly had she deplored in Nannie that marked trait that led her to appear what she was not!

It had exhibited itself in almost babyhood, leading her to smile and appear pleased with attentions that were really a trial to her. This trait, which had been called amiability, had perhaps been unwisely admired and fostered. Certainly it grew and developed in Nannie the sort of girl who said, "Oh, how delightful!" when she listened to a plan that in her heart she thought was a bore. Pity for Nannie that she did not, at the most formative period in her life, come in contact with anyone who labelled this development falseness. Instead it was called common politeness. It grew upon her and had finally borne the fruit that had brought her to the depths of humiliation and almost despair.

Thinking it over and realizing she had faults probably as grave, Helen could yet be sure that temptation in this guise would not have come to her.

And now, when she was all but sinking under the weight of pain and anxiety caused by the various outgrowths of this form of sin, must come John to add his experience, whatever it was! She shrank from it all. Why need she hear anymore? She was tired. She felt she had no more advice to give and that even the vaguest kind of sympathy was almost too much to expect of her.

She had not the remotest conception of what John's confidence might be. She told herself half impatiently that she was too weary to form a theory. Yet a thought had floated through her mind that he must be connected in some way with that disagreeable and altogether unjust will.

She smiled sarcastically over the memory of his surprising statement that he "would not permit any such absurdity!" Probably in his ignorance he imagined that he could prevent it. Yet John wasn't ignorant. She recalled abundant proof that he was remarkably well informed. He was simply a mystery, and she hated mysteries. She was almost sorry she had permitted him to come to her with his story. But even in this unusual irritability that seemed to have her in hand, there was still the solemn sense of responsibility toward every person

with whom she came in contact, especially for
those who asked for her help.

She had struggled with her unwillingness to
shoulder any more "secrets" and had concealed
her annoyance, if not weariness, when she said to
her mother with a wan smile, "John wants to see
me alone for a few minutes, Mother. I told him he
might come at any time after seven."

"More burdens?" asked Mrs. Elliott sympathetically. "Poor little woman! You've had to shoulder
the troubles of others ever since you could walk.
Never mind, dear. Such work has its compensa-
tions. I hope John isn't in any difficulty; I have a
hearty liking for him. If he's ready to confide his
history to you, it may be the dawning of a better
day for him. Anna, bring your book and come to
Father's room. He will enjoy having you read
aloud for a while."

Poor Anna had looked up with a quick, appre-
hensive glance the moment she heard of John's request, and then she had dropped her eyes on her
book again. But they saw nothing on the printed
page. All sorts of incidents filled her with apprehension these days. What could John want of
Helen but to impart to her some fresh gossip about
her that it was necessary for them to know? He
would naturally come to Helen, for her father was
not yet well enough to be troubled more than was
necessary, and they all shielded their mother as
much as possible. There was no need for fearing
that John was himself in trouble. John was good.
She felt she knew that better than any of them.

So Helen sat waiting. To banish as much as possible all disagreeable thinking, she took up the latest issue of a popular magazine and turned to
Stuart King's serial story. She might not approve of

him entirely, but he furnished interesting reading.

And then the sitting-room door opened, and John Stuart entered unceremoniously. He had stood in the hallway for several seconds, being haunted by the silliest trivialities. In the garb of John Stuart King, it seemed natural to think of conventionalities. In his side pocket at this moment reposed his card case, well filled. Under ordinary circumstances, the proper thing would be to ring the doorbell and send in his card by Susan Appleby. But under the current circumstances, how absurd it would be even to knock!

To continue this line of thought would make it impossible for him to talk with Miss Elliott. He hurriedly pushed open the door and as hurriedly closed it behind him. Helen looked up from her book, stared a bewildered second, and then rose to her feet, a startled look on her face.

"I beg your pardon if I'm intruding," he said. "You gave me permission to come, you remember."

Formal expression came naturally to his lips. It belonged, apparently, with his clothes!

"I don't understand," faltered Helen. She was still staring.

The ludicrous side of it became uppermost to John Stuart King and put him for the moment at his ease. "I begged the privilege of an interview, you remember? I felt it necessary to explain something to you."

"But you are not — "

She was about to add "John," but something in his strangely familiar yet unfamiliar face held back the word. It was ludicrous still.

"I am John Stuart at your service," he said, speaking almost merrily. "Pray be seated, Miss Elliott, and I will try to explain as briefly as possible."

She dropped back into her chair, and John Stuart drew a chair for himself, uninvited, and felt the situation had already ceased to be ludicrous. He had, early in their acquaintance, imagined scenes in which he would "explain," but they had never been like this one. If only he didn't care much what she thought of him! He felt the perspiration starting on his forehead.

How he got through with the first of it he could never afterward have told. He knew he stammered something about being a student of human nature and about desiring to understand better certain social conditions, especially the tramp question, before writing about them. It was a lame defense, and he realized it. His listener grew colder and more dignified.

She interrupted him at last: "You claim to be a writer, then?"

"That is my business."

"What do you write?"

He hesitated, and his face flushed. Her tone was that of a person who, not believing what he said, had resolved to entrap him.

"I have written on various lines," he said at last. "Travel and some purely literary papers. At present I'm writing fiction."

"Oh! So you thought you would create some and act it out? It may have been a very clever way, but how am I to be sure which is fiction — or, rather, where fiction ends?"

"You are being hard on me, Miss Elliott!" he said quickly. "I have done nothing to deserve your contempt." Then for the first time he noticed the magazine still in her hand. Her tone and manner stung him, forced him on.

"I see you have the *American Monthly*. It includes what my friends call a very fair shadow of myself on the frontispiece. Can you not corroborate that portion of my story?"

She gave a little start of surprise — was it also of dismay? — gazed fixedly at him for a moment, then turned the leaves rapidly. She looked at the pictured face, then back to his. "You are Stuart King!" she said at last, and it's impossible for mere words to give an idea of what her tone expressed.

"I am John Stuart King. Was it a crime so great as to be beyond the reach of pardon to drop the last name for a time, to come into the country and earn an honest living for myself, doing honest work in, I believe, a satisfactory manner?"

She was looking steadily at him. There was no smile on her face, no indication that she was other than gravely displeased.

"Pardon me," she said at last. "You must be your own conscience. Whether the end in view was worth the weeks and months of deception you have had to practice, you ought to be better able to tell than I. I can't pretend to fathom your motive."

"My motive, Miss Elliott, as I told you, was distinctly in line with my work as a writer. I wished to study certain social conditions untrammelled by the conventionalities that seemed of necessity to belong to my life. In particular, I desired to understand the life of the ordinary tramp and be able to describe it from his standpoint. In doing this, I had a motive that even you might approve. I wanted, if I could, to help solve the problem of how to reach and save him."

"And you found such satisfactory conditions for studying this phase of humanity here in my fa-

ther's quiet farmhouse, where a tramp rarely pene-
trates, that you have lingered on through a large
portion of your exile?"

John distinctly felt the blood surging in great
waves over his face. Once more he had blundered!
"I used the past tense, if you noticed," he said presently in a lower tone. "It was the end for which I
started out. I won't deny that other motives have
gotten hold of me and shaped my later decisions."

It was still a lame defense. He knew that. But it
had in it, either in the words or the manner of ren-
dering them, something that Miss Elliott did not
care to probe further.

"Well," she said suddenly in an altered and busi-
nesslike tone, "I have nothing to do with all this, of
course. You don't have to justify yourself to *me*.
May I ask what it has to do with the matter of
business that seems to have been the occasion of
this revelation? Have you any information to give
with regard to Squire Hartwell's will that has just
been found?"

"Pardon me, Miss Elliott, but are you really not
exempt from the concerns of my situation? From
the standpoint from which you view life, have you
not something to do with it and with me? Am I not
a human being with an immortal soul in which you
are bound to be interested? Will it be of interest to
you, I wonder, to know that, while I believe I was a
Christian when I came into your home, I have received new views of what that word should imply
since I've been here?"

She looked away from him at last, down at the
book she still held, and toyed with the leaves for a
moment. Then she said, "Pardon me, Mr. King, I
don't wish to be hard. But I'm compelled to say
that Christianity has its very foundations in truth."

"I understand you," he said. "You *are* hard on me, but I think you don't mean to be, and I believe I should hereafter agree with you. I have started out now for truth. You asked me a question. Do you not see the relation I sustain to that unjust and foolish will? Have you heard the name of the supposed heir?"

She looked quickly at him, catching her breath. "It is Stuart King! And you are — "

"And I am John Stuart King, distant relative of Squire Hartwell. That complication, Miss Elliott, was not of my planning. It's an accident. But you do not suppose, I hope, that I will allow such an unjust will as that to stand. It was made in a moment of passion, and the maker didn't live long enough to recover his sane mind. It is manifestly unjust, and I shall have none of it. Am I wrong in supposing that I can in that way give you a bit of pleasure? You will like to have your friends remain in undisturbed possession of their own?"

Before he had completed the sentence, he regretted that he had said it. Clearly, John Stuart, her father's hired man, had been on terms of intimacy with this young woman such as were not to be accorded to John Stuart King, the somewhat famous author.

He made haste to change the subject. "Miss Elliott, will you keep my secret for a few days, until I can find someone else to help your father? There are certain matters he has entrusted to me that really require my attention, and — "

She interrupted him. "That will be impossible, Mr. King. I'm sure that my father and my brother, who will be at home tomorrow, would undergo any inconvenience rather than to trouble you further. My father will, without doubt, entertain you as Mr. King if it isn't convenient for you to go away at once. But as for lending my aid to any form of deception, however slight it may seem to you, that's quite out of the question. If there were no other reason, the very recent painful experience in my own family would make it impossible."

"I understand that, too. I will go away at once — tonight if you wish it. But, Miss Elliott, surely I may return? I may call upon you as a friend?"

It was Helen's turn to flush. The color flamed into her face, but she answered steadily, "You make me appear very inhospitable, Mr. King. I must remind you that we are strangers."

"Yet you were kind to John Stuart and friendly with him. You trusted yourself to his care and accepted his help. But the moment he claims equality with you, you become strangers! Nothing has changed but the clothes, Miss Elliott. Do they count for so much?"

A quick flash of indignation filled her eyes. "You compel me to plain speaking," she said, "by utterly misunderstanding my position. It's not a question of equality or inequality. For John Stuart, an honest man, earning his living in an honest way, I had respect and was ready to think and speak of him as a friend. When John Stuart went out of existence, my acquaintance with him necessarily ceased."

John arose. It seemed to him time that this interview should end.

"I will not intrude any longer this evening," he said in his most dignified yet courteous tone. "But it's only fair to warn you that sometime, John Stuart *King* intends to try to secure an introduction to Miss Helen Elliott."

CHAPTER XXV

IN EVERY RESPECT,
SAVE ONE

r. Marvin's prayer at family worship that evening revealed to Nannie that her mother had told him her story. She had shrunken nervously from doing it herself, as it seemed to her that she couldn't bear the look of that pure-eyed, unworldly father when he first heard of his cherished daughter's temptation and downfall. She used that pitiless word in thinking of herself. Rex might blind his eyes to it if he would, and she blessed him for doing it, but she herself knew she had sinned. And her father, who would lose every poor penny he could earn rather than wrong anyone, would be clear-eyed in regard to this thing. She wanted him to know the whole, and she assured her mother that she couldn't sleep until he was told; but somebody else must tell him.

The father's prayer fell like balm on her wounded and sensitive spirit. There was a touch of the divine sympathy in it that Rex had shown and that she had thought no other possibly could. As he prayed, she found herself saying over softly the words, "Like as a father pitieth his children." Then, with a sudden rush of tears that were not altogether unhappy, she cast herself upon the pity of her infinite Father and rested.

He came and kissed her after the prayer, that dear earthly father who had just opened heaven for her. His voice trembled as he said, "God keep my daughter pure. I bless Him for having kept you thus far. Trust Him and He will bring you through to the end in peace. Poverty is not the worst trial that can befall."

"What a strange prayer that was of Father's!" Kate Marvin said as the sisters in their room lingered over preparations for bed. "One who didn't understand the state of things might have supposed that Nan had just had a fortune left her instead of having just lost one."

"Nan seems different, too," said thoughtful Alice. "She has been gentler and less nervous all day than I have seen her for a long time. Perhaps...."

"Well," said Kate, after waiting what seemed to her a reasonable length of time, "perhaps what?"

"I was only thinking that perhaps Nannie, too, had discovered something that Father and Mother have always had."

"What's that?"

"A mysterious power, Katie, to help them over hard places and keep them sweet and strong. Some people find it by praying. Don't you know that Father and Mother do?"

Blessed are those fathers and mothers of whom their children can give such testimony!

It was true that Nannie Marvin found herself more at rest that evening than in weeks — it almost seemed to her years — before. The great strain was over. They were poorer by contrast than ever before. The years stretched between Rex and her, and hard work lay before them all. Nevertheless, as she knelt to pray, her first thought was one of gratitude. God had brought her through, and though years might stretch between her and Rex, there was no gulf between them now.

It seems a pity that dull mornings must so often follow periods of mental exaltation. With the next morning's dawn, Nannie Marvin felt the ordinary side of her life more keenly than she had before. Depths of misery and heights of peace are both more interesting than the middle ground of everyday duty.

Nannie was quiet but sad. The irritable stage had passed, and her voice had recovered its habitual gentle note. But it was hard to go about her room, folding away, out of sight and mind, those pretty wedding fineries she had prepared with such painstaking care. She didn't delay the task. An old trunk in the attic had been brought down almost before daylight, and into it she folded away sundry garments and a dress or two that would be "too fine" for her now.

"It's all horrid!" said Kate, who had been helping her move the trunk. "I'd rather she would scold. It feels as though there had been a funeral!" And she turned abruptly away to hide the tears.

Perhaps Nannie had something of the same feeling. She had slept quietly most of the night but had awakened early to think and plan. Rex would not have all the hard work this time; she was resolved upon that. She, too, would go to work. Helen wanted to give up her position, as her father and mother weren't willing that she should teach any longer. Helen herself wanted to go away for a year of study.

They had talked it all over together in the fall, how Helen would teach for one winter only. Nannie had been secretly glad that, instead of planning to go away for study, she was planning to go to her own beautiful home and make life glad and bright for ever so many people. They had wondered who would take Helen's place in the school and had gone over their list of acquaintances, after which they were sure none of them would quite suit. Helen had said half mournfully, "Oh, Nannie, if it could be you, how delightful it would be for my girls and boys!"

Nannie had laughed and blushed and declared that she didn't see her way clear to take up even such wonderful work. Now her way was clear. She would talk with Helen about it that very day. Helen had said once that, if a suitable person could be found, she would like to be relieved before the spring term. If she was of the same mind now, not many weeks hence Nannie might be at work. It would help a little. There were other ways, too, in which money might be earned.

Although she was grave-faced and a bit sorrowful that morning, she was tingling with energy. Yet she had a tear or two for the wedding dress as she folded it away. She dried them quickly when she heard Rex's voice in the hall below, and she went down to him in a few minutes.

"I had to pass the house on an errand," he explained as he held her hand, "and I didn't succeed in passing, as you can see. This is a bright winter morning, Nannie. How would a brisk walk over to Mr. Potter's place suit you?"

She gave him a quick, regretful look. "Oh, Rex,

are you going to offer your horse for sale?"

"I'm going to tell him he may have her. He has envied me her possession for so long that it seems a pity not to gratify him."

"But that horse is your very own."

"Oh, certainly! She has nothing to do with my uncle's estate. But you know, Nannie, you and I are not going to keep a horse just yet. That's one of the luxuries awaiting our future. Come, the walk out there will do you good."

"No," she said resolutely, "I'm not going to begin in that way. I am to work, too, Rex. I have plans, and I must set about carrying them out this very morning."

"What are your plans? Perhaps I won't agree with them. We must discuss them and agree together for what is best. Mrs. Marvin, please persuade your eldest daughter to accompany me for a walk. The morning is just right for it."

"Is she averse to it?" asked Mrs. Marvin, smiling, as she paused in her transit through the hall. "I would go if I were you, Nannie. It will do you good."

"That's not to be my motto any longer, Mother; I am going to work."

"Ah, but the work can wait for one morning," pleaded Rex. "You want to tell me all about it, you know, and honestly, Nannie, I shall have very few mornings to spend with you after this. I won't hinder you again in ever so long. I have some plans to tell you about that are calculated to hasten the time." The latter part of this sentence was spoken low, for her ear only. Then he suddenly changed his tone.

"Nannie, a caller is coming up the walk. Just hide me in the kitchen or somewhere, won't you? I don't care to be hindered by that man this morning. He'll have a dozen questions to ask if he sees me. What can he want with your father?"

"Who is it?" asked Nannie as she followed rather than led the way to the dining room, Mrs. Marvin having disappeared.

"It's my uncle's lawyer. I placed that paper in his hands last night. I had to wait until the late train before I could see him. He was absent all afternoon, so I merely handed it to him with the statement that it would explain itself. Of course I enclosed a note stating who had found it, and then I came away. It made me too late to come out here last night, as I had planned, so I was even more glad of having a morning with you. He must have taken the eight o'clock train out. His business must be urgent."

"I can't imagine what it can be," said Nannie wonderingly and vaguely uneasy at the same time. "Father has no business dealings with him that I know of. I wish we had gone out, Rex, before he came. I feel as though I don't want to see him."

"Oh, we need not see him," said Rex cheerfully. "I'm not ready for a business talk with him yet. There are some papers to go over first. I told him so in my note. Nannie, if you will put on your wraps, we can slip out this dining room door and be off."

Then Mrs. Marvin opened the door and closed it after her.

"It is Judge Barnard, Rex. He is in search of you, and he says he wants to see Nannie, too, on important business."

Nannie shivered like a leaf and grew deathly pale.

"My dear," said Rex soothingly, "don't be startled or troubled. There is nothing that need annoy you. Some absurd technicality, I presume, that might as well have waited until another time, but the average lawyer doesn't deal in common sense. I'll go out and see him and spare you the annoyance if possible, and I have no doubt that it is."

But he was too late. The door that Mrs. Marvin thought she had closed after her did not latch, and it presently swung open slowly of its own will.

Judge Barnard, who was standing near it, turned at the sound. "Good morning," he said. "Am I to come in here?" Suiting the action to the word, he walked toward Rex, holding out his hand. There was nothing for that gentleman to do but receive him with what grace he could.

"Good morning, Miss Marvin," said the judge again, turning toward Nannie. He had met her once before in Squire Hartwell's library, when she was serving as that man's secretary, and he now bestowed a look of more than ordinary interest upon her. He was a dignified man of more than middle age, and he looked as though he could, on occasion, "deal in common sense." He stood very high in his profession, and it was long since he had attended in person to the minor details of business. The annoyed young man who was watching him couldn't help but think that he had been moved this morning by a vulgar desire to see how both Nannie and himself "bore" the unusual misfortune that had fallen to them. He had to exert himself to speak with courtesy.

"Mrs. Marvin said you wished to see me, Judge Barnard. I suppose there is no occasion for our detaining Miss Marvin?"

"Yes," said the judge with interested eyes still upon Nannie, "the matter about which I have come to talk concerns her also." Then he looked about for a seat.

Rex controlled his inward indignation and brought forward chairs for the three.

"I examined with a good deal of interest the paper you left with me last night," Judge Barnard began deliberately. "An unusual degree of interest, I may say, and following its examination came some very interesting developments. May I ask if the discovery of this paper has, to any extent, been made public?"

Rex gave a swift glance at Nannie before he replied. "It has, sir, to quite an extent. We were rather anxious that our friends should know of the discovery, and of our change of plans, as promptly as possible." He had adopted the plural pronoun in every reference to the subject, though, as a matter of fact, it was Nannie who had insisted upon telling the news as promptly and as widely as lay in her power.

"It's a pity," said Judge Barnard dryly, "because there are people who will talk themselves ill over an affair of this kind, and you might have saved their tongues a good deal of work. I had a remarkable caller last night after I saw you. Some time after, indeed; I think it was nearly midnight when he came. He was none other than the young man in whose favor your uncle drew a will."

"The heir!" said Rex in surprise. "Has he heard of the discovery so soon?"

"Yes, he has been spending some time in this neighborhood, it seems, and making the acquaintance of his friends unknown to them." Judge Barnard evidently enjoyed the bewilderment he was causing. He paused between each sentence and looked from one to the other as if to give them time to absorb his statements.

"In short, he is none other than your neighbor's man of all work. Mr. Elliott's farm joins this one, I believe?"

"John Stuart!" exclaimed Rex and Nannie in almost the same breath.

"That is the name by which he has chosen to be known. But the surprising part of my statement is yet to come. He called upon me for the purpose of saying that he repudiated the entire property. He would have nothing to do with it in any shape except to turn it over, as rapidly as the forms of law would allow, to the rightful heir. He affirmed what we all believe, Mr. Hartwell, that the property by right belongs to you, and that your uncle in his sane mind so intended. The other will was a freak of the moment and has no moral ground to stand on. Therefore, he declares that it shall not stand."

"But I can't have this sort of thing!" said Rex in great excitement. "My uncle made the will and lived for weeks afterward without altering it. We have nothing to do with what *ought* to have been. We must deal with what is. I decline to have my uncle's property on any such ground."

"Then we apparently have two obstinate men to deal with," said Judge Barnard, smiling as though he greatly enjoyed the whole affair. "The other is equally obstinate."

"He will change his mind. Who is he, Judge Barnard, and why has he been posing as a stranger? Is he a laboring man?"

"Hardly! Not, at least, in the sense you mean. I have the climax to my story yet in reserve. He is John Stuart King, the scholar, traveler, author and whatnot."

Their astonishment seemed to satisfy the judge. It was so great as almost to drive personal matters from their minds for the moment.

"Well," said Rex at last, "he has my uncle's property to look after, that's all. You may tell him that I utterly refuse to receive as a gift from him what my uncle did not choose to leave me."

Judge Barnard turned suddenly to Nannie. "Do you approve of such a wholesale renunciation as that, Miss Marvin?" he asked.

Nannie's answer was quick and to the point. "Certainly I do. Mr. Hartwell is not an object of charity. It may be noble in Mr. King to feel as he does. I think it is. But a will is a *will*, and however unjust, people must abide by it."

Judge Barnard leaned back in his chair and laughed. The young people regarded him with astonishment and disapproval.

"Excuse me," he said, "this is quite a new experience to me. There's not much in my profession to afford enjoyment. I told you that the climax to my story was to come, and now you shall have it.

"That paper you found, Miss Marvin, was undoubtedly the last will and testament of this young man's uncle, Squire Hartwell. It is duly signed and dated, and all the forms of law are correct. In every respect, *save one*, it is a facsimile of the one I drew up for Squire Hartwell. But instead of John Stuart King's being the heir, every solitary penny of the entire property is left to Miss Annette L. Marvin on condition that she marry his obstinate nephew, Joshua Reginald Hartwell. Miss Marvin, are you going to consent to meet those conditions, or are you, like the gentlemen, equally obstinate?"

For the third time in Nannie Marvin's life, the room began to whirl around. Judge Barnard, instead of waiting to be answered, went in haste to find a glass of water.

CHAPTER XXVI

DISMISSED

t was very well to appear dignified before Miss Elliott, but never did a gentleman go out from her presence more thoroughly uncomfortable in mind than did John Stuart King on that memorable evening. He was sure he had been a simpleton throughout the interview. He had allowed himself to be misunderstood, to have his motives maligned — in short, to appear ashamed of his position instead of explaining calmly that he had adopted an ordinary business method of action for the sole purpose of studying social problems. It was a scheme of which he had a right to be proud rather than ashamed. This he told himself while he was in a fume.

Later, in a calmer moment, he admitted that no man could really be proud of a position that compelled him to shade the truth a dozen times in a single day. Moreover, people didn't like to be duped, even though the deception had done them no harm. There was something, undoubtedly, to be said for Miss Elliott's side.

He tramped off some of his surplus energy by making all speed to the station. One step of his future was clear to him. He would, without an hour's delay, do what he could to overset that will that by this time he hated. He took a savage delight in the prospect of making it good for nothing. The train was late after all his haste, and he had to march up and down the little platform to keep himself warm, subject to the sleepy-eyed stare of the station agent. It was unusual for residents of Bennettville and vicinity to take a train to town at that late hour.

He came back over the road with slower step, but not with a more cheerful view of life. His interview with Judge Barnard had added a little to his general sense of being ill-used. That gentleman asked many questions and imparted no information. He couldn't even learn from him whether the necessary forms of law could be managed without delay.

Before reaching the farm, however, he had decided upon the next step he should take. He would not leave town that night, notwithstanding his offer to Helen Elliott to do so if she desired. She had not said, in words, that she desired it, and he believed there was a duty he owed to her father, although she had been in too lofty a mood to recognize it.

He had not exaggerated the confidence Mr. Elliott had placed in him of late. On the very next day he was to have driven to a distant town to complete a certain business transaction that required judgment and quick-wittedness. Mr. Elliott had not hesitated to place the matter in his hands. It should have his best attention, as delay would

cause embarrassment and might result in pecuni-
ary loss.

He would start at daylight. If Helen chose, during his absence, to arrange so that he could do
nothing further for her father, that was her concern. For himself, he stood ready to give honorable
warning of his change of occupation. He would be
absent all day and therefore need not disturb her
by a sight of him. Having settled this, he gave a
few hours to restless sleep, during which he continued his interview with Helen with even more
unsatisfactory results than had attended his wak-
ing. Then he roused Susan Appleby at an hour she
considered unreasonable.

"Pity's sake!" she grumbled. "Why didn't you
start last night? I suppose it's your supper you're
hungry for since you wouldn't condescend to
come and eat it." He had packed away Stuart
King's garments in the trunk, and every article of
clothing he wore belonged to the man known as
John Stuart, so Susan felt at home with him. As
usual, she wasn't afraid to speak her mind. He was
very gentle with her. Susan had been a friend to
him. He could recall times without number when
she had advised him for his good. He realized she
had honestly done her best to be helpful to him.

John replied meekly that it wasn't so much
breakfast he wanted as to leave some messages for
Mr. Elliott. It was to be explained to him that John
had made a very early start because he had
learned, the day before, that on Saturdays the chief
man he was going to see generally went to town by
the noon train. By starting thus early, he believed
he could reach him and transact the business before train time. There followed other messages, or
suggestions rather, concerning certain matters that

ought to receive attention during his absence. At last Susan Appleby, who was proud of the evident way John took the Elliott interests to heart, and who faithfully treasured every word he said in order to give an accurate report, grumbled again. Did he think she was a walking dictionary or something to remember all those words? Mr. Elliott had run the farm before he came there, and she thought likely enough he could do it again.

Susan didn't know what a thorn she thrust into the sore heart of John by that last. He felt its truth. He was probably exaggerating his importance even to Mr. Elliott. It really made little difference to anyone except his mother and possibly Elizabeth where he went or what he did.

As he drove into the farmyard late that afternoon, his errand having been accomplished in a gratifying manner, he saw, sitting on the fence that divided the meadow lot from the yard, an individual whose presence gave him a pang of envy. This was no other than Jim, the man who had worked for Mr. Elliott just before his own advent and who had fallen sick, apparently for the deeper purpose of allowing him an opening. He had heard much of this individual. Susan, who thought much better of Jim ill and away than she had of him at work on the farm, had given detailed accounts of his character.

Jim had fully recovered, and he was doubtless in search of his old place. John Stuart had met the youth several times in the village and knew he had a fondness for the Elliott farm. A few words with him as he sat astride the fence corroborated this idea. Jim was hoping there would be an opening, at least in the spring, and had come around to see about it. He had been "talking things over" with

Mr. Elliott. He didn't want to get in any other fellow's way, but, after all, this was kind of his place.
A man couldn't help getting sick.

John assented to it all. Apparently the man had
come in an opportune time, so why wasn't he
glad? Just what step should he take next? It
seemed probable that Miss Elliott had made her
disclosures. Perhaps he could see Mr. Elliott at
once and depart without burdening her with a further glimpse of him. And then Susan Appleby
shouted at him from the kitchen doorway.

"If I was you, I'd find out what I was to do next
before I unharnessed them horses. I shouldn't
wonder a mite if you would have to drive to the
station after Helen. They tramped there this afternoon, her and Nannie Marvin, but it isn't any ways
likely that they mean to tramp out again. I don't
know nothing about it, but I think it's likely that
Mrs. Elliott does. If I was you, I'd ask her before I
did a lot of work for nothing. I s'pose you've heard
the news, haven't you?"

"What news?" asked John Stuart tentatively as
he came toward the house with a view, perhaps,
toward acting upon Susan's advice. Nothing
seemed more improbable than that Miss Elliott
would permit him to bring her from the station,
but it was possible he ought to inquire.

"Why, about that everlasting will. It's going to
pop up in some shape or other the rest of our lives,
I reckon. I don't know what it will do next to make
a hubbub, I'm sure."

"What has it done this time?" John Stuart was
washing his hands now at the sink and reflecting
whether it was probable that Susan had already
heard of the heir's rejection of the property. Apparently she didn't know who the heir was. Susan's

views might indicate how much had already been told; therefore his question.

"Why, that fellow, whoever he is, that folks thought Squire Hartwell left his money to. You've heard of him, haven't you?"

"I have heard his name mentioned several times," said John Stuart dryly.

"Well, I reckon he feels fine today! Only maybe he didn't hear the other story. I don't know how far off he is, but I hope he didn't. I can't help feeling kind of sorry for the poor fellow — having money left him and then not having it, then having it again and then not having it some more. It's worse than never having had a notion of getting any, according to my idea. It ain't his, you see, after all." She stopped in the act of filling her kettle to see the effect of her words.

"That will that Nannie Marvin found and that none of 'em had sense enough to look at but just rushed off to Judge Barnard with — he come up there this morning posthaste and told them it was Squire Hartwell's last will and testament sure enough. But there isn't a red cent of money left to that fellow, whatever his name is, nor to anybody else but Nannie Marvin herself. Only she's got to promise to marry Rex Hartwell or else she can't have it. Easy enough for her to promise that! She's been crazy after him ever since I knew her.

"For pity's sake! John Stuart, what are you dripping soapy water all over my floor for? It don't need cleaning. Didn't I finish scrubbing it not an hour ago?"

"Have I hurt the floor, Susan? I'm very sorry." He transferred the offending hands to the washbasin, finished washing in extreme haste, and got out again to the yard and the horses. It had suddenly become difficult to breathe inside. All his efforts, then, had been in vain! Had he simply kept quiet and allowed things to take their course, all would have been well, and he might be at this moment quietly driving to the station for Miss Elliott. It was a bitter reflection. He hadn't been ready for disclosures; he had made them badly, and now to find them worse than unnecessary!

The repentant Susan came out on the steps and called again. "Come on in and get some dinner. I kept it hot for you. You needn't wait till supper. You must be about starved by this time."

He answered gently again that he didn't feel hungry and would wait.

Susan went in, slamming the door and grumbling, "Pity's sake! If he's goin' to turn so touchy as that, what's the use in trying to do anything? Jest because I scolded a little about his drippy hands!"

He left his horses blanketed at last and went into Mr. Elliott's room. That gentleman was now improving daily. He was sitting up in his easy chair, alone. The moment John Stuart saw his face, he knew he had been told the news. It wasn't a disagreeable interview. Mr. Elliott didn't seem indignant as his daughter had. He said he understood something of what the motive might have been, and he congratulated John on his success in carrying out the scheme. He even laughed a little over his own utter innocence and recalled, with laughter, certain items of advice he had given.

John could sooner have cried. He felt himself parting with a friend. The truth was, he had come in closer touch with a real home here than ever before in his life. Moreover, despite his kindness, there was in Mr. Elliott that little undertone of feeling about having been duped. Like all practical jokes, it had its disagreeable side. No one likes to have his faith in other people played with. John Stuart tried to hint at his willingness to remain until such time as Mr. Elliott could spare him better, but there was no opening for that. It was taken for granted that his reason for making the disclosure at all was his desire to get away. His sacrifice in connection with it had been apparently forgotten.

Why not, since it wasn't needed? Mr. Elliott made light of his share of the inconvenience. Jim had come to him that very afternoon, desiring his old place. It seemed providential. Jim had done very well indeed for so young a fellow, and he himself would be up and around in a few days.

Oh, no, they wouldn't think of asking John to stay. Under the circumstances, it would be embarrassing for all of them. He was sorry John had felt bound to attend to that day's business, but glad, of course, for its successful conclusion. Jim could hardly have managed that. If he would like to take the train that evening, Jim could drive him to the station when he went for Helen.

In short, John Stuart went out from that interview feeling himself dismissed. Despite Farmer Elliott's closing words, half serious and yet comic, "You have certainly served me faithfully, and if, at any time, you find yourself in need of a recommendation as a farmhand, don't hesitate to apply to me!" there was a sense in which he felt himself let go in disgrace. He was almost compelled to leave the farm that night, and it wasn't what he wanted to do. He hesitated with a lingering desire to say good-bye to Susan, then thought better of it and made his way up to the woodhouse chamber just as Jim was responding with alacrity to Mr. Elliott's call.

John didn't go directly to the city he called home. Instead, he bought his ticket for the college town where Corey Elliott was staying. He was in no mood for home just now. He shrank from the thought of Fletcher's probing questions and felt he had no story to tell about his summer's outing.

A vague feeling that Corey Elliott might be in embarrassment of some sort, as well as a desire to be helpful to him, were, as nearly as he could understand his motives, what prompted him to stop at the college town. He had never learned what form of trouble it was that sent Corey home that night so heavily laden, nor how he had gotten out of it as triumphantly as his telegram indicated. It had to do with money in some way, and a boy who was deeply involved in money difficulties didn't usually find his way out so quickly.

Perhaps the telegram was only a skillful effort to lift the burden from his sister's shoulders. The more he thought about it, the more he convinced himself that the boy was in danger — in greater danger, probably, than his secluded sister could even imagine.

If only he, John Stuart King, could secure an influence over him — could win him, perhaps, from dangerous companions, gradually secure his confidence, and help him practically and permanently! If debt were one form of his troubles, wouldn't that be something worth stopping for? It would dignify his more than doubtful experiment and restore to him his self-respect.

Moreover, would it not, in a way that perhaps nothing else could, soften Miss Elliott's feelings toward him and help her to understand that, although he had chosen to masquerade for a time as another character, he was really an honest, earnest man with a purpose in life?

This last motive he tried to put away as unworthy. Miss Elliott had practically insulted him. She had shown him that he was less than nothing to her despite the kindly interest she had taken in John Stuart, an interest that had evidently been growing of late. He owed it to his self-respect to think no more about her. But the boy Corey, who had been uniformly kind to him even when he regarded him with suspicion, he would like to win, watch over and help in any way possible.

Upon his arrival in town he wandered about, valise in hand, in the lower and more obscure portions of the city until he found a lodging house sufficiently humble for his needs and hired a room for the night. From this he emerged in the morning, fully attired as John Stuart King, to the unbounded astonishment and, he couldn't help feeling, suspicion of the sleepy-looking maid who stared after him as he walked down the street. He had taken the precaution to pay his bill the night before and had said he wanted no breakfast. It annoyed him, however, to think of that servant maid's stare. He wanted to be done with intrigue of every sort from this time forth.

He took a car for uptown and, having questioned his way, selected one of the best hotels in the city where he registered at once as "Stuart King," with an extra flourish of his pen about the last name. Then he unpacked his valise and established himself, resolved to give exclusive attention to Reuben and Hannah and wait for Monday and the hope of an interview with Corey Elliott.

CHAPTER XXVII

CITIZEN OR SOJOURNER?

pon my word!" said Corey Elliott, "I don't wonder that my sister was startled to the degree she confesses when you appeared to her. I really don't think I would have recognized you at the first moment had I not been prepared. Is it possible you haven't made any changes except in dress?" He looked critically at hair and mustache.

"It's simply clothes," said Stuart King. "Isn't it humiliating?"

"It's very interesting. You should have stayed and given our neighborhood another sensation. It's fairly boiling with excitement as it is. What with the recovered will and an entirely new heir, or rather heiress, and then your sudden and, to them, mysterious disappearance, I don't know, on the whole, that it could safely have borne anymore."

They were sitting together in Stuart King's room. Corey, who had been at home for Sunday, as usual, and had returned by a later train than usual, hadn't visited his room until night, and then he

had found only Stuart King's card. His curiosity to
see that gentleman was so great that it was with
difficulty he had restrained himself the next day
until his college duties were over before rushing to
return the call. He was cordial in the extreme and
heartily interested in the idea that had led Stuart
King to sacrifice his position in the world to a summer and fall of country life and obscurity.

"I don't know that I understand social problems
well enough to appreciate your work in that direction," he said frankly when Stuart King, with anxious care, tried to elaborate them for him. "But I
can see at a glance that the whole thing would be
great fun, and I confess I don't see the harm in it —
though some people might."

He had made a noticeable pause before conclud-
ing, and Stuart King studied his face for news.
"You, think, then, that some people would disap-
prove? Is that the feeling in your neighborhood?"

"Not to any extent," said Corey, laughing.
"Susan Appleby was the only really cross person I
saw. She considers herself cheated, but she admits
you did it well. The fact is, she believes that the
man who could cheat Susan Appleby 'right before
her face and eyes,' as she expresses it, is a genius.
My father, too, sees the jolly side of it. He laughed
over some of the advice he had given you, and he
says you have the material in you for a first-class
farmer."

Stuart King tried to laugh with him and to make
his voice sound not too anxious as he said, "But
your mother and sisters feel differently, perhaps?"

"Well," said Corey hesitatingly, "my sister
Helen, as perhaps you know, is a worshipper of
Truth. If she had lived in the old days or in some
heathen country, she would have had a carved im-

age named Truth and bowed down to it. I like it in
her. I used to think her too particular, and perhaps
she is in certain directions, but on the whole it's
grand to have a character you can trust, always
and everywhere. Helen is oversensitive in some
lines. She can't help that. She is one, you see, who
looks and thinks truth, as well as speaks it."

Stuart King felt that he need not question further. Helen had criticized him, probably with se-
verity, and her brother had tried to take his side.
He must wait. Meantime, he would cultivate the
acquaintance of the young brother and win him
and, sometime perhaps...well, perhaps what? The
mail had been brought to his room since Corey had
arrived, and on the table before him lay a bulky
letter from Fletcher. It undoubtedly contained foreign enclosures.

He pushed aside all merely personal matters
and gave himself to the entertainment of Corey
with such success that he presently felt he might
safely say, with the most winning of smiles, "And
now that you understand me better than you did, I
wonder if I may renew the offer I once almost offended you by making? In that line or any other, I
would be glad to be called upon. In other words, I
would like you, if you're willing, to look upon me
as a friend. It's true that I'm a few years older than
you, but by no means so many that I've forgotten
my college experiences and the satisfaction that a
frank friendship with a man older than I would
have been to me. Is it too early in our acquaintance
to ask you to take me for a real friend?"

"I thank you ever so much," said Corey heartily.
"I don't feel that you're a new acquaintance at all. I
told Helen that it scared me to think of the great
Stuart King and remember I had actually given

him directions about horses and cows and the like!" He stopped to laugh merrily over the memory. "I said I hoped our roads would never cross again, because I wouldn't know what to say. But you see I rushed away in search of you as soon as possible, and I confess I'm not at all afraid of you. I always liked John Stuart even better than I thought it wise to show him." The half-merry and yet earnest look on the handsome young face was pleasant to see.

"Poor little Annie," he continued, "had a momentary return of her love of mystery and adventure, and she announced that she thought it would be just delightful to meet you as Stuart King, the great writer! I say, Mr. King, we owe you a debt of gratitude that we can never repay for your share in the rescue of that poor little girl. Helen admitted that you were very wise and very kind about that matter, and my mother can't be grateful enough."

This certainly was comforting. Stuart King's heart warmed yet more toward Helen Elliott's brother. Before the interview closed, John renewed his offer to help, approaching the subject from another side and, he flattered himself, with such adroitness that it would not sound like mere repetition.

Corey had risen to go, but he turned back with a bright look shining on his face. "That's very good of you! I recognized it as truly good when you offered help to me before. The only thing I was afraid of was that John Stuart ought not to have so much money!" His frank laugh was fascinating.

"I'm glad to be able to tell you that I have no need of help in that direction. I was in a sea of trouble, but an Infinite Helper came to my aid and carried me through." There was no mistaking his reverent tone. Stuart King waited respectfully for whatever more he might have to say in that line.

Suddenly Corey changed his tone and spoke eagerly, "I do need help, however, in other directions. It seems strange to be asking it of you at this time. It was the last thought in my mind when I came here today, but you've been so kind. My sister Helen told me that you were a Christian man, and I know, by the energy with which you take hold of anything that's to be done, what sort of Christian you must be. I wonder if you would not be just the one to set me at work? I've just started on that road, Mr. King. In fact, my decision dates from the morning following my night of trouble. I was driven into the fold, one may say. A vast amount of coaxing was done beforehand, but I would pay no attention to it. However, I am inside at last.

"Now what I want is to get to work. I'm alive from head to foot with undirected energy. There's work enough needing to be done, I can see that. Among the boys in college, for instance, and outside, in the city, plenty of it. But I don't know how to set about any of it. Could you give me a hint? Sort of start me, you know? What's your line of Christian work in your own city? And what did you do in college? Did you have some system, something I can get hold of? You wouldn't imagine it, perhaps, but I'm a systematic sort of fellow. I have definite hours for definite things and mental pigeonholes filled with them, you understand."

Poor Stuart King! Yes, he understood, but he stood silent, constrained and embarrassed before the bright young face and earnest eyes looking up to him for guidance. What was his line of Christian work? What indeed! Would anything astonish the people of his own city more than to see him at any sort of Christian work? How many times had he spoken to others about the subject? Fletcher, his friend and fellow church member, and he had often criticized sermons together as they walked home from church. But aside from that, he couldn't recollect having held any religious conversation even with him.

He had not been in the habit of attending the midweek prayer meeting of his church. It fell on a night when there was generally a literary lecture of importance in some other portion of the city. Then, too, he had been abroad a great deal and had never fallen into the habit of a midweek prayer meeting, nor indeed of any prayer meeting.

What had he done in college in the name of Christian work? Nothing. If he spoke plain truth such as he had declared to himself that he meant to speak in the future, he would have to use that word. Would it be well to make such a confession to this eager beginner, looking to him for guidance?

He didn't think all these thoughts in detail while Corey waited for his answer. Instead, they flashed through his brain, making a stinging path to his awakening conscience. He was glad that Corey was on his feet and only a moment earlier had explained that he must meet a college engagement.

"These are important questions," Stuart King said, and he was afraid his smile was sickly. "They can't be answered hurriedly. Come and see me again, and we'll talk things over. When will you come? Can you spare an evening for me soon?"

Corey ran hurriedly over the week's program. Tuesday was lecture evening, and on Wednesday he had promised to go with a friend to make a call at some distance.

"How would Thursday evening do?"

"Thursday," said Corey, "is our college prayer meeting evening. I have only recently begun to attend it, but I thought I would not allow other engagements to interfere with it. You think that's the way to begin, don't you? Because, if one starts out with letting other matters push in, there's always something to push."

"Undoubtedly," said the supposed guide. Then there were no other evenings that week. On Friday Corey went home again, and he couldn't know how much Stuart King envied him this privilege, nor how devoutly he wished he could be invited to hold their next conference at the Elliott farm. There was nothing for it but to wait until the following Monday, though he had wanted very much to say certain things to this young brother that he might possibly report to his sister.

Left alone, Stuart King let the bulky letter wait while he gave himself up to some of the most serious, as well as humiliating, thinking he had ever done in his life.

Once more were his plans and, yes, his hopes, shattered! He had earnestly hoped to be helpful to this young man, to win him from careless and probably dangerous ways, to guide him into higher lines of thought and study than his commonplace opportunities had as yet suggested to him. In short, to be such a friend to him that Helen Elliott might one day say, possibly with the grateful tears making her beautiful eyes soft and bright, "I have to thank you for saving my brother so he might become his highest self." And now, behold, the boy was not only safe from the common and petty temptations he had feared for him, but he was also tremendously in earnest and needed leading in exactly the lines in which John Stuart King was powerless to help!

The older man could feel the throb of energy and settled purpose in the boy. He was sure it was no common decision that had been reached. He could foretell that Corey Elliott's religion meant a force that would be known among his classmates and in his boardinghouse. It would grow with his growth and develop as his mental powers strengthened. He would, in short, become such a Christian as Helen Elliott already was, with Christianity being an underlying test to which all acts, however trivial, must be brought.

Could he wish him to be less than this? No, indeed; he drew himself up proudly with the thought. He respected and admired such characters, but he had been content to admire them afar off and to feel (rather than reason) that such a condition was attainable only for the few. Now he discovered that if he would be the friend of Helen Elliott as well as of the boy, he must search after that condition.

He sat well into the night, busy with the most serious problems that can concern the human mind. After a time he was able to put Helen Elliott, and then all human friendships or embarrassments, aside and let conscience speak to his soul. Very solemn questions it asked him. Why should he, a man who had had unusual opportunities for education and culture, discover himself to be actually below a young fellow like Corey Elliott when it came to matters of the most vital importance? He might call it boyish enthusiasm, smile indulgently and give his mind to his studies. He had been doing something of that kind heretofore, he discovered. But some new light had entered his soul and was compelling him, for the time at least, to be honest with himself.

Did he believe that this life at its longest is short compared with the eternity that even the cultured mind can only faintly imagine? Did he believe that one book, claiming to be from God, told us all we actually know about that eternity? Putting aside for the moment the differing opinions of Christendom, did he believe in the general statements plainly made in that revelation? Unhesitatingly his mind answered yes to all these questions.

Then came the searching question: Was his life arranged and managed in accordance with these beliefs? Much of his time since he grew to manhood had been spent abroad. He might in a sense have been said to have lived there. Yet it had always interested him to note that an Englishman or Frenchman seemed to recognize him at once as an American, as a sojourner rather than a resident.

"You are an American?" said (rather than asked) a man in London to whom he had been introduced but a short time before. And then, "I suppose you are like all the rest of them, planning to go home as soon as you can manage it?"

He thought of this as he sat alone with his conscience. Did he impress any person with whom he came in contact as a citizen of another, far away country planning to go home? Had he not rather lived always as though this inch of life were all that deeply interested him, and religion was but an incident, somewhat trifling along the way?

Corey, it's true, had asked his help — confident, apparently, that he would be able to give it. But his clear-eyed sister had not been deceived. And Corey would learn soon that, boy as he was and but just started on this road, he was still — perhaps by reason, perhaps of his lifelong environment — already further advanced than this traveler who professed to have begun the journey years before.

What was he going to do about it? The boy had been drawn to him, had enjoyed the evening and would come again. He could win and influence him, could gradually mold him by what pattern he chose.

Should he try it? His own aims had been high. His life could in no ordinary sense of the word be called a failure, and most parents and siblings of his acquaintance would feel honored by any notice from him bestowed upon their sons and brothers. Would the Elliotts? He would rather hold aloof from the boy entirely than to turn his high aspirations into other, misguided channels. Was there no other alternative?

After a time, John Stuart King got beyond all these and let not only his conscience, but also the voice of God, speak to him. It sent him to his knees.

On the next Monday evening, at the close of a talk with Corey about the home he had just left, he laid a cordial hand on the young fellow's shoulder and said, "My friend, I have something to say to you. I'm not the one to advise you about the most important part of your life. If it were a question of Greek or mathematics, I might be of service, but I'm simply a babe in this matter of practical Christianity. I believe I have yet even to commence crawling." He smiled sadly as he made this confession.

"I don't mind telling you," he added with grave dignity, "that I'm ashamed of my life as a Christian. I mean to have a different record from this time forth, but it's only right to tell you that, much as I would like to help you in the line of which you spoke the other night, I don't know how. You'll have to go to someone who hasn't wasted his opportunities."

The younger man, wondering, touched, attracted powerfully by King's simple frankness and earnestness, hesitated but a moment. Then, holding out his hand, he said eagerly, "Suppose we start together, then, and find out what to do?"

CHAPTER XXVIII

ONE SEASON'S HARVEST

he great stone house, which had belonged in the Hartwell family ever since one stone of it was laid upon another, was ablaze with light. From all the hospitable rooms issued the sound of merry voices. The long-hoped-for, long-deferred social function that had filled the thoughts of Bennettville and vicinity for so long was now in progress. Mr. and Mrs. Reginald Hartwell were "at home" after their wedding journey and had gathered their friends about them royally.

Not one person in the neighborhood who could lay claim to even a slight acquaintance with Nannie Marvin Hartwell had been forgotten. Helen's boys and girls, as the young people from her school were called, were there in force. So also was Susan Appleby, in the dining-room door with her arms akimbo just then, staring about her complacently but doing most efficient service in the kitchen between times.

"I had as good as an invite as the best of 'em,"

she confided in a strong voice to Jack Sterritt. "If I hadn't, I shouldn't have stirred a step to help, but they ain't the kind that looks down on folks the minute they get a little money. Ain't she sweet to-night in that bride dress? I declare for it, I didn't know Nannie Marvin was so pretty. It beats all what wedding finery will do!"

"We'll have them here often," said the bride in confidence to Helen, as they watched some of the country girls who were gazing earnestly at the pictures on the walls. "We mean to have a regular 'evening' for our friends in this neighborhood, and we'll teach them all sorts of little things that will help them without their ever imagining they're being taught. Gradually we'll drive out of the region those games you dislike so much, along with several other objectionable things, just by showing them a better mode of entertainment. Rex says we will try the 'expulsive power' of new entertainments.

"Oh, Helen! We mean to do so many things with this dear old house! Rex has such lovely plans! You don't half know him. We knelt together in this very library, by that leather chair near the grate, and consecrated this room especially to the Lord's work. And Helen" — this with lowered tone and a nervous little clutch of her friend's arm — "I thought then, while I listened to his prayer about what we meant to try to do, what if I had burned that will! I was tempted to do it! What if I had?"

"You never would have done it," said Helen with quiet confidence. "Don't even think of it, dear. God takes care of His own."

She stood later near one of the great leather chairs. She liked to look down into their depths and remember that they had been consecrated. She was feeling very happy. There were lovely possibilities for Rex and Nannie, and through them her dear boys and girls would receive help. Money was a beautiful servant!

Young Dr. Warden moved toward her; he was Rex Hartwell's most intimate friend and had taken a journey at an inconvenient time to act as his best man. It hadn't been difficult to persuade him to take it again and assist at this reception. He was evidently well pleased to be intimately associated with Miss Helen Elliott, the bride's maid of honor.

"I think you told me I was to help you 'feel at home' tonight!" he said, laughing. "Are there many guests left whom you haven't met?"

"Oh, there must be dozens! The entire medical college has come out tonight, I think."

"Then I ought to be doing my duty. I believe I have at least met most of the guests from the college. But there are others equally distinguished, if not more so. Of course you've met the star of the evening? He came late, however, after we had ceased to receive formally. Perhaps you really haven't met him? What an oversight!"

"How can I know until you name the wonder?" laughed Helen. "Who is the star? I thought there were several."

"Ah, but this one is of the first magnitude. His last book, just out, is creating a furor. I mean Stuart King, of course."

At that instant someone tapped the doctor on the shoulder and spoke a few quiet words.

"Certainly," said Dr. Warden. "Miss Elliott, allow me to make you acquainted with my friend, Mr. King. Excuse me, Miss Elliott, but Mr. Hartwell is summoning me" — whereupon he disappeared in the throng.

Stuart King and Helen Elliott stood confronting each other. There was a moment's hesitation as though she were trying to determine what to say. Then she laughed, a low, rippling laugh full of merriment.

"I am acquainted with you after all," she said. "Clothes are not so important as we supposed."

"But you said we were to be strangers."

"I know I did. I was hard on you, Mr. King. I've realized it since. My father, who is quite fond of you, has reminded me earnestly that the gospel is a message of grace. I've been studying and praying much to develop that side of my Christian life. My brother also takes care that we shall not, in the family, forget your name. I like the work you and he are doing."

"It is he who's doing it," said Stuart King. "I've only been able to help a little with the organization. I couldn't enter into it as I should like to do because I'm going home so soon."

It was a very different conversation from any of the numberless ones he had tried to plan since he first knew he was to have this coveted opportunity. He had been anxious, if she would talk with him at all, to make her listen to his defense of his fall campaign. He felt that, while his own opinion of it wasn't as high as it used to be, he could yet convince her that he had been thoroughly in earnest in his effort to understand a form of life about which he wished to write. He also meant to ask if she wouldn't read his book and see if she didn't find evidence that he understood some points better than he could have done without such an experience.

But after that first laughing sentence she utterly ignored their past acquaintance and went straight to the center of their present work, his and her brother's. She was eager for details, for suggestions about what he would try to do if he were to continue in the college town. She had certain plans of her own to propose and was anxious to learn, through him, whether they would be feasible for her brother to add to his. In short, she showed him as plainly as words could have done that she had chosen to think of him as Stuart King, the Christian friend of her brother, and was trying to put the deception of John Stuart behind them.

For the next few weeks, he had certain opportunities to study this phase of Miss Elliott's character. At least he made the opportunities. His invitation to call had been sufficiently cordial, and he improved it. Twice during the week following the reception at the stone house came invitations from certain of the wealthier families of the surrounding neighborhood. People who had never noticed John Stuart by so much as a glance were more than delighted to have the chance of receiving John Stuart King into their homes. On both of these occasions, he went down by an early train and called at the Elliott farm.

Early in the ensuing week he persuaded himself that courtesy demanded the making of a few calls in the neighborhood — notably, of course, upon the bride and bridegroom, but also at the Elliott farm. On Friday night he went down by Corey's hearty invitation and stayed through Sunday. Certainly Helen Elliott had decided he was not a stranger. She was frank and gracious, was as deeply interested as ever in the enterprise he and Corey were managing, and showed herself to be an efficient helper.

Farmer Elliott had recovered from his slight sense of annoyance at having been made the subject of a practical joke and was quite cordial. As for the quiet mother, she had never been other than kind and friendly. Poor Anna, who hadn't recovered from her frightened air and timidity in the presence of others, yet received him most gratefully. Only Susan Appleby held aloof.

"Humph!" she said when his position in the literary world was explained to her. "How do you know he writes books? He may have borrowed 'em like he did his work clothes. Who knows what he'll do next? I shouldn't be surprised to see him turn out a circus man or something."

This estimate so amused Corey that he couldn't resist the temptation to repeat it to Stuart King, who laughed with him genially and hid a sense of shame and pain. Did Susan voice in her rough, uncultured way a lingering suspicion shared by Helen Elliott? In other words, did *she* trust him fully?

There came a time, just as the spring was opening, when Stuart King steadily yet with infinite pain to himself declined Corey's earnest invitation to go home with him.

The older man had held stern vigil with himself the night before, and he knew that honor demanded his staying away from the Elliott farm. Not for Helen's sake — and therein, with strange inconsistency, lay the deepest pain. She continued to be friendly toward him, but he knew that mere friendliness was so far from satisfying to him that at times he was ready to declare he would rather they should be strangers.

Yet what did such a state of mind prove? It was humiliating to a degree that he hadn't thought he could endure. But he must face the facts, and he must be a man of honor if he could, and at the same time a man of truth.

It was late in the night when his decision brought him to the writing of a letter. It was early in the morning before that letter was finished, although it wasn't long. Three times he tore the carefully written sheet into fragments and commenced anew. He had never spent so much time in writing a letter to Elizabeth, nor had he ever thought to write this kind of letter to her or to any woman. What a humiliation for a man of his years and his character to have to admit he had made an irreparable mistake — to admit that the woman he had asked to be his wife didn't occupy the first place in his heart!

More than once he laid down the pen and hid his burning face in his hands, telling himself he couldn't write it, then telling himself sternly a moment afterward that he must. Honesty demanded it. Elizabeth could hold him to his pledged word if she would; he didn't deny her right to do so. He was ready to abide by the mistake he had made, but to go with her to the marriage altar hiding the facts would be adding insult to injury.

It was vain for him to go over his past and groan at the folly of a boy playing at manhood. He had allowed himself to drift into an engagement when, had he understood his own heart, he would have known he had only a friendly liking for the woman he asked to be his wife.

He thought of his mother and the interest she had taken in the entire matter and the influence she had used. Then he put those thoughts sternly aside, assuring himself that he might have been a manly man, had he chosen to, and that he couldn't blame his mother for his own bad decisions.

At last the letter was written, sealed and started

on its journey across the ocean. It remained now to wait for a reply. Worn with his night of self-humiliation, Stuart King had just strength enough left to decline Corey's invitation. Miss Elliott might consider him only a friend, but he knew his own heart well enough now to be sure it would be dishonorable of him to try to see her.

Corey went away vexed. He was growing extravagantly fond of Stuart King, and there seemed no possible reason why that gentleman should not prefer a visit with him at the farm rather than a Sunday alone in town.

When the next Friday night came and his pressing invitation was again rejected, Corey was puzzled and all but angry. There was evidently some mystery about Stuart King, as there had been about John Stuart. He professed to be so fond of the farm and of "Father and Mother," and he was so ready, even eager, to hear about every little detail of their family life. And this time, at his instigation, his mother had sent her own genial invitation to him to come down, yet he had refused.

In the evening, while Stuart King sat alone, weakly wishing it had been right to go to the farm and sorely missing the bright-faced young man who grew daily nearer to him for his own sake, the foreign mail was brought to his room. There was only one letter, and that from his mother. It couldn't possibly be in response to anything he had written, not yet, but his face flamed as he tore it open. What would his next piece of foreign mail have for him? This one commenced ominously.

My dear Stuart,
    I hope you feel satisfied now with the result of your method of managing! I am

sorry for you, of course. A mother's heart always remains the same, no matter how foolish her son may be. Yet, while I don't for a moment admit it to Elizabeth, I can't but feel that you have yourself to thank. No girl of spirit will endure such tardy letter writing and such prolonged and unnecessary absences as you have treated her to. She has written you all about it, I suppose; at least she promised four days ago that she would. This wretched little Englishman may be going to have a title, but he is, in my opinion, anything but a gentleman. He knew months ago that Elizabeth was engaged. I told him so myself, but it evidently made not the slightest difference to him. I have never liked the creature. He is too fulsome.

Elizabeth pretended he was paying attention to me. The idea! She knew better all the time. Well, this is like all my other plans in life — for naught. I must say you have thwarted me in one way or another ever since you were a baby, but I suppose you cannot help it. You're like your father.

I am too much provoked with Elizabeth just now to have heard any particulars, but I suppose the wedding will be soon. It's just like him to rush. I shall come home as soon as I can. I will write again when I know what's to be done.

Your affectionate
Mother
P.S. It's just a case of pique on Eliza-

> beth's part. I have no doubt but that you
> could make it all right again if you
> would, though I have no faith to believe
> that you will.

Stuart King sat and stared at the letter like one in a dream. Elizabeth was engaged to be married, and he — *free!* By degrees he took in that tremendous fact. He didn't have to wait for the foreign mail and for a long series of embarrassments and humiliations, all of which, even at the best, would be terrible to explain. Elizabeth had deserted him, and he was free! He need not have written that humiliating letter; he might have spared her so much. There seemed to be so many things he need not have done if only he had been willing to wait!

With renewed hope he sat up again that very night to write another letter. He couldn't wait! He was losing ground every day, and Dr. Warden was gaining. Twice during his calls at the Elliott farm he had met Dr. Warden there. Moreover, Helen liked frankness, so he would be frank. This letter was long. It confessed everything but was very humble in its claims. It asked only for time and opportunity to prove the sincerity of the writer.

Helen sat quietly by the window, staring out at the Western sky where the sun was slipping to its nightly rest. On her lap lay the letter. She had mused at length over the words of Stuart King.

What was she to think? He had changed so abruptly, yet he was no different, she acknowledged, from the man who had taught her boys so eagerly at the school those nights nor from the man who had put aside his own interests and rescued her sister from a serious plight.

The scheme he had carried out before her family,

before everyone, was clever. His motive at the start had been a good one — she could see that. But why couldn't he have achieved it by some other means? And why didn't he abandon the disguise at the first opportunity, perhaps the night they rode home from the meeting with Rex and Nannie, the night she had suspected something was not quite right with him?

Wasn't he expecting too much of her, writing as he had? The others — Corey, Anna, even Nannie — she could easily forgive them and love them as much as ever. Perhaps it was easy because they had asked only for her forgiveness and nothing more.

Why was it so different with him? True, she had known the others nearly all her life. But why did she find it so difficult to accept him as he was? He had confessed to his failure to follow the truth and more than once admitted to his genuine sorrow over the consequences of his actions. She believed him to be sincere; she had seen the remarkable change. Must she abandon her love of truth and all that she stood for, simply to —

Oh, why couldn't he just return to his former life, instead of presenting himself to her in this way?

Question after question pushed its way through her weary mind, until at last only one remained, refusing to leave unanswered: Why couldn't she forget John Stuart King? Finally she took up her pen, knowing she could not put on paper what her heart had at last acknowledged.

Stuart King received an answer to his letter more quickly than he had dared to hope — a frank, kindly letter. She had been sorry more than once, Helen wrote, for those hard words she spoke to him on that first evening. She was so astonished and had been so tried that she didn't realize what she was saying. She would be glad if he could forget the part he called "hard" and look upon her as a friend.

Stuart King sat longer over that letter than he had over any other. He read it through a dozen times, read it until the words burned into his heart. Because of his evidently genuine concern for her family, she had developed a growing respect for John Stuart before he was revealed to be a sham, and she knew his better qualities were also Stuart King's. Furthermore, she was trying hard to take her father's words about grace and forgiveness to heart. But trust is a precious thing, she said, not easily given and even more difficult to extend when once it has been betrayed. Perhaps, after she had some time to think things through, they might start over afresh.

She agreed with her brother, however, that it had been too long since he had come out to visit the family; she urged him to accept Corey's next invitation.

As he pondered her words, he could understand her reluctance to trust him when his whole life before her in the beginning *had* been a sham. For a moment he placed himself in her position. How very difficult it would be to accept, then trust. But she was, at least, willing to begin again.

He would wait for Corey's next invitation, but he needed to go home in the meantime and attend to some pressing business matters. And he had his own thinking to do — and praying.

He was settled in his old rooms, seated before his old secretary, with sheets of paper strewn around and two pictures mounted on easels, in their old places, looking down on him. One was a photograph of Elizabeth. He hadn't put it away. Elizabeth was his cousin, and her photograph had stood there ever since he occupied the room. He had only kindness in his heart for her, but perhaps he would find another place for it. The other was the pictured face of Truth. The eyes were certainly very like Helen's, he told himself, gazing at it earnestly, but they didn't do her justice.

Seated in his old place near the south window was Fletcher. He had been there all evening; he had asked a thousand questions; he had been answered heartily and with apparent completeness. Yet there was something about his old friend that Fletcher didn't understand.

He has taken strides, he told himself. He's changed. It evidently improves one to become a tramp! I feel as though he has gone out of my vision, or up out of my horizon. I wonder what it means.

"Did you make any acquaintances that will last?" Fletcher asked presently, continuing his cross-examination. "Any kindred spirits, I mean?"

"A few that will last through all eternity."

Fletcher's eyes had followed his friend's and were resting on the pictured face of Truth, their old subject for discussion and disagreement.

"Did you convince yourself of the folly of finding such a face as that in flesh and blood?" he asked whimsically, simply for the sake of recalling old times. "Especially the eyes," he continued, as his friend was not ready to answer. "They seem to look through one. I'm glad that there are none such in real life. They would make one see his own shortcomings as a fine mirror does."

Stuart King wheeled around in his chair to look full upon his friend.

"Fletcher," he said earnestly, "there *are* such eyes. They belong to people who do remind one of his mistakes and failures, but who at the same time lift him up to a higher plane. I'll tell you something in confidence. The woman I hope will one day become my wife has eyes much like those."

OTHER BOOKS BY
ISABELLA MACDONALD ALDEN
IN THE ALDEN COLLECTION

———————

The King's Daughter
A New Graft on the Family Tree
Ester Ried's Awakening

Available from:

Creation House
'190 North Westmonte Drive
Altamonte Springs, FL 32714
(407) 862-7565